THE
HUNGER
BETWEEN
US

MARINA SCOTT

THE
HUNGER
BETWEEN
US

FARRAR STRAUS GIROUX

New York

Farrar Straus Giroux Books for Young Readers
An imprint of Macmillan Publishing Group, LLC
120 Broadway, New York, NY 10271

fiercereads.com

Our books may be purchased in bulk for promotional, educational, or business
use. Please contact your local bookseller or the Macmillan Corporate
and Premium Sales Department at (800) 221-7945, ext. 5442, or by email at
MacmillanSpecialMarkets@macmillan.com.

Library of Congress Cataloging-in-Publication Data

Names: Scott, Marina, author.
Title: The hunger between us / Marina Scott.
Description: First edition. | New York : Farrar Straus Giroux Books for
    Young Readers, 2022. | Audience: Ages 12–18. | Audience: Grades 10–12. |
    Summary: When her best friend disappears in the summer of 1942,
    Liza resolves to rescue her no matter the cost, entangling herself in an
    increasingly dangerous web with two former classmates, one a member
    of the militia and other other forced to live in Leningrad's tunnels.
Identifiers: LCCN 2022013829 | ISBN 9780374390068 (hardcover)
Subjects: CYAC: Survival—Fiction. | Conduct of life—Fiction. |
    Starvation—Fiction. | Saint Petersburg (Russia)—History—Siege,
    1941–1944—Fiction. | Soviet Union—History—1925–1953—Fiction. |
    LCGFT: Historical fiction. | Novels.
Classification: LCC PZ7.1.S336853 Hu 2022 | DDC [Fic]—dc23
LC record available at https://lccn.loc.gov/2022013829

First edition, 2022
Designed by Veronica Mang

Printed in the United States of America

ISBN: 978-0-374-39006-8
1 3 5 7 9 10 8 6 4 2

For Bryan

THE
HUNGER
BETWEEN
US

LENINGRAD, SUMMER 1942

1

I DIG MY MAMA'S GRAVE AT DAWN.

Drops of perspiration trickle down my spine as the air shifts. The cemetery smells of newly turned dirt, fresh grass, and rot.

The whole city smells of rot.

I pause to wipe the beads of sweat pooling between my brows and steal a glance at Mama's ashen face. Her body lies on a muddy sheet that used to be white. In death, my mother looks healthier, even younger. She's still worn out, battered by exhaustion and constant hunger, but her face has smoothed.

She won't ever look at me again or stroke my hair or call me by my name. The realization of loss is so deep, so sudden, it hits me like a shovel to my chest.

Liza, keep on digging, my mother's voice orders.

A strong gust of wind whips my reddish-brown hair across my face, and I groan. My legs are already shaking, and I can't feel my arms anymore. Our last meal was two days ago—an allotted piece of bread, washed down with some water. Generous in the beginning of the war, the allotment of bread dwindled with time. The initial rationing was 400 grams for children and 600 grams for most of the adults. By November, the rations were cut repeatedly. Now all we get is a thin slice of bread of 125 grams, carefully measured on scales.

In the winter months, grain was delivered by the Red Army trucks across the frozen Lake Ladoga. Leningrad's bakeries, using sawdust and bran as fillers, baked loaves of bread overnight. The food lines were long. People were angry and desperate. Many died of starvation in those lines. Many were robbed and killed on their way home.

I remember the first time we got our new reduced allotment. Mama, her bony hands shaking as she broke her slice in half, chewed on it slowly. As if she was savoring the taste of sawdust. Her voice was furious when she asked, "Liza, how long do you think people will last eating like this?"

As the winter proved, not long.

The ice on the lake melted in April. But by then, the position of the Red Army was improved, and food deliveries were more consistent, bags of supplies dropped off the planes. At least temporarily. Until the summer months came and the Red Army fell back and the Fascists moved closer to the city, closing the circle. Boats and barges carrying supplies still cross the lake, but we never know when the next delivery will happen.

Last night Mama gave me her half of the bread, and I ate it. I didn't know she was about to die.

I swallow a sharp lump in my throat and try to inhale deeply, but the stench of death makes me gag. I should be used to it by now—in the heat of summer, the breeze from the Neva River does little to conceal the reek.

I have to hurry; the city is waking up, but my strength is diminishing with every breath I take.

I pull the hair away from my face, tie it into a loose bun, and jab again into the solid ground with the shovel.

"I'm going to dig for some roots. Maybe cook a soup later." I'd concocted that lie last night after Mama took her last breath. It slipped easily off my tongue when I asked my elderly housemate to borrow a shovel.

Yelena's faded gray eyes pinned me to the floor, and her old mouth twitched. I knew she didn't believe me, but she gave it to me anyway. Did she guess Mama was dead?

Now my legs are so weak I must lean on the shovel. What if Yelena turns me in? I'm committing treason by not reporting Mama's death to the regional bureau of food and hanging on to her ration card until it expires at the end of the month.

I can't think about that now.

When the Nazi siege started last September, my mother declared, "It won't last long. The Red Army will come soon. We just need to last a couple of months." Her brown eyes gleamed when she talked, and her jaw was set. Most of us—there were quite a few neighbors alive then, ten months ago—felt the same way.

The man I call Kaganov, the only other person besides Yelena now left in our communal apartment, called my mother's unfaltering belief in the Red Army naive.

"I'm not naive," she told him with a small shake of her head. "I'm optimistic."

Look where that optimism brought you, Mama.

I wipe more sweat off my face. Or is it tears? Then I dig.

The Germans cut us off from the world. They bomb us from the air and shell us from the ground. But mainly they just strangle us from all sides. Starvation, the deadliest of soldiers, has invaded the city.

I sit down and close my eyes. Let myself breathe. Inhale. Exhale. Repeat. Listen for a distant roar of Fascist planes and blaring sirens signaling an upcoming air raid. Wait for the post-explosion ashes to fall on my face. Nothing.

Maybe I made a mistake coming here by myself. I'm too weak for this. Maybe I should've asked Kaganov for help. But how could I? After what he asked Mama to do?

Don't think. Don't talk about it.

It's too much to remember. My focus should be about survival now. The war has taken everything from us—our decency, our bodies, our minds—and left us drained and withering. We've turned into ghosts—silent and dangerous. It destroyed my father, and now it's killed my mother.

My lips tremble. I press them together, try to empty my churning mind and direct my attention to my body's movements. My breathing. Anything but the black void of loss. It seems like everyone I know is either dead or about to die.

Far away, the cemetery gates creak. Someone else will be digging a grave today. People don't leave their dead to decay in the summer heat. During the winter months, people stopped taking the deceased to the cemetery. It took too much. Energy became a precious commodity. Bodies of men, women, and children littered the streets.

The Communist Party Committee had to convert the Church of the Savior on Blood into a morgue to have somewhere to put them all. The glorious building towering proudly over the river with gilded, bright domes used to remind me of a colorful folk costume. Now I just think about the dead rotting inside.

Don't look and don't think. Always keep on moving. My mama trained me to just walk on by.

I listen intently but hear nothing. No one else is nearby. I take two deep breaths before I tell myself it's time to move. One more minute of rest and I get up.

A bird croaks loudly over my head. A crow?

When was the last time I saw a bird? I'm hallucinating. I'm getting sick like my mama. The birds left the city last fall. Aka's grandfather said they took their wings to the German lines where food was in abundance. Lucky birds. At least they were able to flee the death and hunger of the city.

I inhale. There is no bird. There is no bird.

Indeed, there is no bird.

Exhale.

I take a swig of water from an old flask and check my watch. I've been at it for an hour. An hour? My muscles tell me it's been ten years.

I go back to digging the god-awful hole for my mama. If I rest any longer, I'll fall into the grave and won't get up.

The ground is solid and unforgiving. By the time the earth is ready to accept Mama's body, my hands are bleeding from blisters formed and burst. I pull myself out of the hole, get on my rubbery legs, and walk over to her. I wrap her in the dirty sheet. There are big rips in the middle, and they threaten to tear it apart. I jerk and tug, pulling Mama to the hole, and roll her body over the edge.

Another hour and it's all done. I look over the small mound of dark soil under which lies my mother—sad, starved, and stubborn. And soon rotted from inside. Should I say something? The smell of decay and loneliness seeps into my nostrils. Pressure in my chest builds, and I press a palm over my mouth to suppress a sob about to burst out. I can't do this.

I stand in silence, my mind blank. To avoid collapsing, I turn away from the grave, pick up the shovel, and start toward home.

I don't get far.

A dark outline moves in the corner of my eye. Then someone's right there, on top of me. They push, and I drop my shovel and slam into the ground, landing on my back, a man's body hard on top of mine. My lungs won't expand under his weight. Why is he so heavy? I try to wriggle out from beneath him, but my body doesn't listen to me anymore. I can't fight. I have no strength.

One arm pins my chest while the other feels my pockets. I dig into his flesh with my broken fingernails, and the man gasps.

"Ration cards. Give me your ration cards and I'll let you go." A putrid whisper into my face.

I frantically pat the grass around me. I must get to the shovel. As if reading my mind, the man tightens his hold on my chest. My hands fly back to his arm to try to push it away. His weight is strangling me. Red and black spots dance around, cloud my vision, and turn my brain into mush. My weak muscles are strained so tightly I might snap in half at any moment.

"I don't have cards on me." A strangled breath is all I muster.

Everyone carries ration cards, a precious treasure to be guarded day and night. We pin them to our inside pockets or sleeves. We stash them away in our socks and shoes. We know better than to leave the cards at home. Apartments get broken into daily. People search for money, food, wood, and ration cards.

"Money, then," he growls. The man's dark eyes turn murderous. He's now straddling me while his hands restlessly slide up and down my body searching for valuables he can take. My feet kick violently. My ration cards are folded inside my socks. To get to them, the man will have to remove Mama's old boots from my feet.

That is, if he knows where to search.

He lifts his hand, curls it into a fist, and I know he's going to hit me, shatter my bones. He's going for a kill. His mouth opens, and the stench of excitement, the expectation of my death gusts over me. There is nothing I can do, and suddenly I don't care. This is it, the end. My last sight will be this man's hungry eyes and crooked yellow teeth.

A rustle. Then a thud. Something warm splashes my face, and the man rolls off me with a weak moan escaping his lips.

"Come on, get up," a low, husky voice commands, and a skinny arm reaches out to me.

I scramble to my feet.

My best friend's chestnut curls—almost identical to mine—spill out of the blue scarf on her head. Her eyes are wild, but the sight of her brings a slow smile to my face. The unexpected release of all tension makes me light-headed.

"Did you kill him?" I nod at my assailant, a small pool of blood beside his head. His pale skin is tight, almost translucent across his facial bones. He lies very still, except for the soft rise of his chest with each shallow breath.

"No, but he'll probably be out for a while," Aka says, and stumbles, dropping the shovel. "I need to rest for a minute. I'm not feeling well." Aka's movements are heavy and slow. She probably spent the last of her energy walking through the city to the cemetery and saving me from my attacker.

I sit down by her side and take her small hand into mine. "How did you know where to find me?"

Aka's blue eyes brush over my face. "I came to your apartment. Yelena told me you left with a shovel to go foraging for roots. I knew your mama has been sick for a while . . . and I guessed." She sighs and whispers, "I'm so sorry, Liza."

"Do you think Yelena guessed it, too?" I ask.

Aka shrugs. "I'm not sure. Maybe."

Aka knows that I'm not reporting my mother's passing and that I'm keeping the ration cards. She and I talked about it months ago and decided that survival justifies everything. Even treason. "You did that all by yourself?" Her sharp chin points at the grave.

I nod. In the early-morning hours, while the city was asleep and the militia were too drunk to patrol the streets, I dragged my mother's body to the cemetery. Our summer nights, White Nights, never get dark. The twilight never comes because the sun doesn't descend below the horizon. My mama loved this time of the year, when you can barely distinguish dusk from dawn.

"I don't understand. No help at all?" Aka narrows her eyes. "Why didn't you ask—"

I shake my head. "I haven't told him. I'm not going to. Don't ask."

Aka and I share almost everything, but I haven't told her what happened between my mother and . . . and Kaganov, two weeks ago. I blink hard, trying to erase the memories.

Aka slowly shakes her head, and a dim shadow catches her familiar features: the sharp cheekbones, the pointy chin, and the gentle slope of her nose. It's not just our appearance that makes us look like sisters. There's something about the way we move, the way we laugh that tricks people into thinking we're related. "Don't worry about Yelena. She's how old? A hundred? She doesn't stand a chance against you." Aka snickers. "Anyway, she won't report you to the regional bureau. It would be cruel."

My throat tightens at her words. Cruelty is an everyday occurrence in the city.

"Look what I've got." Aka rustles in the pockets of her dress and holds up a rectangular piece of bread. "What do you think about that?"

I gasp.

The piece is thicker than our 125-gram allotted slice distributed through stores. So much thicker I might as well be dreaming. I take it into my hand and hold the crust to my nose, inhaling the scent of sawdust and mildew. Despite the smell, my mouth floods with saliva.

"Where did you get this?" She must've stolen it from someone. Aka's known for lifting small things. Along with showing me how to flirt with boys, she taught me how to steal. "A redistribution of wealth as Comrade Stalin commanded," Aka said when she lifted a small silver brooch off one of the teachers in the seventh grade. A smile tickles my lips. "Did you steal it?"

"You give me too much credit. I wouldn't know where to steal so much bread. And I don't go around attacking people for ration cards or food." She jokes about it because the alternative is too realistic. It lies on the ground not far away from us.

I consider rolling my eyes at her, but I don't have the energy. "Where's this from then?"

Her expression darkens. "This is why I was looking for you. Another girl I met. She looks so well-fed, it's disgusting. Last night I went to see her and to ask, point-blank, where she gets the food. Guess what she was doing when I knocked at her door? She was slicing a loaf of bread. Can you believe it?" Aka swallows hard, her pale throat moving up and down. "A whole loaf!"

"What?" It's impossible. No one has access to so much food . . . Except the NKVD, the People's Commissariat for Internal Affairs, and pilfering from the secret police is punishable by immediate execution. A chill slides down my spine, and I grab Aka's hand. It's just skin and bones, and yet it feels strong. "What has she done?"

"Are you going to eat it or what? Someone might come along." Aka nods at the bread in my hand.

I break the bread into two perfect halves and give one to Aka.

"Oh, no, I had my share. It's all yours," my best friend says quickly. She turns to face me and watches me shove pieces of bread into my mouth. "Don't choke." Aka giggles. "All right, listen. I asked the girl where she got the bread. She told me there's this house, a mansion really, not far from the Haymarket. Militia and NKVD officers who are stationed there have plenty of food, and they allow girls

15

to come and . . . and entertain them. They pay with food, actual food," Aka says quietly.

Entertain? The word feels wrong, and I try not to think about it, but a cold rock forms in my heart and settles there. "What do you mean *entertain them*?"

"You know what I mean, Liza. Don't make me say it." Her words are harsh, and they burn like a slap across my face.

"Singing and waltzing?" I ask, irritated.

Aka doesn't reply.

"And this is how she got this bread?" I push, and my voice breaks. Should I eat it? Does it matter where it comes from? I've heard about that place before. The Haymarket is full of rumors.

"Yes." She turns her face away from me and looks at my mother's grave.

"It's not right," I say.

"What we do in the market isn't right, Liza. We take away people's money and food. From people like us. Hungry people."

"What about the girl's family? What would they say if they knew about her offering herself up for a piece of bread?"

"She's doing it for them." Aka's blue eyes flash. "Besides, they're too weak to have an opinion."

I swallow, desperate to change the subject. "How are things at home?" I ask.

"Grandpa barely moves now. But he still shaves every single day." Aka chuckles darkly. "Imagine that! It breaks me to watch him shuffle to the window and scrape the rusty razor down his dry skin. Then he stumbles back to bed. But this morning, he asked me to do it. He couldn't get up. And Mama . . . Mama spends her days standing in the queues, trying to get food. Most days she comes back with nothing. Even if we make it through the summer, I don't know how we'll survive another winter." Aka turns her head away.

My lips tremble, and I pull her into an embrace. "I have Mama's ration card. I'll share it with you."

Aka shakes her head, and her lips curve into a smile, but they quiver slightly. "It doesn't matter if you have ration cards. It doesn't even matter if we have money. There's no food."

Like Mama, most of us were naive in the beginning of the war. When the Germans decided Leningrad was not worthy of the direct attack, we rejoiced. The Nazis were not going to waste their precious ammunition and soldiers on us. We believed it wouldn't be too bad. But then the Fascists surrounded the city, cut the food supply, and trapped us.

"Maybe we can hunt rats. I've heard of people who set snares underground. In the tunnels. Maybe with enough salt, rats will taste all right."

Aka looks at me as if I'm speaking a foreign language. "Liza, there are no rats left in the city. And the tunnels are dangerous. You know this. Cannibals live there."

I pull myself upright. When there's nothing to eat, people turn to the unthinkable. I should know this. I saw what this war had done to Kaganov.

"Aka, I saw a bird when I was digging the hole. Maybe we can go hunt down that bird."

"You sound crazy." Aka puts her head on my shoulder, and the muscles in my body relax. I tuck a stray dark tendril of hair behind her ear. A vein on the side of her neck throbs, a pale blue lifeline on a perfect sheet of marble.

We sit and think about life and survival.

The man on the ground stirs and moans, breaking the silence.

"We'd better go." Aka jumps to her feet, grabs my hand, and pulls me up.

I grab the shovel, and we escape as fast as our weak legs can manage.

2

THE AIR IS SO QUIET I HEAR THE BRANCHES
move. Our breathing is louder than a breeze. It's not just us.
The city itself has turned into a silent ghost.

"Aka, come home with me." I pause by the cemetery gates.
The shovel in my hands pulls on my shoulders. "I don't want
to be alone. Not today." I count the beats of my pounding
heart and try not to think about the apartment, the emptiness that's waiting for me there. What will never be there
again. I know now what the war does. It takes away everyone we love, and it doesn't offer us a replacement.

She reaches out and moves a strand of loose hair away
from my eyes. "But you're not alone, Liza," Aka says. "You
know that—"

I don't let her finish. I put my hand up and shake my head
so violently I'm surprised my neck doesn't snap.

"Don't say anything. I don't want to be in the room alone.
Without Mama. There is so much of her left. Her scent.

Her dresses. Her perfume on the piano." My voice breaks. "Just come with me, all right?" I force my trembling lips to stretch into a smile and add, "Please?"

Aka shuffles her feet and nods. "I can stay for a little bit. But I promised my grandfather I wouldn't be long. Look what he gave me." Her hand goes to a thin silver chain I hadn't noticed before. A small crucifix dangles between her fingers. "Grandpa called it the protection cross. See, he carved an *A* into the center on the back. For better protection, he said."

I cock my head toward this unexpected piece of jewelry. "I didn't know your grandfather is religious."

"He isn't. This crucifix is his father's. Leftover from the czarist times. He gave it to me this morning." Aka gently drops the chain inside her collar.

"Wait. Let me see. What is this?" My fingers fly to her neck and I pull away the lapel of her dress. My breath hitches when my fingers graze against the fabric. "Is this silk?" I inspect a purple silk undershirt. "Looks rich."

A small smile plays on Aka's lips when she steps back and readjusts her dress. "Found it in the market. Slipped off a stall, it seems."

We start walking again, arms around each other, steps matching steps. Neither one of us says a word.

A few long Leningrad blocks later, I unlock the front door and we stumble inside. Our *kommunalka* is silent. The communal apartment greets us with a murky light and random dust motes floating in the sun. Three families, including ours, once shared three rooms, a kitchen, and a bathroom. Now, instead of eight people, only three of us are left— Yelena, Kaganov, and me.

In a *kommunalka*, silence can be deceiving. Even at night, it doesn't mean everyone's asleep. Someone's always listening. Someone's always watching and reporting to the NKVD. People used to watch one another before the war. Half were busy trying to figure out who'd read forbidden books, who'd spread antipatriotic gossip, who'd socialized with the wrong people. The rest of us were trying to decide who reported their neighbors to the secret police.

Now we watch one another for different reasons. Our life is all about food. We want to know who's eating what and where they're getting it.

Down the hallway, the low clank of a cup makes both our stomachs grumble at the same time. This constant grumbling never ends. Understandably so. We're always hungry.

Aka nods toward the sound and we creep down the hallway.

In the kitchen, my elderly housemate, Yelena, sits at the table by the window. Her skinny body is tightly wrapped in a thick brown shawl. A black scarf hides her snow-white hair, and her jaw moves slowly as if she's chewing on something rubbery. A crow busy with her breakfast. Her beady eyes focus on something only she can see.

A small steel cup is squeezed tightly between her scrawny fingers. Aka and I freeze in the doorway. There's a cube of white sugar on a saucer in front of the old woman. She takes a sip from her mug and then picks up the sugar and sucks it. My jaw goes slack, and I blink rapidly. It's impossible to get sugar. Not even in the Haymarket, where almost anything can be found if one looks close enough. People would kill for it. Aka gasps, and her eyes turn into the icy-blue slits I know way too well. Like me, she's wondering what Yelena has done to get sugar.

Yelena takes the half-eaten piece out of her mouth and gently places it back on the saucer. I step closer to Aka and squeeze her hand. We gape at the rounded, melted corners of the sugar cube.

The scent of strong black tea floats in the air.

"Good morning," Aka croaks, and swallows. There's a hint of anger and longing in her voice.

"Yelena Stepanovna, I brought your shovel back," I say. "It's in the hallway by the door."

Yelena inspects us with a steady gaze. "All is well, then?"

It's an odd question, and I don't know what to say. Mama is dead and nothing is well. I nod, drop Aka's hand, and smooth the sides of my dress.

"Did you find any roots?" Yelena cocks her head like a bird, appraising the object of her curiosity.

I shake my head. "No such luck."

"That's what I thought." She rolls the words on her tongue. "I haven't seen your mother for a while. Is she all right?" An all-knowing look in the old, hooded eyes. Is she baiting me?

Chills crawl down my neck. "Mama's quite all right. She works nights at the hospital now and is sleeping there during the day. They need her there."

Mama used to stay overnight in the infirmary. Last winter, when death became a mass event, the Communist Party Committee issued an order to convert the old Hotel Astoria into a hospital. They even established a morgue in the basement where dead bodies found in the streets were taken. My mother was a classically trained pianist. Music was her life. That's why we all were surprised when she quit playing and volunteered to work at the hospital. "They need help. And we need food," she said. The hospital was providing double rations of bread to their medical personnel. The first time Mama brought the hospital bread home, she handed me one half of her ration. "Save it, Liza. Always remember to save some for later."

That was the kind of person Mama was—always taking care of me.

"She says it's safer that way," I say to Yelena. "She doesn't like walking the streets at night . . . and then, there's curfew, too." The words burst out of me in a rush as I shift from one foot to another. My eyes roam around the kitchen, trying to find an object to focus on. Our big, empty kitchen gets tighter, more claustrophobic as I speak. But there's no reason for Yelena to doubt what I'm saying. No one's allowed to walk in the streets after curfew. I wipe my palms on the sides of my dress. I must get out of here and into my room before Yelena asks more questions.

"You want *kipyatok*?" I offer Aka boiled water. "I have no tea."

Before Aka gets a chance to reply, I move to the big white cabinet stretched along the wall above the *burzhuika*, our small woodstove with its makeshift chimney vented out the window. A piece of wrinkled yellow paper is glued to each section of the cabinet, fat numbers in black ink indicating ownership. Not that we need to know which section belongs to whom now that there are only so many of us left in the apartment.

I scan the shelves, locating Mama's kettle, feeling Yelena's eyes drill into the back of my head. I fill the kettle from one of the pots that contain water from the Neva River. To replenish our water supply, Kaganov and I lugged buckets of water a few days ago. Even though spring and summer gave us hope, some things haven't improved. Plumbing is not fully functional, but there's a limited supply of electricity. *Pravda* is printed again, and the post office delivers mail. The other day, Aka and I took a short ride on one of our streetcars. It felt almost normal. I try not to think how long it will all last and what will happen to us if the Germans advance again.

"People get sick in Astoria," Yelena says with a heavy sigh. "A lot of people are dying in there. If it's not hunger, it's pneumonia or typhus. I hope your mother's safe."

Slowly, I set the kettle down on the *burzhuika* and pick up a few sticks of kindling we keep by the stove to bring the embers to life. Was that a hint? We used to talk about death all the time. But that was last year, in the beginning of the war. Now we don't. We move through our days like tired flies, about to expire. Death is always by our side, watchful and ready to collect. We pretend it's normal. It makes it easier to ignore it. If Yelena's bringing death up now, she must suspect my mama is gone and she wants her ration cards.

"Where did you get tea and sugar, Yelena Stepanovna?" Aka's voice fills the silence. "Such a rare thing."

I turn around and inspect Aka's hollow face with the sunken cheeks. Her dress hangs on her skinny frame, skimming over her protruding hip bones. She winks at me.

"In the Haymarket. You never know what you'll find there. I traded a few possessions in exchange for this." Yelena points with her crooked finger at her mug and sugar.

"What did you trade?" I ask. I have some money. I also have a silver candleholder I lifted the other day off a man who had it ineptly stuffed in the pocket of his jacket. I bet he was shocked to discover half a brick tucked in its place. He should've protected his belongings better. Silver's too valuable to be neglected like that.

The first time I brought a stolen wallet home, my mama was horrified. "We're not criminals," she said, and took the wallet away from me. I told Aka how ashamed I was. Mama didn't talk about it for a long time. Months later, I found out she kept the wallet. When we sold all our valuables and still didn't have enough money to buy food, Mama pulled out the wallet and gave me a few bills. "See what else you can find in the Haymarket." She gave me a pointed look.

I understood it then. To survive, we must shift our moral compass. Just a bit. Just enough to get us through the siege.

The candleholder and a few silver teaspoons are hidden under the floorboards in my room. I wonder what I could get for them. Saliva floods my mouth at the memories of strong, bitter black tea with a hint of cinnamon and sugar. A roll of bread. A couple of eggs if I'm lucky. Maybe a potato.

Yelena looks up from her cup, and for a moment, her deep-set eyes transfix on my face. "Three porcelain cups and two hundred rubles for a piece of a pancake made from lard and leather. I think it was boiled leather. This piece of sugar cost me a bottle of vodka," she says. "Whatever you take there, make sure to barter. Hard. Or you'll get ripped off."

It's nice of Yelena to say that. Maybe she isn't as bad as I think. And she's right about one thing—bargaining is an essential tool. Even though I'm skinny and weak, I can handle myself. The man in the cemetery was an exception. He took me by surprise.

Yelena wipes her lips with a corner of her shawl. "The market's a dangerous place for a young girl like you. Ask your mother's permission first."

My chin starts to tremble at the realization that my mother won't tell me what to do ever again. I'm on my own now. I bite down on my lower lip, and the metallic taste of blood brings me back. Then I gather my tattered composure and force a smile. "Mama will go with me when she has a day off."

The old woman takes a long slurp from her cup, slowly sucks on her sugar cube, and doesn't say anything.

She knows I'm lying.

"Good morning, ladies." A deep voice interrupts us from the entryway. Piotr Kaganov leans against the frame, smiling. Despite his willowy stature, his broad shoulders block the door. "A lot of ruckus so early in the day." His eyes glint like he knows something we don't. His gaze latches on to the tea and the deformed sugar cube on Yelena's saucer. "Ah, morning tea with sugar. How unexpected." His sharp face darkens. "Especially in times like this."

Inky shadows burrow into the corners of our kitchen. I grab Aka's hand, and she shoots me a startled look. Then she turns to Kaganov. "Good morning, Piotr Andreyevich."

The air gathers around me like a sticky cloud. If I could back out of the kitchen, jump out of a window, anything to get away from Kaganov, I would. But all I do is stand and stare.

"Good morning to you, too, Aka. How is your family?"

"Like everyone else's, I guess," Aka replies with a heavy sigh.

Kaganov's usually stern face softens. "Everyone's struggling. I'm sorry to hear it."

"Well, Grandpa barely moves now. He manages to shave every single day, though. Mama's weak yet still goes to stores. But our neighbors on our floor are all dead. Only a few remain in the building."

"You didn't tell me about that." My voice shakes.

Aka's gaze settles on my face. There's so much sadness in her eyes it hollows out my chest. "Everyone loses someone almost daily."

My heart swells with so much love for my friend. I want to pull her into myself and promise we'll survive this war together. But I don't move.

Kaganov's attention switches to me. "You all right, Liza?" A wrinkle as deep as my mama's grave forms in his forehead. "You don't look well." He steps to me and presses his inner wrist to my temple. "You're burning up. How long have you had this fever?" He leans in closer to me as his voice deepens. He reaches out, but I step back, forcing my body not to flinch. My hands clench into fists, and I school my face. I've been feeling hot and cold all morning, wondering if I contracted Mama's sickness. Now that he mentions it, I feel as if I'm slowly roasting in the stove.

"I am fine," I croak.

"Your mother used to make a special tea to reduce fever. You have her *travka*?"

Mama's herbs. Memories slice into my mind. My thoughts are too frenzied under his unblinking eyes; I can't allow myself a single unguarded moment.

Before I get a chance to reply, Yelena cuts in. "She probably traded her herbs for food a long time ago, Piotr." She huffs. "Liza's mother is working day and night at the hospital. What are you doing to help the country fight the Germans?"

Before I say a word, Aka says, "Liza, go lie down, and I'll bring us some boiled water. Unless your neighbor will spare some tea for a sick girl?" Her hands planted on her bony hips, she stares down at Yelena.

The old woman pushes herself from the table with her scrawny hands and gets up. She turns to me. "Go, Liza.

Tell your mother I'm thinking of her. And thank her for me for her service to the Motherland. She's a true *proletariat*, unlike some of us." Her words are pointed and firm and directed at Kaganov. "You rest. I'll help Aka make some tea. I don't have much left, but I'll give you what I have."

I struggle to breathe, totally stunned by Yelena's kindness. I didn't think she even liked me. She certainly never missed a chance to point out a spot I overlooked when cleaning, over-flowing soup that spilled into the stove, dirty tracks in the hallway from my shoes. I guess the war has changed us all.

"Well, I need to go," Kaganov says, ignoring Yelena's jab. "I've heard fresh bread will be distributed on the Volodarsky Prospect. I'll bring us some." Kaganov looks my way, one dark brow raised as if he's expecting me to thank him.

My stomach growls at the thought of bread, and I press my hands against it. Too late. Everyone heard it. Kaganov's shoulders droop, and Yelena shakes her head. There is so much hunger inside me. It's all-consuming. I doubt there's any room left for bones or muscles in my body.

Kaganov waits for my reaction as seconds tick past.

"I don't want anything from you," I finally say.

Aka gasps.

"I'll get you tea, girls." Yelena walks out of the kitchen without looking at us.

The silence lingers longer and heavier than is appropriate.

With time, you'll forget and forgive. My mother's words buzz like annoying bugs in the air.

Now you want me to forgive? Not likely, Mama. Time won't make anything easier. Memories don't erode with time, they become sharper, take form, and turn into a living being. You suffocate under its weight, and forgiveness becomes impossible.

I watch Aka take the kettle off the *burzhuika*, and go back to my room.

There, I drop down on my bed like a log. I close my eyes. The fever raging through my body consumes the last of the strength I had. Time expands and the world blurs at the edges. Curling into a tight ball would be nice, but I'm too tired to move. My breath is heavy, hoarse like my mama's in her last days. Is that what's happening to me? Her sickness? My thoughts slow down. Maybe I'm just worn out. A few seconds of rest is all I need.

———

The smell of strong black tea floats in the air, wraps around me, and forces me to get up. A heavy tray is placed by my bed. Where did it come from? I pick it up and carry it to the table in the middle of the room. Its sharp handles dig into my skin. Aka sits at our dinner table, fork in hand, waiting for me expectantly. A freshly roasted whole chicken surrounded by baked apples serves as a centerpiece. I'm not sure I want to know where this came from or what Aka did to get it.

Suddenly my mother appears in the doorframe. "It's time to remember the living and honor the dead," she says, sitting down across from Aka.

I wake up with tears running down my face and the taste of roasted chicken in my mouth, its perfectly crisp skin flavored with salt, pepper, and sage. Drops of grease slide down my chin, and I'm about to wipe them off when my mind flickers to the surface, and the taste of rot and ashes returns.

I dream of food every night—feasts in the Throne Room of the Grand Palace at Peterhof, now occupied by the Fascists, where we went on a field trip two years ago with my class, and where a boy named Luka in the grade ahead smiled at me for the first time. I dream of the wide tables covered with heavy white linen. Striking chandeliers hanging high beneath the painted ceiling framed by gold molding. Tall windows looking out into the formal gardens laid out by Russian czars and tended by the serfs. And piles and piles of food. Roasted lamb and potatoes; *blini*, my favorite pancakes, filled with cream cheese and raspberry jam; platters of bread and apple pie.

The apple pie is a constant presence. Before the war, my mother used to bake a scrumptious pie in a deep ceramic dish. She used *Antonovka* apples because they were sour and gave such a nice contrast to the sweet dough.

For a few seconds, I let myself think the war never happened and Mama is alive and well. The memory chews on my empty stomach. Slowly, I turn my head to the side. It doesn't get dark during the White Nights, and there is already enough sunlight in the room. My mama's empty sofa bed is by the wall. It's bare, stripped of the sheets. Her thin blanket is folded neatly, the white pillow tucked away in the corner.

I must've slept through the night. I prop myself on one

elbow, my arm shaking. The fever has broken, but I'm weak and exhausted and utterly alone in our family room. I smell like dirt and death. I need a bath.

But I would have to heat the water in the bucket in the kitchen, then drag it back to the room. It would take forever. Just thinking about the process makes me tired, and I stay in bed a little longer. The tension that's building inside me tells me I need to get up and try to find some food.

I roll out of bed, pull an old cotton shirt over my skirt, fold the ration cards back into the socks, and stick my feet into my mother's boots. I smooth my unruly brown curls down with a brush.

And then my mind clears. Aka. Where is she?

I remember a thick darkness in my dream. A creak in the floorboards and someone leaning over me, a gentle hand checking my burning forehead. And later, her fragile shape at the threshold, closing the door behind her as she stepped outside.

My mother's kettle stands on the chair by the bed. A white piece of paper is tucked under a cup with cold tea.

Sorry not to wake you. You're burning up, and I can't wait any longer. Going to get us food. Aka.

There's no food in the city, and the Haymarket isn't even open yet. Aka's tone in the note is too confident, though, as if she knows exactly where she's going.

A twinge of dark panic races through me.

3

AKA'S MOTHER OPENS THE DOOR. HER FACE
is hollowed. Her stare is blank. As if she doesn't recognize
who I am.

"Good morning, Olga Ivanovna. Is Aka home?" I lean on
the doorframe. Even though the fever's gone, my legs are
shaky from the climb up the stairs. Stale air seeps from the
apartment into the hallway. The smell of something foul
lingers around us. Something old and desperate and dead.

Aka's mother's gaze slides past me, eyes skipping around,
as if trying to understand where my words are coming from.
"Aka? *Dochka?*" Her voice is weak, almost a whisper. A
concern scurries across her face. "I thought she was with
you, Liza. Aka hasn't been home since yesterday." She scru-
tinizes my face. "Isn't she with you?"

Here comes the part I know I'll regret later. I don't want
to do it, but I must lie, because Aka should've been home
by now.

Did she go to the Mansion? If so, something must have happened that kept her from returning. What was it Kaganov said yesterday? A bread delivery on Volodarsky?

"Aka was with me. She must have stayed the night, but I fell asleep. I think she went to check the stores. We've heard bread would be delivered today. In a corner bakery, on Volodarsky. I just thought she'd be back by now. Perhaps the lines are long." My voice trails away as I catch a glimpse of Aka's grandfather stumbling into the hallway.

"Aka, is that you?" The old man's voice is muffled, feeble. He supports himself with both arms, pushing against the wall, his bony shoulders threatening to collapse under his weight. He squints at me, and his arms shake uncontrollably. "Aka," he calls out to me. "Where have you been? You missed our evening tea." He chuckles and rubs his jaw.

He doesn't recognize me. He believes I am Aka. The hunger has affected all our minds. It has changed the way we think. The way we process information. I faced it myself this winter. A fog descended, slowing down my thoughts and obscuring the world around me. Mama said it was caused by the lack of energy to feed our brains. Our minds are delicate and fade away fast if not sustained. The hungrier I am, the thicker the fog.

Olga Ivanovna gives me a surprisingly clear stare. "Tell Aka when you see her to come home. She shouldn't be wasting her time looking for bread. There is no bread." She shakes her head. "We need her home." Her voice cracks. Before I can say anything, Olga Ivanovna shuts the door in my face.

I turn toward the wall on the other side of the hallway. The muted green wallpaper is pulled up. The plaster has splintered and chipped. Underneath the cracks, the dirty dark flesh of the building is peering back at me.

Why was Olga Ivanovna so curt? Might she know if Aka has gone to the Mansion? No, it doesn't make sense. Aka wouldn't say anything to her mother. But she wouldn't make them worry like this, either.

What happened to her?

The thoughts nearly break me. I push them away. I can't think about Aka's absence. Or the deep concern in Olga Ivanovna's eyes. The best I can hope for is Aka's timely return from the Mansion. And that she's bringing some food for her family. She'll be fine. She can handle herself. In the meantime, I must concentrate on the problems I can do something about. Like going to the market and getting some food.

Above me, the clouds shift and let warm rays of sunshine through. My stomach twists and turns with emptiness as I make my way through the decimated streets of the city, walking around bomb craters and piles of garbage and rubble no one cares to move out of the way. Leningrad's tall buildings loom over me, their walls a washed-out, murky gray against the pale blue of the sky. Maybe I should go down Volodarsky Prospect and check the bakery by the Arts Square. Just in case there's bread. And maybe Aka is there, too.

But I'm not sure my weak legs can carry me that far.

Resting, I pause in front of one of the gigantic posters

beckoning to defend the city of Lenin with all our might and proclaiming that the Fascists will be beaten. On the poster, two Red Army soldiers, Defenders of the People, are holding machine guns and our red flag. The men's faces are stern; their chins are strong. They're fierce in their undying determination to destroy the enemy and defend the Motherland.

Two young girls are coming toward me. Their bony hands are wrapped around each other for support. Their skin is sallow and sagging, and when one of them speaks, I see there's not a tooth left in her mouth. But their soft whispers and small smiles remind me of Aka and myself.

For a moment, my eyes sting with the threat of tears, and I push down a lump in my throat. I should've insisted on sharing my ration cards. Aka never would've considered going to that awful place. I gasp for air as my throat closes in a spasm. I've failed my friend.

I'll find something to eat—I'll steal if I have to—and then I'll go home and see if Aka has returned. We'll share the food, and I'll make sure she never has to go back to that place where human life equates to a piece of flesh—if that's where she's gone.

———

An hour later, I finally get to the Haymarket, a desperate place for starving people located in Sennaya Square in the center of Leningrad. One side of the square is a cluster of now-empty officers barracks built in the nineteenth century to accommodate the army. The opposite side opens into Sadovaya Street, where a maze of streets and alleys runs between St. Isaac's Square and the back of the market.

I trail between stalls, tattered tents, and wooden kiosks that somehow survived the winter, pausing to appraise the offerings. Watchful eyes of the sellers track my every move. Their gaunt faces tense in anticipation when I slow down to inspect the scattered goods on dirty rags spread out on the ground. There are stacks of worn leather shoes, long wool coats with patches, some with bloody spots and burn holes from the previous owners, killed by shrapnel from Nazi bombs, bullets from militia, or NKVD weapons. I pass by handmade scarves and bins filled with children's clothes. A stall with rifles and shotguns scattered on the tabletop. Bullets of different sizes are neatly packed in boxes. Only the military can carry guns. And, of course, the militia and the ever-watchful secret police. This trade is prohibited in the city. But no one cares as long as law enforcement is not in sight. I pause by the gun stall. Maybe I should buy one for myself. Considering what happened in the cemetery the other day, I might need it.

I can't eat bullets.

I move on.

A soft breeze flutters through the rows and flaps pieces of paper on the tables. The background hum of people arguing, asking for a better price or berating greedy sellers, is a soothing noise.

I don't make eye contact with the sellers. I don't make eye contact with anyone. The hunger in my eyes makes me vulnerable. Exposed. Slowly, I trek between stalls. The smell of leather, spoiled cabbage, and boiled glue lingers in the air.

A man appears in front of me. His teeth are rotten, and his putrid breath brings a wave of nausea. He works a stand full of jars with yellow jelly. "Look at this, girl. Hundred rubles for a jar of pure *zhir*," he announces enthusiastically, and thrusts a disgusting jarful of fat in my face. I turn away. I don't want to know what he used to produce this.

The sour, salty tang of fish pulls me forward. I haven't had fish soup in months. Not since Aka and I shared a bowl of fish soup and a potato salad in a café on Nevsky Avenue at the beginning of last summer. The salad had peas and carrots as well as potatoes. All freshly cut and mixed with smoked ham and pickles and eggs. We sat outside in the sunshine and gossiped about Luka and his impossibly blue eyes. The night before, he had shown up at Aka's birthday party with one of his older friends. Aka was so giddy when she dragged the other boy into the kitchen and left me standing alone, by the wall, helplessly gazing at Luka. For a brief moment, I dared to dream he was going to ask me out. Instead, moments later, his friend walked out of the kitchen, reached for me, and asked me to dance. I batted him away, as if he were an annoying fly. I remember Aka wiping the salad off her lips with the back of her hand and giggling while I told her what happened.

A few months later, Luka died in the bombing. It was a

different life before then. Before the Fascists, bombings, and deaths. Before the relentless, feral hunger occupied the city and our bodies.

"What fish is this?" I ask the old woman behind the counter. She's wearing a long green dress and a headscarf, the pale skin of her face tightly wrapped around her protruding skull bones.

"It's fish," the woman croaks, her glittery eyes trying to assess what a skinny girl like me could offer for a smelly fish.

I gape at the river goods, glistening in the sun. "It doesn't look fresh," I say, and wrinkle my nose.

"If you're not interested, move aside." The witch waves into the distance, beckoning me to move on. "Others might want it."

I check over my shoulder, hoping someone else will come to the stall. No one is in my immediate proximity, but there is a man standing across the path by another table. He's turned away from us, leaning over the stand in front of him as if something on the counter is of a great interest. I can't see what it is he's studying, and I turn back to the woman. Maybe if I wait a little longer, he'll come over to us. For what I'm about to do, I need an audience.

I point at the biggest and smelliest. "How much for this one?" The woman has six fish spread across the stand on a piece of old, yellowed newspaper.

"Three hundred."

That's extortion.

Before the war I could've bought a whole stall of fish for fifty rubles. Now a 125-gram piece of bread costs a hundred rubles. The woman and I glower at each other. She probably guesses I have little bargaining power. But she isn't sure, because she shuffles her matchstick-skinny legs and frowns.

"Too much." I turn away from her. Where are people when you need them? The man is arguing about something with the other seller. But I see a woman with a small boy making their way toward us. I decide to linger a little longer.

"Two hundred. Or two pieces of bread," the fishmonger says.

A gold watch can buy you a crust of bread. Two hundred rubles can buy you a rotten fish.

Lips pressed together, I pause. I can almost smell my future dinner—a fish soup—and the aroma is amazing. Hot, with the right amount of salt and a tiny bit of the sorrel Yelena grows in pots in her room. I saw Kaganov hauling cabbage from somewhere two days ago. That cabbage can be a nice complement to the fish. But the last thing I'm going to do is ask him to share. If anything, I can steal it later tonight. I have no qualms about stealing from *him*. Aka and I will have a feast.

I take a step to the side as if readying myself to leave. The woman watches me closely.

The man from the other stall trails my movements, but he doesn't come over. He looks familiar, but I cannot place him. Did I see him in one of the food lines? In the bomb shelter? The haze in my mind is too thick. All I can think about is the fish soup. The man's hair is dark. His frame is tall and skinny. He says something to the man behind the stall and runs his fingers over a small jar. The seller mumbles a few words I can't hear. The man snaps his head, as if he's angry, and a vague memory floats through my mind. Something about the way the man moves makes the hair stand up on my arms. The sounds of the Haymarket vanish, as if the humming of voices, the occasional rustle of paper, the never-ending buzzing of flies suddenly have been smothered by the heavy cloud in my head. Something's wrong, but I can't figure it out. Maybe later, when I have some fish in my pocket, I'll think about the man again.

The woman with the boy stops by the fish stall. They look like two walking skeletons with their thinning, greasy hair and hollowed-out eyes. "How much?" the woman asks, and sways, her legs barely supporting her.

Finally, an audience. I turn around and refocus on the scene in front of me.

"Two hundred rubles. Or two pieces of bread."

"Your fish is rotten, almost inedible," I say in a loud and clear voice. "The smell alone can kill." I wink at the boy and point at the smallest fish, my fingers lingering over the oval shape with its small gray lips and unseeing eyes.

"Get the hell away from me," the fish hag hisses.

I take in a deep breath through my nostrils and raise my voice higher. "Why are you selling rotten fish to people?

Don't you know it's poison? The Fascists are killing us. Are you trying to make things easier for them?" I pause and swat flies away from my face. "Are you a Nazi collaborator?"

It might be too much, and I feel almost bad for using such harsh words. But I need a distraction, and it was the only thing that came to my mind.

I look at the walking skeletons next to me. The boy's poking every fish on the newspaper with his scrawny finger. "Petya, don't touch it," his mother says. She still looks unconvinced by my charade, but her eyes dart around the fish as her brain undoubtedly assesses my words. The inky black bags under her eyes get darker when she finally nods. "It does smell bad."

"And she wants two hundred rubles for it. She really shouldn't be selling it," I say. "The fish is old. Look at all the flies. They know it's garbage. Should we call for authorities?"

"How dare you say I'm a collaborator. I lost my son at the front." The fish seller's voice is piercing now, deafening. People start to gather around the stall, watching us.

"What is that smell?" someone asks.

Murmurs louden as a small crowd grows around us.

"Fish shouldn't stink like this," another voice adds.

The seller pales and her lips form a scowl as her eyes dart around the group of people behind me.

This is all I need. I shrug, turn away from the stall, and slide the closest fish into my pocket.

Like a phantom, I slip into the small gathering of onlookers. The seller is explaining something about the fish and her son and Nazis, her voice trembling as she speaks. She is afraid someone will decide to call the militia and they will confiscate her fish.

I walk away slowly; each step is measured. A pang of guilt floods my veins, but I ignore it. The old hag will be fine. She'll talk her way out of the situation, and by the time it all settles, it will be too late to catch me.

In my pocket, the fish bounces against my hip.

4

A SHARP CHILL SPREADS DOWN MY NECK AS soon as I enter the streets behind the Haymarket. I'm being watched. Did someone see me lift the fish? Mama never liked coming to the market. It attracts too many desperate people. And desperate people do desperate things. Yelena's always going on about crimes committed around this area, too.

My fear intensifies, but I manage to increase my pace. I should've been better prepared for this trip. A kitchen knife tucked inside a boot would've kept me calm. Why didn't I think about it earlier?

I glance back. The man from the market is not far behind me. He lifts his head, scowls at me, and I gasp. I recognize his skinny, feral face, his missing teeth and broken nose.

My attacker from the cemetery.

He glides across the street, and the distance between us diminishes at an alarming speed. The way he moves toward me, with determination and fury, tells me he isn't after my fish. He's after me, and he'll probably kill me. The fish in my pocket is just a nice bonus.

My brain tells me to run, but my weak legs won't obey the command. I half walk, half jog down the empty, narrow streets. Destruction and desolation are everywhere in the back alleys. I pass by scattered, abandoned cars; empty lots; and bombed-out apartment buildings with crumbling walls and gaping, dark holes for windows. I follow the dirt-packed alley that leads me to the backyards of a residential street. There's no one here. Through the holes in the building, I spot the far end of the main avenue.

The man's heavy footsteps echo behind me.

I should've taken Sadovaya Street out of the market or turned to the always crowded St. Isaac's Square. I shouldn't be here, in the backstreets, even though someone in the market once mentioned the Mansion was somewhere around here, and I hoped to find it. I should've known what dangers empty alleys and small backyards hold.

Too late now, and I push forward. My skin feels hot one second and is prickling with icy pins the next.

Another minute or so, and I'll reach one of the main streets with people and safety. He won't attack me there. Here, with no one around, my only hope is a random militia car patrolling the streets. But the militia doesn't patrol backstreets. No one wants to waste precious fuel on stupid people who wander the back alleys.

I leap over a lonely bucket that suddenly appears in my way and almost lose my balance.

"You won't get far," the man barks, his voice terrifyingly close.

Another quick glance over my shoulder. He's gaining on me. Where does his strength come from? He looks thin and weak, and yet he's fast. I'm running now, but Mama's boots are too big, and I skid to the side, losing my balance. I drop to my knees, slamming them hard into the concrete.

A few seconds is all it takes for the man to catch up.

Something hard slams into my back with such force I'm propelled forward, and then I'm on the ground. It takes me a few frantic heartbeats to realize the man shoved me, knocking me down. It takes a bit longer for the pain in my scraped knees to register.

I twist away, scramble to my feet, and turn around to face him. I won't go down without a fight. My breathing is thin, and dark spots are jumping in front of me. If I want to survive this, I must pull myself together.

"Why would a grown man chase a skinny girl down the street?" an oddly familiar male voice asks. "Go after some-one your own size."

A tall blond boy steps out from the shadows of the trees. It takes me a second to place him. My heart flies up into my throat. *Luka.* It can't be, can it? Maybe my fever is back and I'm hallucinating. I'd heard his whole family died. Their building destroyed in a fire. I thought he was dead, too.

The man reels back, and the boy steps in front of me, shoves me behind his back, and faces the man. His right hand is curled into a fist. His left hand is missing a pinkie and ring finger. My breath is loud and shaky. I blink a few times to make sure I'm not seeing something that isn't there.

My attacker doesn't reply, his eyes fused to the boy's right hand. A boy with a fist is by far more dangerous than a weak girl with a half-rotten fish. Without a word, the man slowly turns away from us and hobbles into a side alley. Hunting me down must've taken a lot of strength from his depleted body.

We watch him disappear between the buildings.

"You shouldn't be walking here alone, Liza." Luka smiles at me, ear to ear. "Stupid and dangerous."

My own smile breaks out. Never in my wildest dreams would I have thought Luka Petrov would be saving me from criminals in the streets of Leningrad.

"Why was that man chasing you?" Luka asks, tilting his head.

He looks genuinely concerned. A warm ripple spreads in my chest when I meet his eyes. He was the first boy I ever noticed in school. Luka never looked at me the way I gazed at him. I was always the one desperately trying to catch his eye, and he was the one who slipped between my fingers like water, leaving me sad and uncertain in his wake. Once Aka, worn out by my desperation, had suggested I ask him out. When it came to boys, Aka was a master of alluring smiles and flirtatious words. I was a creature of contemplative stares and delicate sighs. But with Luka, I couldn't muster a coherent sentence. The thought of asking him out made me want to sink into the ground. I was sure he'd laugh at me. Now the boy who used to haunt my dreams is looking at me like he thinks I have something important to say.

"We've met before, this man and I. It didn't go well for him the first time around. I could've taken him down again." The words come out heavy and awkward. I close my mouth, horrified.

Brows raised in a perfect arch, Luka appraises me. He thinks I'm bragging. "You planned to take him down with this?" He nods at the fish on the ground. I must've dropped it when I fell. He picks it up and makes a show out of sniffing it, wrinkling his freckled nose and recoiling from it theatrically, almost dropping it back on the ground. He catches it swiftly and holds it away from his body. "I see. It can be used as a weapon. The smell alone might've knocked the man down." He chuckles at his own joke.

I suppress a smile and extend my hand to Luka. My fingers tingle slightly and my hand shakes. What if he doesn't give the fish back? The siege and the hunger have changed us all. He lost his family. His home. He lost his fingers. What if Luka has changed in some cruel, unimaginable way? Would he consider slashing my throat and disappearing with my fish before my body hits the ground? I didn't know him well before the war. I knew he played the piano. He came to the same parties as Aka and me. He always left early. He never smoked or drank. We never exchanged more than a few polite words. I know nothing about the boy I used to like. Just because he saved me doesn't mean he'll return the fish. Maybe it was his plan all along—save the girl, eat her food.

Luka puts the fish into my hand. "You're bleeding." He points to my knees, and I look down, surprised I forgot about the pain. My knees are scraped raw, and blood trickles down my legs.

"*Chyort!*" I swear. Left hand cradling the fish, I use my right hand to wipe off the blood. Streaks of red decorate my pale legs above the boots.

Luka steps closer, kneels down to my knees, and my breath hitches. A sudden rush of excitement, fleeting and fragile, sways my mind. His blond hair makes me think of dandelions in the spring.

What is wrong with me?

He has never been this close to me before. Not even at Aka's birthday party where he walked around the room not talking much to anyone. He always was a loner, a mysterious boy who wished to join the Leningrad Radio Orchestra. The war damaged his hand and annihilated his dreams. I want to ask how he lost his fingers, but I don't dare for fear of offending him.

He blows on my wounds, and goose bumps spring up where his breath touches my skin.

I jerk away from him as a flush creeps up my neck and makes its way to my face. "What are you doing?"

He looks up, his face relaxed, no tension at all. "My mother used to do this when I was a kid. She said it cools it down and makes the pain go away."

A laugh bubbles up, and I open my mouth to say something witty, but I can't come up with anything. My cheeks are burning now.

He inspects my face with an expression I can't read. "You need to disinfect those scrapes. Do you have any alcohol?"

What an odd question. Alcohol is a precious commodity. Same purchasing power as bread. Sometimes even more, depending on the buyer's state of desperation.

I shake my head.

He waits a beat, contemplates something, and then he whistles.

I jump. "What are you doing?" My words come out as a hiss.

"What?" a voice asks from behind me, and I turn around. A girl has appeared out of a dilapidated building on the corner. She's small and skinny, and she has the same bright blue eyes as Luka. Her blond hair is tied into a messy ponytail, though dirty locks hang loosely around her face. She can't be more than eleven or twelve, but she has lost so much weight, her face looks older. "What is it?" A big rucksack is slung over her shoulder and beats against her sharp hip bone.

"You still have that vodka Galina gave us to trade in the market the other day? She needs to wash her wounds." A nod at my bleeding knees.

I didn't know Luka had a sister. She must've attended a different school, because I'd never seen her in ours.

The girl pulls out a half-empty bottle from her sack and hands it to me. "You don't need much."

I sprinkle the cloudy liquid over my knees. My world shrinks from pain, but I bite down on my lower lip. I won't show them any weakness.

They look down at my burning knees, expectant and curious.

"Do you feel the germs dying an agonizing death?" Luka asks.

I smile despite the fact I'd rather cry. "A very painful death for sure." I return the bottle to the girl. "Thank you."

"We'll escort you home," he says. "Flaunting your food around while walking with bleeding knees isn't safe." He's right. The man might be watching us from the side streets, waiting for me to get away from the strange pair. "Well," he says, an eager smirk on his full lips. "Where are we going?"

The unexpectedness of the situation overwhelms me. The boy who barely knew I existed is offering me help. In the past few minutes, we have exchanged more words than we did during ten years of school. And, of course, I can't come up with a single word to say. Aka will be thoroughly entertained when I tell her how Luka saved me.

We study each other for a few seconds.

"You two should stop staring at each other and move. That man might return and bring his friends with him," the girl says. Her arms are crossed over her chest. "So where are we going?"

"We're going on an adventure, Katya." Luka smiles at me as if he sees the brightest star in the sky.

"It's all right. I can manage on my own," I mumble, but I

already know I'll let him walk me home. I drop the fish back into the pocket of my skirt. "I'm not a damsel in distress."

"You *are* a damsel in distress. I saw what happened. Without Luka, you'd be dead," Katya says. She looks at me sideways and tilts her head. Her blue eyes look silver in the dim light of the alley. "Where do you live?"

"Liza . . ." A pause, as if he's unsure it's my name. I cock an eyebrow because I won't make it easy for him. But the invisible wall between us breaks as he continues. "If I remember correctly, Liza lives six blocks away from here. Her house is not too far from the Arts Square."

He knows my name. He knows where I live.

"Why don't you lead the way then?" I ask.

He waves down the street, and we take off.

"What are you going to do with the fish?" Katya asks. She walks by my side; her stride is long. Her back bones are clearly visible under the yellow summer dress, her shoulder blades as sharp as knives, threatening to cut through the cotton.

"*Ukha*," I say, and hope she doesn't ask to have some.

Luka blows out a long breath of air. "I haven't had fish soup since last summer."

I don't respond to Luka's words, following one of my mother's rules—when you don't want to say too much, take a pause.

Neither Luka nor Katya say anything, but Luka's shoulders sag. My chest tightens, and I bite down on my lower lip. I should be nicer. Kinder. I should invite them to dinner.

Be careful, my mother's voice whispers. *You don't know what they do to survive.*

We walk in silence.

After a few minutes, I steal a glance at Luka. He's about five to eight centimeters taller than me, and broad shouldered. His pale skin doesn't look gray, which means he probably ate recently. He's skinny, but he looks stronger than his sister. His features are sharp, but there is nothing delicate about them. I keep wondering what happened to his hand. Where do they live? Questions I'm not going to ask because I don't want them asking any questions in return.

"You said you've met the man before," Luka says, breaking the quiet. "Do you think he's following you?" His voice is raspy and deep. But it flows unexpectedly, like music.

"What? That man has been following you?" Katya's eyes are round and serious.

At first, I don't say anything. There's a long, awkward pause as we stop walking. Katya turns her head to the side, reminding me of a cat. They obviously won't let it go.

"He attacked me in the cemetery the other day," I say. "Then he followed me from the Haymarket. I didn't notice him until it was too late. It's my own fault for not being careful."

Now that all the excitement of the fight is fading, my hands hang limply to my sides. The fish in my pocket weighs at least a hundred kilograms, even though a few minutes ago it was as light as a dove's feather.

"What were you doing at the cemetery?" Luka asks in a low voice.

My face goes slack, and I push down a sharp lump in my throat. "I buried my mother." The tightness in my chest hasn't loosened since the moment she died. The memory of her last labored breath edges to the corners of my mind, but I ignore it.

I don't say anything else, and Luka doesn't ask for more.

"At least you got to bury her," Katya says. "Our parents died in the bombing in January. Our building collapsed. Luka hurt his hand that night." Her face falls. Neither of them looks at me. Their grief seeps into the air like humidity from the Neva River. It bleeds into my own skin. There is so much death in the city. So much loss.

Where do they live now? On the streets? It would explain their presence in back alleys. They probably sleep in one of the abandoned buildings.

"Your mama . . . was it hunger? Something else?" Katya asks, her voice insistent.

"She contracted pneumonia in the hospital," I say. "She worked there."

"We're sorry," Luka says, and shoots a brief glance at his sister, probably giving her a sign to not ask any more questions.

He pities me because my loss is fresh. He thinks my pain is sharper. For one short moment, we look at each other and everything feels almost serene. The hunger, the war, the city itself recedes, extra air fills my lungs, and it's just Luka and me. I want to hold on to this feeling of peace for as long as possible.

"I'm sorry, too," I say, shattering the moment.

We don't say anything for the rest of the walk.

5

AS WE GET CLOSER TO MY APARTMENT, MY jaw tightens. I can't invite them inside. If Aka has managed to get us some bread, it won't be enough for all of us. We already have to divide it in four—for Aka and me, and then she will take some to her mama and her grandpa. Then we'll make *ukha*, but it's not going to be much, either. We can feed only so many. Aka and I used to cook together before the war. When my mother was touring the country with the Radio Orchestra, Aka helped me make dinners. Yelena always wrinkled her nose at the smell of burnt chicken that wouldn't leave our apartment for days. Before the war, I loved good company and I enjoyed cooking. I was raised around people, loud dinners, and classical music. It's different now. I'm different now. I can't invite Luka and his sister to join us. I don't have enough food or energy for everyone.

Survival is a lonely business, Liza. They'll understand.

Luka catches me staring at him and smiles. "Would you

like to come in?" The words are out before I stop myself. Apparently, my brain doesn't communicate well with my mouth anymore.

He turns to face me, surprised at my invitation. "You sure?"

"Yes. My friend Aka is probably waiting for me inside. Why don't we all spend some time together? It might be fun." Why am I trying to persuade them to come? If Aka is back, she won't like my bringing additional mouths to feed. But we don't have to tell them we have food, do we?

"Aka?" he asks uncertainly.

"Akulina Riabina. Don't you remember her? You came to her birthday party two years ago."

"I don't think I remember her. Someone probably dragged me to her party." He scratches at his chin. "Wait. The flirty girl with a thick braid who used to hang out with you all the time?"

"Yes. That would be Aka." With a small smile, I open the front door to the apartment. "Be warned—I have odd neighbors."

Katya shrugs. "Ours are mostly dead." Her voice breaks on the last word. With a short sigh, she turns her head away from me.

Inside, the door to Kaganov's room is ajar and the window is wide open, letting a warm, sluggish breeze seep into the hallway. His heavy blackout curtains move lazily.

Kaganov himself lingers at the kitchen threshold, appraising me. His pinched face tells me he's annoyed. "I was waiting for you." He notices the pair behind me. "You brought company, Liza. Does that mean you're feeling better?" he asks, stepping forward and extending his hand to Luka. "Piotr Kaganov."

"I'm Luka. This is my sister, Katya." Luka smiles at Kaganov and looks at me. I keep my face even.

"Are you feeling sick?" Katya asks me. "Maybe we should go."

"No, stay, please." My voice is high-pitched. It bounces around us and off the walls. The thought of their leaving me alone with Kaganov is daunting. "I wasn't feeling well last night. I'm much better now."

"What's this?" Kaganov asks, his eyes scan my frame. "Is it fish I smell?"

"Fish from the Haymarket," I say, and pull it out of my pocket. "Should be good for a soup. Is Aka here?" I quickly scan the hallway, peeking over Kaganov's shoulder into the kitchen, but I don't see any signs of her. "She was supposed to come back here and wait for me."

Ignoring my question about Aka, he says, "The fish doesn't smell very good. Are you sure you should eat it?" All the questions. Never-ending efforts to get closer to me. I step away from him. Why can't he just keep to himself?

"Yes, I'm sure," I say as my gut tightens queasily. "What about Aka? Was she here?"

He pauses a moment, then shakes his head. "I haven't seen her since yesterday. I think you were sleeping when she left."

She should be back by now. My throat tight, I swallow so hard I'm certain everyone can hear it. She's at the Mansion; I'm convinced of it. Doing whatever she thinks needs to be done to earn a piece of bread.

Kaganov steps closer. "Liza, can we have a word alone, please?"

I sway lightly. Luka's strong hand steadies me. He doesn't smell of dirty clothes and rot like Kaganov. Instead, he smells like June itself—spicy, warm, and promising. He reminds me of the pine forest, sunshine, and currants I used to pick with Aka. Ignoring Kaganov, I take Luka's hand in mine, entwining our fingers. His skin is warm under my touch. When Luka gives me a confused stare, I say, "Let's go to my room."

Kaganov trails us down the hallway like *domovoi*, a house spirit. He knows he's not welcome in my space. I open the door and let the siblings pass me, then I shake my head at Kaganov. I hope the look in my eyes burns him down. He halts midstep, his shoulders slumped. Relieved, I enter the room and shut the door.

Pages of *Pravda* and a few chipped plates clutter my table. I pull the biggest plate into the center and place the fish on it.

Luka and Katya slowly walk around the room, past my unmade bed, the old brown sofa my mother used as her cot, the chair by the window, my mother's old wardrobe. Luka stops in front of the grand piano, my father's wedding gift to my mother.

"I remember you playing in the same talent concert as I

did. A couple of years ago. You were wearing a long red dress and white shoes. You played Mussorgsky." His hand brushes over the smooth wooden surface and rests on a deep dent in the corner. His fingers inspect it, as if it's something worth studying.

My thoughts begin to wander to places that turn my blood hot and cold at the same time. Luka remembers many things about me. It means he paid attention when I thought he didn't. "I didn't know you heard me play. I listened to you, though." I shut my mouth. I'm rubbing salt into a fresh wound.

"He still plays, you know," Katya says as if reading my mind.

"Where?" I look at Luka, but he turns away from me and starts smoothing his pants with his hands. His shoulders hunch a notch.

"So where is your mysterious friend Aka?" Luka blows a soft breath, bouncing on his heels.

How do I explain in front of Katya? "She . . . she thought she could get us some food." A knot of unease is stuck in my throat. "She went to this place called the Mansion. She should've been back by now."

"The Mansion? Are you sure?" His eyes dart around, not settling on anything in particular.

"I'm sure." I pointedly look at Katya, who is intently listening to our conversation.

"That place—Aka shouldn't have gone there."

Something in his voice makes my heart skip a beat. "You've heard of it? Do you know where it is?"

"People talk."

"You know the address? Can you tell me?"

He shakes his head, points at Katya with a slight nod, and my voice trails off. Of course, we shouldn't be talking about this sort of thing in front of Katya.

He flips the music stand open, and his fingers gently stroke the piano keys. He grabs hold of the only chair in the room, sits down, shuts his eyes, and lets his long, pale fingers fly over the keys. A beautiful, fierce melody shatters the silence. He taps his right foot to keep the beat.

I listen, hypnotized by the sound. Memories dig into my mind and pull me back into the past. Sunday family dinners. Aka's ringing laughter. A low rumble of voices gathered around the piano. And my mother, imperious and withdrawn, in a black velvet dress, her fingers pressing on white and black piano keys.

When Luka stops, no one speaks for a long moment.

"What a beautiful piece." Kaganov's voice floats to us from the door. He obviously ignored my unspoken message. "I've never heard it before. What is it?" The tentative smile on his lips softens his face.

"Maurice Ravel," Katya and Luka say at the same time.

"Ah, Ravel," Kaganov drawls. He looks to me as if he's searching for something that is out of reach. "A nice surprise to hear you play, Luka. Thank you for that." He leaves the room before anyone has a chance to respond.

Katya smiles. "Liza, you're crying."

My fingers fly up to my face and brush over my cheek. It's wet and cold to the touch. How embarrassing.

Never cry in front of strangers.

A hot wave of shame singes my cheeks.

"My talent has this effect on people," Luka says, a wide grin spreading on his face. "Imagine me playing with the Philharmonic. Rivers of tears would flood the building."

I can't help but smile back. "The Radio Orchestra is still around. Some of them are alive. You should rehearse with them. They need musicians. And they pay a little, too."

Luka and Katya study me with a question neither of them asks.

"I know because my mother used to play with them," I explain. "She dreamed of playing in the Philharmonic Hall." My voice shakes, and I turn away from them to hide more tears rolling down my face. When I was ten, I got an awfully painful ear infection. Right on the day when Mama was supposed to perform a solo concerto. It was everything she ever dreamed of—her first concert in front of a sold-out audience. Instead, she stayed with me and let her understudy take the spotlight. I chase away more unwelcome tears. I need a few more breaths inside this memory to see if the emptiness in my heart finally fades away.

"That fish really doesn't smell good," Luka says. He shakes his head, and his left hand presses against his nose.

Katya flips open her rucksack. "We can eat our food." She pulls out a small paper bag. "We have a potato." She puts an oddly shaped spud with jagged edges and dark spots on the table by my rotten fish.

I try to push down the rising feeling of gratitude mixed

with confusion. They saved my life, and now they're offering me their food. I want to sweep Katya into a hug and press my face against her wild hair.

Don't trust anyone. Especially those who offer to help.

"It's all right. Keep your food. My fish isn't rotten. It's carp, a trash fish. Carp never smells good." As soon as I hear myself, shame prickles through my skin. I lied to the woman in the Haymarket when I told her the fish was rotten. The fishmonger most likely didn't know the fish and couldn't defend herself against my accusations. I used the bad smell to my advantage. And now the old woman probably won't be able to sell them for the price she wanted. "I'll be fine. Here." I hand the potato back to Katya.

There's a long pause. A silence so heavy I can feel it forming around us into a cloud.

"I guess we leave then," Luka says. He turns to the door. "Katya, let's go."

6

IN THE EARLY-MORNING HOURS, I WAKE UP
with tears on my face.

Last night, I heard booming shots followed by a familiar
roar of planes in the distance. A burst of gunfire, no more
than ten to fifteen kilometers away, followed by silence. I
guess the Fascist planes were brought down either by the
Baltic Fleet or the Red Army fighters. I'm never sure how far
away our military is. The Germans always seem to be closer.

Murky light seeps through a tiny crack between the blackout curtains, creating odd, twirling shapes on the walls.
Before she got sick, Mama used to pull the curtains open,
complaining how heavy they were. She loved the morning
light. Despite there being plenty of openings in the apartment due to the war and death, my mother decided we should
stay in here. She believed our room was the brightest and the
warmest.

Now I feel entombed inside it. I crane my head and look at her empty bed. Shutting my eyes, I inhale and feel her hand smoothing down my hair. Then I exhale, and she leans over to kiss the top of my head just like she used to do on school days. The room is breathing with me, and I feel a little less trapped.

Yesterday, after the siblings left, Kaganov got an unexpected visitor. A woman came to see him. I stood in the kitchen, cleaning my fish, and watched the unusual commotion. She looked skinny, but not as malnourished as the rest of us. Her face was familiar, but I couldn't remember where I'd seen her. As she glided through the hallway into his room like a spirit, she turned her face away, her steps light and hurried. She obviously didn't want to be recognized.

Later, after she left, Kaganov dawdled in the hall like a scarecrow—thin-lipped and wavering on his feet. His hands were shaking. He couldn't meet my eyes. A visible redness crept up his neck and settled onto his face. I wanted to scream and call him names, but I kept my mouth clamped. I couldn't believe what I had witnessed. As it turns out, he is no better than the men at the Mansion.

I push my thoughts and memories aside and slide out of bed. Arms shaking, I pull on my mama's boots, shove a few bills and ration cards into my socks, and slip into the kitchen. If I can just locate Yelena's tea from the other day, it might keep my head clear until I get to the market.

"I thought you were resting in your room, but here you

are. Doing what exactly?" Kaganov's voice says from the door. His words are sharp, honed by some hidden meaning.

"Yelena said I could have some of her tea," I say, meeting his gaze.

"If it's food you want, I have three slices of bread and two potatoes. I even have two small eggs. Pure luck, I guess; I found them in the market. Let me make you and your mother breakfast." He takes a step into the kitchen.

That's a lot of food. The fish soup didn't turn out so well last night. It tasted as bad as it smelled. I had only three spoonfuls before I threw it away. "Was there bread on Volodarsky yesterday?"

"No. That was just rumors."

"Where did you get all that food, then?"

He shrugs but doesn't look at me. "I traded a few ration cards in the market."

He's obviously lying. He's trying too hard to look relaxed. Eggs don't exist anymore. And there's no bread in the Haymarket. Hasn't been for a while now. The city ran out of grain last winter. Red Army trucks are sometimes able to cross the blockade, but the supplies they bring back are sparse, and the German planes bombed the last grain delivery. No one knows when the Red Army will send us more. Stories of possible deliveries spread every day, but like yesterday, most of them are just that. Stories.

"You traded ration cards? Whose?" I ask.

"The cards. You know. The ones your mother brings from the hospital."

The kitchen seems to shrink as a nagging suspicion drills into my brain. "My mother brought ration cards from the hospital? How did she get them?"

Kaganov's head jerks back, and I realize my mistake. Past tense. I should've been more careful, but it's too late now.

"I assumed . . . you knew," he notes slowly as if he's thinking about something else entirely. "Your mother . . . the sick and the dead . . ." He stops midsentence, his skin gathering into wrinkles around his eyes. It almost looks like he's about to cry. "I really thought you knew."

What did Mama do with all the cards she pilfered? The heaviness of his words weighs me down. Did she share the cards with *him*? I don't want to believe she trusted him more than me. I think of my mother, blood on the handkerchief in her hand, and the words that followed.

You must survive at any cost, Liza. The war will end, but you won't.

"Why don't you ask her to explain," Kaganov says.

That would be impossible, I want to say.

"It doesn't matter," he continues. "What matters is that I've got food for us." He walks up to the stove, pours water from the bucket to fill a pot. The long cupboard that used to hold rows of plates and pots is now empty except for a few chipped pans and a scratched skillet. Anything that could be sold was sold a long time ago. We kept only a bare minimum. "I'll boil us potatoes. Sit with me." It's an order, not an invitation.

Without a word, I run out of the kitchen, out of the apartment, down the stairs, and burst into the streets of the city. I should've known Mama had her own reasons to drop the music and go work in the hospital.

Survival, Liza. I wanted us to survive.

Then why, Mama, why didn't you? You took all that risk of stealing the ration cards and for what? You committed treason. People are shot for lesser crimes, but you went ahead and did it anyway. Did *he* force you to do it? You always told me you wanted what was best for me. And then you left me alone. Unprotected and starving.

My head is dizzy, but I ignore it and force my shaking body to walk.

It's July, but the day is not as warm as a summer day should be. The sky hangs like a dusty curtain, and the air smells of dead things festering. Aka's apartment is a few blocks away. What will she say about her time at the Mansion? Suddenly, the collar of my dress feels tighter, as if it is about to strangle me. How much do I really want to know?

I turn onto a side street. I know I should take the route through St. Isaac's Square instead of the backstreets, but it's twice as long and I don't want to look at all the damage the bombs have brought onto the once beautiful place. The dome of St. Isaac's Cathedral used to be gold and bright. Now it's painted in a dull, awful gray to not attract Nazi aircraft from above. It reminds me of death and war and everything we lost.

I enter Gorokhovaya Street, once lined with majestic old birches. With the trees leafless and blackened or cut down altogether, this place is unrecognizable, too, but it's easier to look at it than the ugly gray of the dome. I stop and lean against the wall of a building. Aka and I used to skip down this street on our way home from school. Now I can barely make it from one end of the block to the other. Hunger has deteriorated my muscles and turned my legs into two soft and rubbery stilts. It has thinned my bones and dulled my hair.

A breeze is whipping a few scraps of paper against the walls across the street. I marvel at how they are suspended in the air for a few seconds before tumbling down to the pavement again.

A harsh squawk sounds above my head, and a pair of black crows abandon their branch in a nearby tree. I blink and watch the two black dots against the pale blue sky. This is not possible. Yet two crows slowly disappear into the distance.

Has my fever returned? The air suddenly turns hot. It smells of burnt wood and ruined buildings, shattered lives. My footsteps echo in the empty side roads, and I walk as fast as my body allows. Taking back alleys is not smart; I might be attacked again, and this time there will be no Luka to save me. I push myself to pick up my pace even more.

A few minutes later, I'm at Aka's front door. It swings open and Aka's mother looks at me with such longing, I step back, ashamed I can't fulfill her expectations.

"Is Aka home?" I ask, but I can already feel myself bracing for the answer.

Olga Ivanovna clutches her thin arms to her chest. Her shoulders curl forward at an odd angle and tears pool in her dark eyes. "Oh, Liza, I hoped she was with you." She slowly shakes her head. "She hasn't been home for a couple of days now. I looked for her everywhere—asked around, went to the Haymarket, checked the empty buildings around our block. I can't find her anywhere." She rocks slightly on her heels as she talks. Her eyes search my face for the answers I don't have. The fierce desperation in Olga Ivanovna tells me how deep her worry for Aka is. "Liza, do you have any ideas where she might've gone? The streets are not safe for young girls."

I take her trembling hand in mine. "I'll find her. I'll bring her home."

"You know where she is?"

I can't tell Aka's mother about the Mansion. "I have a guess. I should go now, Olga Ivanovna. I'll find her, I promise." I take a step back. Tears run down her face in thick rivulets. "Don't worry, I'll make sure Aka comes home." I turn around and slowly walk away.

Anxiety mixed with fear rises inside me as I march through the streets. Why *hasn't* Aka returned yet? What's keeping her in the Mansion? Or who?

My hands are clammy, and my muscles quaver. I don't know if it is from the exertion or fever. Maybe I need to go home and get some more sleep. But what about Aka? I reassess my surroundings. The Haymarket isn't that far away. Someone there must know about the Mansion. All I need is the address.

A piercing scream breaks the silence, and my insides tighten. A girl. What if it's Aka?

A rumble of voices begins to swell not far from where I'm standing. I rush toward the noise. Another scream turns into a wail. A wounded animal on the brink of death. I round the corner. A small group of people are gathered around something.

A metallic smell lingers in the air. The strange thing on the ground is pure white. What *is* it? I've never seen such blinding whiteness before. It lies smooth and unmoving. When the answer hits me, I want to run, but my body is full of lead and I can't move.

It's a severed arm in a pool of blood.

My hand on my mouth, I step back. My legs feel wobbly, barely able to support my weight. I scan the area, searching for the rest of the body. Nothing. Just a severed arm. Stubby fingers curving into themselves.

My insides twist violently, but I can't stop looking.

Everyone around me is deathly still.

"Do you recognize it?" someone asks behind me.

Are they talking to me? Why would they ask me this? The arm is wrinkly, skinny, and unbearably pale. The nails on the soiled fingers are darkening.

Someone groans. A low moan filters through the silence. Is it me? I shake my head so forcefully my neck cracks. "No," I whisper. "I don't recognize it."

The woman across from me swallows convulsively.

She mumbles words I don't understand, her face twisted with so much pain my breath catches.

I stop breathing. She knows whose hand it is.

An older man by my side shakes his head. His long, crooked finger points at the arm. "It's cut. A very clean cut."

We all go silent at his words. Everyone's heard the stories of people hunting people, butchering corpses and consuming the meat.

"*Lyudoedy*," a woman croaks. She wipes tears from her deeply wrinkled face. A black scarf on her head sits low and askew. "Probably got spooked by something and dropped it."

"Hunters," a young man says. His face is almost as white as the small limb on the ground. He shoves his hands into the pockets of his pants.

The Hunters. Cannibals. People who target the weak and the sick. They stalk their prey in the streets, mostly at night. I've heard hushed whispers in the market that they live in the unfinished metro tunnels, secret passages, underneath the streets. Easy to hide. Easy to hunt.

"We must report it." My gaze darts around the street, half expecting to see the Hunters. "Maybe the militia or the secret police can find whoever did this."

The woman with the black scarf gives a short, cackling laugh, like a crow in the trees. "The police don't care. No one does."

She's right, Liza, no one cares.

I must keep moving. I take a step back, but the limb in

front of me keeps me rooted in place. I wish I'd never seen this. Never stopped to look. The image of an arm on blood-soaked asphalt will stay imprinted on my brain forever.

I turn around and slowly walk away. I must find Aka and bring her home.

Fueled by a surge of adrenaline, I make my way to the marketplace.

7

CITY FOLKS CROWD THE STALLS, HAGGLING
and trading family silver, ration cards, and money for
clothes—some of which were picked off corpses the night
before. Someone is already offering floorboards for the
winter. I pass by the rack of leather belts. People boil
them for food. The price for a belt is a bottle of vodka
or three hundred rubles. Small pieces of what look like
meat jelly are laid out on a yellowing newspaper. I keep
on walking.

I stop in front of a table offering candy made of glue from
book covers.

The bony teenager behind the stall scowls at me. "What?"

He probably doesn't think I'm here for his candy. Almost
no one ever buys it. No one in their right mind would trade
anything for a piece of glue boiled with some sweetened
water. I'm not here to buy it, either. Aka once told me the
boy trades a different product under the cover of candy, and
that's why I'm standing in front of his stall.

"How much for an address?" I ask. I have two hundred rubles in my pocket. Hopefully, it's enough.

"Depends what you're looking for. Might be one hundred rubles. Might be more." The boy presses his lips together. His freckles, like gold dust, stand out against his pale skin.

"I need to find the NKVD headquarters." I pause, and when the boy doesn't react, I add, "Or . . . the Mansion?"

The boy looks down at his hands, fingers knit together tightly. "Five hundred rubles," he whispers.

Does he think I'm stupid? Five hundred rubles can buy me a stall of fish along with a few solid floorboards.

I wrinkle my nose and sigh. "I don't have that much money. I have twenty." I pull out two ten rubles' worth of crumpled banknotes from the pocket of my dress. My left hand inches toward a candy in the corner. I'll get the address, and then I'll have a candy. All I need now is for the boy to focus his attention on the money in my hand.

"A girl like you can make more money there." A sly smirk stretches his mouth.

I almost choke as disturbing images flash through my mind. "I'm not going there to work. I need to find someone. One hundred rubles." I clear my throat. The boy's face is closed off. He's listening half-heartedly. I raise my chin and lean forward. "It's just a piece of information. It's not a piece of bread." My tone inches a notch higher.

"Stop yelling. I can hear you just fine. Are you here to cause trouble? Again?" The boy nods at the fish stall across from him. It's empty now. "You stirred up a lot of problems here the other day."

"Wasn't me," I say with a wide smile. He can't possibly remember me when so many people pass through the Haymarket.

The boy shakes his head. He scratches his jaw and steps back, increasing the distance between us. "You're hard to forget. Loud and pretty," he says.

I shrug. "Even if it was me, why does it matter?"

"It doesn't matter to me. As long as you don't cause *me* any trouble." His eyes scan our surroundings. "Five hundred and not a ruble less." The boy pauses, rubs his freckles with his palm. "Pretty girls like you do well at the Mansion," he adds in a low voice. "You'll find your friend, and you can earn your money back by tomorrow morning."

Pushing away nauseating thoughts, I take a sharp breath and hold my head high. "I don't have that much money. Why won't you help me?"

"Why won't you indeed?" a voice behind me says. "Why don't you sell the girl some candy?"

I turn around to face a tall young man in the militia uniform. His dark blue jacket shows off broad shoulders, and a holstered gun rests snugly against his hip. His eyes are so green my breath hitches.

I recognize him. He went to a different school, elite and military, nothing like mine, but a couple of years ago, he came to Aka's birthday party. He asked me to dance, but I refused. He asked me again, and I waved him away. He must have graduated a year or so ahead of me. He's now, what? Eighteen or maybe a year older, too young to serve in the *militsiya*. Before the war, no boy got to wear a uniform like his right out of high school. But the war has changed the established order of things. I'm not sure about his rank, but by the looks of his clean and crisp uniform, I guess he might be a sergeant or a lieutenant.

"Another minute of this, and I'll confiscate your goods." He raises a perfect brow at the boy, and his full lips war between a smile and a scowl.

Then he winks at me. What is he playing at? And how much did he hear?

I slightly shake my head at the candy boy, an unspoken understanding falling between us. Assuming he hasn't heard our previous exchange, the officer doesn't need to know what we talked about. What I asked for. It's time to pretend I wanted to buy a candy and the boy was jacking up the price.

"He was about to sell me some," I say. "We just couldn't agree on the price."

"She offered me twenty rubles," the boy hisses. "It took me five hours to boil this batch."

I shrug and turn to the officer. "It's okay. I don't really need a candy."

"You don't?" The corners of his mouth curve a little. "I think twenty rubles is a fair price." He turns to the boy. "What do you say?"

The candy boy's nose twitches. He scratches his cheek. Then he holds one palm up and out. My rib cage shifts when I put money into his hand. "Twenty rubles. Everything is fair nowadays," he says coolly. "Pick one."

I just lost twenty rubles. But neither the boy nor I dare to argue in front of the officer.

"A fair warning: It tastes like glue and paper. I've had a few on a dare. Have you added sugar to dilute the taste?" When the boy nods, the officer points at a round piece of candy, a little bigger than the others. "Get this one. More sugar, more energy."

Most likely, the boy used Badayev earth, plain dirt dug up around the Badayev warehouses that burned down last year. Liquefied sugar poured into the dirt during the fire. I've heard people still dig around the site. But most of it was excavated last winter.

I pick up the candy and bring it to my face. My nose wrinkles involuntarily at the smell. I've tasted it myself. Last winter, Aka's grandfather took a couple of books from his own collection, ripped off the covers, scraped off the glue from the books' spines, and boiled it. Aka's mother melted the frozen dirt and ran it through a cloth to separate the molten sugar from the soil. We added it to the glue. It was the most disgusting candy I've ever had. Later, Aka's grandfather burned the rest of the books in the stove for warmth.

"It's better than an empty belly," the officer says with a smile.

I hold his gaze for a few seconds. "I remember you. You came to my friend's birthday."

He gives me a small nod. "I remember you, too. You were too busy with your friend to grant me a dance. Liza, isn't it? And your last name—"

"Good memory," I cut in, and force my lips to stretch into a smile. The less he knows about me the safer I'll be. "It is Liza."

"You wore a black velvet dress two sizes too big," he says. "Was it your mother's?"

It was. My cheeks flush. Aka had been so excited that the older boys came to her party. "And your name?" I say, trying to recall.

"Maksim," he says, and steps closer. A scent of wood, cinnamon, and tobacco fills my nostrils, surprisingly fresh for the middle of summer. People don't waste their precious energy on bathing. Or laundry. I guess being a militia officer changes everything. By the looks of him, I bet his food rations are nothing like ours. His strong shoulders and thick arm muscles contrast well with his narrow waist. He is handsome, and the obvious care he takes with his appearance tells me he knows he's good-looking.

Maksim holds his hand out to me. His skin is soft and warm beneath my touch. His grip is firm. "Nice to see you, Liza. Again."

I look at the candy in my hand.

"Well, now that you have candy, what's next?" He's cool and flirtatious, and a flush of red builds at the nape of my neck.

The smart response would be something along the lines of "I'm going home now," and then walk away from the stall and Maksim. But all I can think about is his crisp uniform. And that Maksim can get me the address I need. Even better, he can take me to the Mansion. Maybe I can use this boy's interest in me to my advantage.

I run my fingernails along the sleeve of his uniform. "You're kind." My voice wavers. "And you look dashing. But I must go and find something else to eat. Something better than candy." The words catch in my throat, but I push them out. Am I overdoing it? "And I'm not feeling well. I should hurry before I spend all my energy."

A breeze blows a lock of hair over his forehead, giving him a less formal appearance. He suddenly looks like the boy I remember from the party, young and eager. "You should've saved your money. A candy won't help you feel better."

"I had to start somewhere." Sounds stupid, but I can't come up with anything else.

He turns to the candy boy and asks, "How much for all the candy?"

The boy's eyes bulge until I'm afraid they'll fall out of their sockets. He blinks rapidly, processing Maksim's question. "Two hundred rubles," he finally answers in a shaky voice.

"Wrap it," Maksim orders, and pulls a stack of rubles out of his coat's pocket.

My breath catches somewhere between my lungs and my throat. I've never seen such an obscene amount of money in the Haymarket.

The boy wraps the candy, hands shaking. Most likely from the excitement of getting two hundred rubles for glue and dirt.

Maksim shoves the paper packet into his uniform pocket and turns to me. "Ready?" With a grin, he throws his shoulders back and stands even taller. Then he bends his arm at the elbow and offers it to me. His grin expands when I wrap my arm around his.

Behind the stall, the boy meets my eyes, mutters a few words under his breath, and shakes his head before he dismisses us.

People part in front of us as we walk. Having an officer by my side has unexpected advantages. I feel safe, maybe even feared. "Thank you for helping me. I doubt he would've sold me candy for just twenty rubles," I say, and shove the piece of candy into my mouth. "I needed it."

Walking to the Haymarket has left me feeling like a damp rag wrung out too many times. My legs are weaker than ever, and my breath is shallow. I sway, and his arms hold me up.

"Let's see if we can find something more substantial than candy. I have an idea," Maksim says with a smile.

Sharp thoughts scrabble against my mind like tree branches. I don't want to waste time in the Haymarket. I need him to take me to the Mansion. I lean on Maksim's arm. "I feel dizzy," I whisper, and push into him even more, as if I want to melt into his strong frame. "Is there somewhere we can go where I can rest? My home's too far from here."

An arm holds my waist, gently yet firmly. Maksim turns me toward him, pushes strands of loose hair away from my eyes, and holds my face between his hands. He looks down at me as if he's making sure I'm feeling as bad as I told him.

Afraid he might see something he isn't supposed to, I push his hands away, press my head into his uniformed shoulder, and cling tightly to his firmness and strength. "Give me a second," I whisper. I close my eyes and try to figure out what else I can do or say to make him take me to the damned place. He should've offered to do it by now. What am I doing wrong?

I look up at him. His eyes soften, and he flashes his wide grin at me. "You'll be fine. I've seen worse," he says. "Why don't we find you some bread? Something else, maybe eggs. How about an omelet?" He's talking crazy. Where would we find that? There are no eggs, no butter, no milk left in the city. Does he think imaginary food will sustain me? "I know a place with lots of food." His arm wraps around my waist as he steers me through the people and stalls of the Haymarket.

I suppress a breath. Finally. My body is as light as the balloon my father used to buy for me every Sunday when I was little.

You're making a mistake.

My mother's voice rings a warning in my mind. But Mama doesn't get it. I must find my friend and bring her home. And in the meantime, if I get something to eat, how wrong can it be? If I must kiss and flirt to get the food, I'll do it.

It won't be just kissing.

Am I willing to do that? Maybe I am. Aka is doing it. Other girls are doing it. Survival justifies anything, Mama. You said it, remember? Or was it Kaganov who said it? It doesn't matter now who said what. Before the war, I could never imagine selling myself for scraps of food. Even earlier, when the candy boy told me I could earn a lot of money, I couldn't bring myself to think about it without retching. But now? With Maksim by my side? This boy isn't that bad of a choice. He's handsome and charming, and he makes me feel wanted. Even if it's more than kissing, it can't be too bad.

A slow smile threatens to break out on my face, but I bite the inside of my cheek to chase it away. My body releases all the tension, and I stumble. Maksim catches me, holds me closer to his well-fed body, and I let him lead me out of the market and into the back alleys of the city.

8

"WHERE ARE WE GOING?" MY VOICE IS wheezy. We've been walking for a while now, and the back of my dress is soaked in sweat, but I'm shivering from the cold. My breathing is labored. The fever must've returned. "I need to rest." I stop. Exhaustion is building, and I'm having trouble thinking straight. "I can't do this anymore."

I want to sit down on the sidewalk, but Maksim holds me up, pressing my body tightly against his. "Almost there," he says.

I hang like a rag doll in his arms. If he'll only let me rest. If I could close my eyes for just a few moments. I need my strength for the Mansion. For myself. And for Aka.

Maksim lets me go, and I sway. He searches for something in his pants pocket. "Here." A candy lies in his wide palm. "Eat this."

I chew the candy slowly. "It's not too bad," I mumble. It

really isn't. The taste is sweet and bitter. Acidic, yet filling. I'm eating dirt and actually liking it. I swallow and wait for my body to respond. It doesn't. The sounds around me are muffled, and white spots jump behind my closed eyes. "I can't walk. I need to sit down."

"As I said, we're almost there." His strong arms slip beneath my back, and he picks me up with ease.

My whole body is on fire. I writhe in Maksim's arms. "Put me down. I'll walk." My voice is raw.

"I don't think so," he says as he carries me across the street. "If I let you rest, you won't get up. Food is around the corner. You just have to hold out another minute."

I take a deep breath. The desire to resist has burned off, leaving me shaky and weak.

Maksim's fingers tense around my back and hold me tighter. "Good."

———

"We're here." His voice wakes me up.

We stand in front of a three-story building made of bright yellow-and-white stone. White columns support the structure. The red flag above one of the tall onyx windows moves slowly in the breeze. Two security guards study my face, my dress, my boots.

I can't draw enough air under their scrutiny.

Maksim nods at the guards and pushes the door open; we step into a front foyer with a sky-high ceiling and a massive golden chandelier dangling from above.

He takes my hand and leads me into a front room filled with laughter, whoops, and hollers, where a group of officers—the NKVD by the looks of their dark olive jackets—sits around a big round table playing cards. Two ashtrays full of old cigarette butts serve as centerpieces.

Our steps reverberate through the room as the parquet floor creaks under our feet.

The smell of vodka, tobacco, and cheap perfume is heavy in the air. A few girls, wearing nothing but silk slips, sit on two leather couches by the wall-high windows. Some of them are staring outside. Others just sit on the edges with their backs rigid and their eyes glued to the officers at the table, as if awaiting orders. Most of the girls are covered in bruises. Most of them are my age or younger.

None of them look at me.

None of them is Aka.

In the farthest corner, an old piano stands against the wall looking out of place. A tall silver candlestick perches on top of it, yellow wax spread on the polished surface like raindrops. A big mirror above it reflects the window across the room.

The room falls silent.

Maksim's hand tightens around mine, and he pulls me closer as the officers' attention trails us. Most of them are well-fed, arrogant, and drunk. How did Maksim earn his slot in this violent and dark world of the secret police? The militia fights street crimes. The NKVD hunts enemies of the State. These two organizations are not known for collaboration. But I guess the war has brought us all together in the most unimaginable ways.

"Look at that," one of the men at the table says. A thick scar runs down his chin. His white shirt is unbuttoned, exposing a bare chest covered with thick orange hair. "We were wondering when the boy would finally grace us with his presence. Daddy has been worried." A slight wave at the end of the table where an older officer, also in the blue militia uniform, sits silently. "And here you are. Finally. And with a new addition." He lets the words hang for a few seconds. "Well done, Maksim." Scarface smiles, and the predator peeks at me through his wicked grin.

I try to yank my hand away from Maksim. "Please, let me go," I mutter, and take a step away only to be pulled back to his side. I can't fight Maksim's strong grip on my arm.

"Olga, come here." Scarface waves at a girl sitting on the couch with her legs folded underneath her.

The girl's gaze slides across the room and settles on my face. She hits me with a smile. It's bright, wide, but it doesn't reach her eyes. Her long blond hair frames a small, heart-shaped face. She walks over to the officer and sits on his lap. He buries his face into the curve of her neck, and his hand slides under her silk slip, pulling it up the girl's legs, exposing gaunt, pale thighs.

I don't want to look anymore, but my eyes are glued to the

girl's smiling face, to her mouth whispering into the man's ear, to her exposed breast under his palm.

Someone laughs. Someone else whoops and whistles.

Maksim shoves me behind him and salutes the officer. "As it was duly noted, I have a guest with me, Comrades." He nods over his shoulder. "I'm taking her to my room."

"For a private interrogation?" someone says, and the room fills with obnoxious laughter.

I study the slats of wood under my feet, my chin resting on my chest.

Maksim points at the door on the other side of the room. "Let's go." His voice sounds almost breathless.

I don't argue. Going with Maksim to his room might be dangerous and stupid, but I want nothing more than to get out of this room, away from the ogling and the desperate, hungry looks of the girls.

Before we leave, I glance at the girl on the officer's lap and shudder at the dead blackness behind her eyes.

A maze of brightly lit and winding hallways leads us to Maksim's quarters.

His room, shaped like a narrow box, is bare. The walls are white, and there's no window. It would be depressing if not for a small round mirror over a chipped porcelain sink, reflecting the brightness of the walls. It's furnished with two upholstered chairs standing on the opposite side of the room. A pair of shiny leather boots is placed under one of the chairs. A white *gymnastiorka*, a pullover shirt with small brass buttons, is draped neatly on the back of the other. I'm surprised to see a few books stacked on the floor by the window. Obviously, Maksim didn't need to burn them last winter. A narrow bed with a dark cover stands by the wall.

"You're chalky white," he says.

"Just like the walls," I snicker, and wave around me.

"Worse," he says, and shakes his head. "I'm going to get you something to eat." He hesitates by the door, his hand suspended in the air by the doorknob, and without looking at me says, "I'm going to lock the door."

"Why?"

"So no one can get into the room."

"Is that really necessary?"

Without a word, Maksim walks out and closes the door behind him. The lock clicks. The trap is shut.

The white walls start to swim around me, and I drop to Maksim's bed. I must rest, let my body relax. A few minutes, that's all I need, and then I'll figure out where Aka is and get both of us out of this wretched place.

———

A loud bang behind the wall jolts me awake. I sit on the bed, my hands clutching the sheets, and try to orient myself. Still alone. Still in the Mansion.

Loud, vile laughter. A scream. A slap.

I tense as a horrible suspicion creeps into my mind. I wait and wait for the sounds to stop. Another horrible slap of flesh, a gasp followed by a whimper, then muffled moans of pain. My hands curl into fists. The girl's voice sounds painfully familiar.

It's Aka.

The man on the other side of the wall groans loudly. A few seconds later a door opens and closes. Heavy footsteps recede down the hallway.

I get up from the bed, creep to the door, and slowly turn the knob. It's still locked. Of course it is. My pulse pounds like a church bell in my head. I pull a hairpin from my braids, straighten it, and stick it into the lock. My breathing is hard, and my hands are shaking. Every nerve's alive and buzzing like a wire. I wiggle the pin until the lock clicks.

I grip the doorknob, fingers pressing hard into the metal, and turn it. Then I slowly open the door and look out into the hallway. I tiptoe to the room next to Maksim's and knock. "Aka," I say in a low voice. "It's me, Liza. Open the door."

Nothing. Not a sound from inside.

I inspect the hallway, to the left and to the right. Then I take in a deep breath and place my ear to the door, listening for some signs of life on the other side. Still nothing. I shove my fears into the depth of my mind and push the door open.

The girl on the bed looks small and frail. Her body is bruised in various places and there's what looks like a fresh bite on her shoulder. When she sees me, she pulls a sheet over herself and sways like a piece of tall grass in the wind. The smells of stale vodka and something sour bite at my senses.

It's not Aka, and I don't know whether to be disappointed or relieved. This is so much worse than I imagined.

I push myself away from the wall and step forward, my feet uncertain and knees shaking. I reach out to the girl and take her small, cold hand in mine. "Do you know Aka? Akulina? She came here not so long ago. A tall, dark-haired girl. People say we look alike. Is she still here?" I hold my breath, waiting for the girl to respond.

The girl looks at me, but her eyes are misty. Her silence is all the answer I need. She doesn't know what I'm talking about.

She shakes her head and murmurs, "Leave, please."

I nod and step outside into the hallway. I need to check every room in this house. Aka must be in one of them.

"How did you get out?"

I turn around and face Maksim. He's holding a silver tray in his hands. A bowl of steaming cabbage soup and two sizable pieces of bread are placed in the center.

I might as well tell him about Aka. He might know where she is. "I picked the lock. I thought I heard my friend in there. I had to go and check. You know her, too. You came to her birthday party. Remember Aka?"

"Was it Aka in the room?" A slight nod at the door.

"No. Have you seen her? Do you know where she is?"

"I have no idea where Aka is." His smile is all sharp edges

and unspoken words. It's too deliberate to be true. "Come back to my room, Liza."

I follow him inside.

I go back to the bed and sit down. How do I get him to help me find Aka?

He sets the tray carefully on the bed. "Vegetables and bread," he says. "Not too heavy for an empty stomach."

My hand flies up to my throat. "This is all for me?"

He nods.

"I have money," I say, and search my dress pockets. "I'll pay." I hold out a few banknotes.

Maksim pushes my hand away. "I don't need money." His words seem a warning that money doesn't buy food here. A different payment matters more. "Eat, and don't worry about it."

I don't believe him, but if I want to find Aka and get us out of here, I need to eat. Hunger taught me how to prioritize. There is food, and there is everything else that isn't; and it can wait because nothing else matters more at the moment than getting my empty stomach filled.

The soup is hot and delicious. Big chunks of potatoes, some with the scabby skin on, melt in my mouth. I chew on soft cabbage, and my taste buds refuse to believe the incredible aroma. It reminds me of my mother's savory soup. The bread doesn't taste like sawdust. It's a dark, slightly bitter rye bread made with real flour and sweetened with molasses and spiced with coriander. *Borodinsky* bread. It feels like one of the dreams I have at night.

I finish the plate of soup and one piece of the dark brown sourdough. The other piece remains on the plate. I'm close to bursting.

"Thank you." I smile at Maksim, who sits on one of the chairs by the wall. "It was the most delicious food I've had since . . . since I don't even know when."

He stands, removes the tray, and puts it on the floor by the bed. "Since before."

"Yes, since before." I get up as well.

We stand in front of each other, and I swear the room darkens.

"Do you want me to pay for the food?" My voice croaks.

Beneath the green, there are flecks of dark gold in Maksim's eyes as they travel to my lips, then to my neck and, finally, back to my mouth. "It's up to you."

Maksim steps in front of me and brushes a strand of hair away from my face. The touch is soft and unexpected, but my body tenses anyway. "I won't force you to do anything you don't want to."

A spark of hope stirs inside me. My head fizzes with relief. I might get out of here, after all. "Can I leave?"

He chuckles. "Already?"

Is it another warning? An electric current cuts through me, and I snap, "Are you going to stop me?"

"Not if you kiss me."

A kiss? It can't be that easy, can it?

We appraise each other. Waiting for the other to make a move.

His warm hands cup my cheeks. "One kiss, and I'll take you home."

Is it really all he wants? Can I trust him? "A kiss," I agree because I don't have a choice. Better Maksim than the men in the front room.

His hands dip into my hair, pull my head back, and his lips lightly brush over my closed mouth, trailing the outline of my lips. The skill of his touch is nothing like my first kiss behind the school with a boy who starved to death last winter. He sucks softly on my lower lip, and I gasp—a short, frightened sound. The world sways around me. He pulls me in closer, so close I feel the tightening of his core muscles.

In response, every bone, every nerve in my body tenses.

A loud knock on the door makes me jump.

He pulls away and flashes a wide smile at me. I'm breathless and lost in all the odd sensations running through my body. The disappointment at the distance between us. The lingering touch of his full lips. The pull of his hands on my hair. I'm shocked I want more. The audacity of it is staggering, and a sweltering heat slowly creeps up my neck.

"Who's there?" Maksim asks, his eyes never leaving my face.

"Major wants to see you," a deep voice says from behind the door. "Your friend's here."

"Coming," Maksim says. He strokes his hair and tips his chin, pointing at the door behind me. "I'll be right back," he whispers. "Don't go anywhere this time." He walks around me and pauses by the door. "This place isn't safe for you."

After the door closes, I'm alone. Again. I have no idea what I'm going to do or how I'm going to get out of here. I take the piece of bread and shove it into the pocket of my dress. For later.

Back on the bed, I sit and wait.

A few minutes go by before fierce, rich, and haunting piano music trails down the hallway from the living room. My heart lurches violently as I recognize the melody. I heard it not so long ago. The tune seeps into my bones, triggering memories that I can't quite put together.

The music is enough to muffle the voice of reason. It's enough to propel me toward the door. I try the knob, and this time it turns. In his rush, Maksim must have forgotten to lock it. As if hypnotized, I walk down the hallway, the melody growing louder as I enter the room.

The piano player turns around and looks at me. He goes completely still, his damaged hand hanging down at his side.

The echo of Luka's music floats in the air like lingering light in the darkest of the shadows.

9

THE ROOM SEEMS SMALLER WITH LUKA IN IT,
more crowded than before, and it buzzes with men's loud
voices and oily laughter. He gets up and turns to the officers, yet I can tell he's tracking me with a sidelong glance.
His shoulders stiffen.

So that's what Katya meant when she said he still plays.
Yet when I told him about the Mansion, he looked me in
the eye and pretended not to have any information. And all
along, he not only knew about this place, about the girls,
but he actually works here. Fury rushes through me, but I
clamp it down as a new thought appears.

Does it mean Luka can help me find Aka?

She must be locked in one of the rooms, because I can't find
her familiar frame among the girls.

My eyes settle on the table, still surrounded by the same
men as earlier. The cards are gone, and instead, plates over-

flowing with food have been placed on the dark wooden surface. The men eat and drink with gusto. Saliva fills my mouth at the sight of hard-boiled eggs and cubes of cheese no smaller than a thumb. Pieces of dark rye bread are surrounded by fresh red tomatoes and dark green cucumbers. A plate of fried fish and what looks like sliced beef are pushed into the center. Several bottles of vodka serve as an odd ornament to the arrangement.

I bet the girls are expected to be thankful. Grateful to be fed and alive. And what about the people, most of them children, beyond the walls of this Mansion dying from hunger? Losing their homes to Nazi bombs? What makes the men in this room so special? Their uniforms and guns?

Let them see me. Let them read the fury and disgust on my face. Spittle builds up in the corner of my mouth as words, biting and cold, move to the tip of my tongue.

Then Luka's by my side, and my rage is replaced by annoyance. "What?" I say. He's a liar and a poacher. He's no better than the men in this room.

"Don't," Luka whispers. His face is red. "Whatever you're about to do . . . don't do it."

I step away, but I nod. I won't misbehave.

"Ah, here's our new girl," a deep voice from the table says. "Grand entrance with an interruption." A soft chuckle. "She looks upset. Maksim, introduce us."

I turn away from Luka and face the room. My ribs seem

to shift and narrow around my center in response to the smirks, too direct and obnoxious not to hurt.

"This is Liza." Maksim appears by my side. He takes my hand and leads me to the table. I'm in the middle of the room, holding on to Maksim's hand as if it's an anchor rooting me to the floor. "Liza, this is my father, Major Nikitin of the Leningrad militia. I'm sure you've heard his name. He's in charge of the security in the city."

That would explain how Maksim became an officer at such a young age. I search the man's face but don't find any resemblance to Maksim. The glint in the major's cold eyes tells me what lies behind his evaluation. He's deciding if I'm worthy of their attention. The way he grimaces tells me I'm a lesser person than the men in here. I'm insignificant and small. Like all the girls in the room, just a fixture that will be forgotten as soon as it has served its purpose.

He gestures me to step forward. "How do you know my son?"

"Through school," I say.

"Welcome," he says, and nods at Maksim. "Perhaps you can stay for the best part of the night." He throws a pointed look at his son, as if the invitation is just for him and not me.

"We'll stay," Maksim says.

I don't want to stay, but I can't leave without Aka, either. And I don't want to know what the *best* part of the night means.

"Music and dancing," Maksim says as if reading my mind.

"It's the best part. I usually patrol the streets, but tonight is different."

Waltzing and singing. My own words ring through my head.

"I don't hear any music," Scarface growls from the table. His shirt is still unbuttoned, but the girl, Olga, is back on the couch. Her eyes are red, and her upper lip looks swollen. "I didn't like the piece you just played, boy. The girls want to dance. Play something jolly for them."

"But he can't, can he?" another officer says, clawing the air with a hand on which he's extended just his thumb and first two fingers. Harsh chuckles rip the air. "Why did we hire a mangled musician? We should've invited the symphony."

"Most of the symphony is . . . not available," Maksim says. A careful choice of words, considering most of them are dead from starvation.

Maksim points at Luka. "He's a damn good musician. Auditioned for the symphony before the war."

He's lying. No one can audition at such a young age. But the officers don't question it, their minds clouded by vodka and lust.

"He was playing with only one hand." Scarface puts his empty glass down with a loud bump. The sound is as sharp and painful as a slap. "Not much of a musician, I reckon. We should find someone else. I'm tired of his music. Sounds foreign, not *proletariat*."

What an ignorant fool. "The piece he just played was written by Maurice Ravel. It's the Piano Concerto for the Left

Hand. An educated man would know this piece is meant to be played with one hand." The words spill out of me in a torrent.

You're your own worst enemy. My mother's irate whisper cuts me in half. *Apologize while you still can.*

Everyone's eyes settle on me.

The girls on the sofa move in unison, curling their backs and bracing their hands around their middle as if preparing for an impact. Like the alcohol and the bread, I can taste the fear in the air, greasy and sickening.

"Did she just call me an imbecile?" Scarface barks. The threat is obvious in his voice.

"No, Comrade Commander. She meant if I tried to play the piece with two hands, I'd sound like a fool," Luka cuts in as he moves in front of me, shielding me from Scarface. The genuine smile makes him so handsome my chest aches. "Let me see . . ." He pinches the bridge of his nose as if thinking about something extremely important. "I know a jolly waltz, sir. I hope you'll like it." He nods, shoots a quick glance at me, and goes back to the piano.

"Dance with me," Maksim urges.

Is this a joke? I shake my head.

"I'm not asking." His voice is full of urgency, and I sense a deep feeling of unease. He opens his arms, and I step inside his embrace. I don't have a choice but to put my arms on his shoulders and let him spin me into the center of the room. I'd rather dance with him than with any of the other officers.

He's a good dancer—confident, strong, and fluid at the same time. I, on the other hand, am stiff and clumsy.

Maksim twirls me while his eyes glide over the room. "If you listen to me, I'll make sure you're safe," he says into my ear. "Don't address anyone again or I can't guarantee anything. But you have to be nice to me." His voice dips. His mouth brushes over my earlobe. I know what he means by *nice*. Everything comes with a price. "Now, smile at me."

I respond by stepping on his toes and stumbling over his feet, but his strong arms keep me from falling, and we continue to spin.

"Liza." Maksim's voice is harsher than a few seconds ago. "Be nice."

The tune picks up. I plaster a smile on my face. Maksim pulls me closer and, when I look up at him, hits me with the brightest grin.

"Much better," he says.

"Do you know where Aka is? Can I talk to her?"

"Maybe." He's holding me much too close to his firm and strong body. His abdomen is pressing into my rib cage. I can feel the fold of rubles in his pants pocket.

"Maybe you can help me find her," I note, and shift a few millimeters to the right. Closer to the bulge of bills. "And I can be very nice." I pull away as far as I can without being too obvious to anyone who's watching us.

"Why don't I believe you?"

"Just because I can't dance well doesn't mean I can't repay in kindness."

Maksim chuckles. "Kindness is different from being nice." He tilts his head, exhales deeply. "Don't you think so?"

"I don't know what to think," I say, trying to keep my voice even. How long are we going to play this game? When I look up at him, his eyes gleam with a challenge.

"I'm sure you do." His mouth moves so close I can almost taste him. I try to pull away again, but his hands press into my spine, and I'm trapped in his arms.

Maybe if I let him kiss me again, he'll let me go. Maybe if we kiss, he won't notice my hand in his pocket. Maybe if I concentrate on doing what I'm good at, my mind won't wander to the boy at the piano and what he thinks of me. I bite down on the inside of my cheek. Why do I care what Luka thinks? He's here, too, doing exactly what? Is it just playing the piano for scraps of food or does he participate in the officers' parties? I glance back at him; the muscles in his shoulders have tightened and he's playing with more force. He can't see me, but something tells me he can feel me, swinging in Maksim's arms.

I brush my lips over Maksim's. Probably not quite the kiss he hoped for. It feels better than expected, and as our lips touch, my hand slips inside his pocket and my trained fingers lace around the bills. I lean into Maksim, closer, so much closer, and press harder against his mouth, but he draws away. I use his movement to pull the money out and shove the wad into the sleeve of my dress.

His eyes travel over my face. His expression is hungry. Ravenous even. His arms remain locked around me, snaking up my back and holding me tighter.

Our chests pressed together, we swirl.

"How do you know Luka?" he asks a few seconds later. "You seem pretty close." There's a pinch to his voice and it makes my breath stagger.

"He was in my school. And yesterday, he saved me from some lunatic from the Haymarket," I say.

Maksim pulls away. "You were attacked at the Haymarket? And yet you went back today?"

I shrug. "One must do what one must do."

He chuckles.

"My mother used to say it," I explain.

"Used to?" His voice is low and careful.

I swallow hard. I shouldn't have said that. Now he knows my mother's dead. He might ask about the ration cards. I need to get out. I need to find Aka, give her some of the money, and make her promise to never come back to this place.

But how am I going to do that when I'm caged in Maksim's arms?

He searches my face. "Has she died?"

I nod. "Pneumonia."

A slow clench of his jaw, then lines form across his forehead. With his eyes a shade darker, and his jaw set a notch tighter, he continues to lead me, moving with unrushed steps across the room.

"Girls, time to show us how you dance," one of the officers says.

Olga obediently goes into the middle of the room, puts

her arms above her head, and starts to sway and whirl. She looks pale and fragile, but her moves are sharp, deliberate, and professional. As if she knows how to follow the music. As if she's danced before.

Other girls follow, until we're surrounded by ghosts in silk slips.

"Can we leave?" The bundle of rubles is burning my skin under my sleeve. What will Maksim do if he finds out?

He flashes a wide smile at me, carefree and playful. "Soon."

I don't believe him.

"I need a few more minutes," Maksim says. "I'm getting you out, I promise. We'll go and find Aka."

I just nod politely and take a steeling breath.

Scarface joins Olga. His hands fall on her skinny shoulders, and she flinches as if she's in pain, as if his hands are about to crush her.

"He's hurting her," I say.

Maksim swings me. A frown appears. "Maybe we should go now." His voice is so low I barely hear him.

A movement to my right side, and I turn as Scarface slaps Olga across the face. She reels backward, her body slamming into the wall behind her. Scarface curves his mouth into a scowl, and he moves closer. The girl's body is limp and small, bones as thin as matches. Her face has gone chalky white. Only her cheekbones, sharp as razors, burn a bright red color.

She turns to me, her eyes wide and wild, and shrills, "Get out of here while you still can. What they do to us, what *we* do . . . you don't come back from this."

Her words bring us to a halt. Maksim's arms fall away from my back as he pauses by my side.

The music stops.

"Being here is a privilege only a few are allowed," Scarface says, slowly walking toward the table. He picks up a knife, puts the tip of his thumb on the edge, testing its sharpness. He smiles, a smirk from a monster planning his next torture.

Then he walks over to Olga.

She presses her back against the wall as if she's trying to melt into it.

"Being here is an honorable service to the Motherland." He stands in front of the girl and shifts the knife in his hand. "Only a few patriots are allowed to serve our fearless leader Stalin and the Communist Party alongside my brave comrades."

Scarface smiles at Olga pressed against the wall. "Look at you." His harsh chuckle is piercing in the room filled with fear. "You're not a patriot."

Olga gathers the sides of her thin slip as Scarface grabs her by her hair, tips her head, exposing her pale throat, and starts hacking off her locks with the knife.

I hear labored, panicked breathing. Most likely my own.

The silence is broken by someone striking a match to light a cigarette and Olga's painful, strangled gulps, the sounds of an animal confined in pain. Her beautiful blond hair scatters across the carpet. A breeze moves the curtains, and the sunlight reflects like liquid gold in the strands.

What if they did this to Aka? Maybe this is why she hasn't come back. She's alone in some room, hurt and terrified. And there's no one to protect her from these savage animals. The urge to act swells inside me. I leap forward and grab the silver candlestick standing on the piano. "Damn you!" I shout, half a growl, half a desperate cry, and swing the heavy candleholder with both of my hands.

The crack echoes in my ears, and Scarface crumples to the floor.

The officers scramble to their feet, shouting at me while the girls huddle in the farthest corner of the room, making themselves small and invisible, as if they're hoping if they're not seen or heard, they won't be punished.

The ringing in my ears makes me incapable of reacting to the agitated moves around me, but in two big strides, Maksim is by my side. He rips the candlestick from my hands and throws it to the floor. Then he turns to Luka, who has appeared right behind me. "Take her and run." His gaze meets mine for a desperate moment. There is no fear, only a plea to leave. Then Maksim turns to face the officers and stands in front them, upright and rigid, his breath catching in the back of his throat.

Luka grabs my shoulders. "Go," he says. His face is as pale as winter snow. He pushes me toward the door. When I don't move, he drags me to the exit.

We race down the hallway to the front entrance.

The air around us is thick as we push past the guards and down the street, away from this forsaken place.

"*Stoyat!* Stop!" a guard yells to our backs.

Luka freezes. Composed and in control just a few seconds ago, he's as terror-stricken as I am. Stumbling on, I haul him down the street.

Up ahead I spot a narrow alley. "In here. Quick."

I'm leaving Aka behind. She'd never do that to me. The thought nearly breaks me, but my feet propel me forward.

We don't stop. We don't look back.

We run.

10

WE COLLAPSE AT THE SAME TIME ON A SMALL
lawn in front of the bombed-out city library. Huge holes
open a sad view into the belly of the eighteenth-century
building. A vast staircase leads up to the second level and
ends abruptly in a jagged, blackened edge. The stair ban-
ister has been vandalized, all the wood cut out, only the
metal frame left. The filing cabinets are scattered in the
middle of the room and covered in dust, ash, and pieces of
rubble. The bookshelves are empty, the books used for fuel
last winter.

The fear and fury that propelled me into action are
replaced with fatigue and an odd sense of calm. I press the
back of my head into the soft ground and inhale the smell
of grass and ash.

"I can't breathe," Luka gasps for air beside me.

Side by side, we observe the blue sky above us. Now that
the tension and adrenaline are gone, my legs and my core

start to shake. The scorching hot anger is coming back. I can't believe what just happened. What I did.

I glare at Luka. Why didn't he tell me he plays piano at the Mansion? Everything could've been so different if I had known what I was walking into.

"Why were you there?"

"It's a job." Luka's eyes are closed. "They give me food afterward . . . or whatever they decide is good enough for me."

"Why didn't you tell me?"

"Why do you think?" He swallows. "I don't like to talk about it. It's not something I'm proud of."

"I've done a lot of things in the past year I'm not proud of."

"That's hard to believe." A small smile on his face chips away at my rage. "Your sense of danger is skewed." Luka opens his eyes and finally looks at me. "Significantly. You must do something about it."

"What do you suggest I do?"

"Stop hitting people."

I shake my head. "He deserved worse. And you have no right to give me any advice. You lied to me."

He sits up and his eyes search my face. "I didn't lie. I just didn't tell you the truth."

"It was important to me. I told you about Aka and that I was looking for her. I told you she went to the Mansion."

"How did *you* end up there?"

"This is not about me. You could've helped me to find

Aka. If you would've told me about your pathetic piano concerts, things might've turned out differently. For all of us. Have you thought about that?"

"I have," he says in a steady voice, but he's as tense as a piano string. "God knows, Liza, I wish I had told you. I was embarrassed to admit where I go to work. I'm so sorry." There is genuine pain in his voice. The reflection of my own. My anger shrinks back further.

"I tricked Maksim into taking me there." My breath constricts when I brace myself for my next question. "Have you seen Aka there? She still hasn't come back."

"I haven't. She must've been in one of the back rooms." He pauses. "I don't go to the rooms."

I shove away a vision of Aka in a silk slip.

"Maksim didn't warn you?" A rasp in Luka's voice turns my head. "About the place?"

"No."

Luka straightens his back. "That bastard."

"Isn't he your friend?" Suddenly I remember Aka's party. How Luka said one of his friends had dragged him there that night.

Luka nods, and his face hardens. "We used to be close. Before the war. Last year he just disappeared. I ran into him by accident. Told him about what happened to us, and he offered me a job, to come and play for the officers."

"Did he tell *you* what place it was?"

"He warned me." Luka looks at me. "If it wasn't for Katya, I wouldn't be able to bring myself to play there, but she's my responsibility. I must take care of her. And the Mansion provides us food."

"How is it even possible to have so much food in a city that has nothing?"

"The government takes what they want of the food the Red Army brings into the city. Only leftovers go to the people."

"Nothing goes to us. There is no food." My voice is hushed. The government is committing a crime against its own citizens. So much for defending the Motherland.

"For people like us, there is no food. For people like . . . *them* . . ." He never finishes the sentence and just watches me for a moment. Then he turns away and waves a hand. "The officers think they deserve it because they protect the city, the streets. Protect the people. They think it's justified because they need their strength."

"That's what Maksim said," I whisper. But protect us from what? The Nazis? The Hunters? I've heard rumors the Hunters are free to roam the streets at night, after the curfew, because the government doesn't care about them. All the government cares about is the government.

Luka lies back down on the grass. "I was supposed to get food tonight. Katya is sick. She's weak and coughing continuously. And now . . . I won't be able to go back to the Mansion. Our supply is cut off." His frustration is almost a physical sensation tearing through him and spilling over on me.

What he doesn't say is clear. I'm the one who caused Luka to leave the Mansion without food. Because of me, he lost his job and now neither of us can ever go back. Somewhere in the city, Katya is wasting away while Aka is locked inside the Mansion. Her family must be a nervous wreck by now. And it's all because of me.

I take his damaged hand into mine. "I'm sorry, too. Both of us made a lot of unnecessary mistakes." I wait for him to withdraw from me, but he doesn't move. "I should probably go home."

He doesn't take his hand away, but he doesn't reply, either. The silence expands and fills the air around us.

I tap Luka gently on his hand. "I'm not sorry for hitting that awful man. But I'm sorry for dragging you into this mess." Despite everything that happened after, I'm glad I knocked Scarface down.

There is a heaviness to my heartbeat while he's silent. His doubts and frustrations are captured in the quiet that settles between us.

"It's all right, Liza. I'll figure something out," he says finally, and looks at me, a muscle pulsing in his set jaw.

My sleeve is full of money. We *can* figure something out. I angle myself away from Luka and slowly shake the bundle of money out of my sleeve.

Remember, he lied to you once. You can't trust him.

My mother always stayed vigilant. I quickly shove the money into my left boot. I'll figure out a way to help Luka later.

"Did you hear what I said?" Luka's voice breaks through my thoughts, and I realize I stopped listening.

I look down at him. His face hardens around the edges.

With a sigh, I murmur, "Sorry."

"Do you understand what you did back there? What the punishment is for assaulting someone like that?"

"What?" I narrow my eyes at Luka, assessing if he is joking. It's not like I killed anyone. I expect to see Luka smile, but he's serious. Of course, he's right. I didn't just hit a policeman, I hit an officer of the People's Commissariat. That's not just a crime, that's treason, an assault against the state, punishable by death. I can't go back home because the NKVD will find out where I live and come for me. "You're right. I can't go back home. I can't go anywhere." Kaganov's face floats up to the surface of my mind. My neck prickles when I think how he'd react to officers coming to arrest me. Would I see a sad, pleading look in his eyes? Or would he be cold and judging? My chin begins to quiver, but I clamp my mouth tight.

"I know a safe place," Luka says softly. "And Katya won't mind your company."

"A safe place?"

"Yes," he says with a smile.

"You just helped a fugitive on the run. You're as guilty as I am. We won't be safe anywhere."

His fingers brush over my hand. His warmth is soothing against my cold skin. "It's a place close to here, but far away enough for you and me to be safe."

He's talking in puzzles. Why doesn't he just tell me where this place is?

Just because you're stuck in this horrible situation

together, doesn't mean you can trust him, my mother's voice reminds me.

Your worries wore you down, Mama. You risked everything to get those ration cards but never even told me what you were doing. Then you turned around and handed them over to Kaganov, of all people?

She doesn't respond, and a thought creeps into my mind. Kaganov could have stolen the cards from my mother before she had a chance to give them to me. My chest aches. It was all for nothing.

I look up at the sky. The sun is slipping away, and dark clouds are settling above us. Summer twilight is coming soon. It won't get dark, but it means the curfew's approaching and I need to decide if I trust this boy.

"We'll go to the tunnels," he says. "The people who live there will give you a place to stay for a few days. No one ever raids the tunnels."

I jerk my hand away. Fear, wild and cold, starts to uncurl inside me, driven by one thought. Luka's not talking safety. He's talking food. I'm his ration. "The tunnels?" My voice is shaky. I sit up and my body sways as if my muscles and bones stopped supporting me. "I'm not going into the tunnels."

"Why not?"

Doesn't he know about the rumors? "*Lyudoedy*. The Hunters. They live in the tunnels," I snap at him. My heart tells me to trust Luka, but the tunnels? No one dares to go into the dark passageways underneath the city.

Luka turns his head toward me, and his mouth twitches at

the corners. "Don't believe everything you hear. I live there. Katya lives there."

"Then who are these people in the tunnels?"

"Men and women who helped us after we lost our home. Former neighbors. They're good people." He shakes his head and chuckles. "The Hunters. Whoever came up with that story didn't know what they were talking about."

Before I can answer, a loud rustle above our heads stops me mid-breath. A small murder of crows explodes out of the trees. The sound of beating wings fills the air around us as they take flight.

My neck tipped back, I gape at the departing flock.

When they disappear, Luka gets up, turns to me, and slowly releases a breath. His eyes scan my face. "We need to move. Are you rested enough?"

I'm not rested at all. If anything, I'm as worn out as my mother's old boots, but I drag myself to my feet. "I'm all right." My voice wobbles. Not convincing. Not at all.

Luka clutches my hand with such force I almost lose my balance. "You look like you're about to fall down."

I already collapsed once today. Not happening again. "I'm all right," I repeat, this time firmer.

A thought flickers across his face. "When was the last time you ate?"

I'd been asked the same question earlier. The day seems to repeat itself. "A couple of hours ago. Maksim gave me some food in the Mansion." My cheeks start to burn as Luka takes a step closer.

His expression turns hard. "What did you have to do for it?" His voice is hollow.

I set my jaw, but my voice is steady and low. "Nothing."

"Nothing?" He crosses his arms, his lips a flat line. "Maksim took you there to share food. I know for a fact they don't give it for nothing."

"Maksim never asked for anything." A bit of truth. A bit of lie. I loathe myself for saying this, but there's no way I'm telling Luka about the kiss.

Luka holds my gaze for a long time. Did he see the kiss, after all? But a few breaths later, his jaw muscles relax, and he tosses me a grin. "Maksim didn't have time to ask for anything, I guess. The candlestick got in the way."

"Why does it matter to you what I did for the food? *You* take it from *them*. You do exactly what they ask. You have no right to judge. Or act like you care."

"I do it for my family. Just like you do it for yours. Or for Aka. And I'm sure Maksim believed he was doing you a favor, but look where it got you."

I don't blame Maksim. He saved me from passing out in the streets. "He didn't do anything wrong. And he never lied to me. Instead, he helped me survive the day. That's all."

"Not everything's about survival," Luka snaps, and kicks a nearby pebble.

Not everything's about survival, my mother notes calmly. *For him. For you, it is.*

I swallow thickly. Why is he so angry with Maksim? With

me? He was the one who lied when he could've helped. If he could have put away his pride and ego yesterday, we wouldn't be running away from the NKVD. I don't want to talk about it anymore.

"Which way are we going?" I surprise myself with my own words. I guess my mind has decided to go to the tunnels. I don't really have a choice but to trust Luka and follow him into the underground. All I need is a bit of time, a night or two away from home, and maybe the NKVD will forget about me. I don't think I killed Scarface. His head might hurt for a day or two, but there shouldn't be any serious damage, should there? I'm not that strong. And why chase one girl when there's an abundance of food and other girls?

"It's not far from here." Luka nods in the direction of the Haymarket. "Ready?" He rocks back on his heels.

A sharp razor of unease scrapes the back of my neck. I'm abandoning Aka. But not for long. All I need is a bit of time, and then, when we're back in my room, I'll tell her everything that happened to me. She'll laugh it off and call me silly. She won't need to go back to the Mansion because Maksim's money can buy us food when it becomes available at the Haymarket. In a couple of days, after the next delivery, all will be back to normal.

I straighten my dress. "Let's go. Curfew's coming."

"We'll take the backstreets. Better to stay away from main boulevards." Luka runs his tongue over his teeth. "In case they're searching for you."

I nod and trail after Luka. A few blocks later, we approach

a tall, nondescript brick building, and for a few long seconds we stand in front of our escape route, a wide steel door. Luka places his hand on a wooden door handle and twists it. The door opens, its hinges creaking loudly, and he walks into the beckoning void of a long hallway. The smell of stagnant water and decay hits my nostrils.

My heart drops. The only sound I hear is the blood thumping in my ears.

What if Luka's leading me into a slaughter? What do I know about him? Fear flushes through my veins. Luka lost his parents, his home, his fingers, and his future as a pianist and now his—what did he call it?—supply. I've seen a constant pain hidden deep in his eyes. A sorrow floating around in there like dust motes in the air. Luka has saved my life twice now. Katya offered me their only potato. I don't think Luka would put me at risk. Not intentionally.

I boldly step through the door and follow him into the tunnels.

11

——

THE DARKNESS PAIRED WITH THE SILENCE
of the tunnels is eerie.

I step forward, then pause. How are we supposed to move through this thick blackness? Like a living organism, it wraps its cold tentacles around me.

Luka picks up a flashlight hidden in a pile of dried leaves not far from the door. A secret stash only those who live in the tunnels know about, I guess. He lights it, and the beam flickers on the concrete walls. The narrow space in front of us is shaped like an elbow. A couple of pipes run horizontally above our heads. Black mildew creeps along cracks in the walls. This space was probably meant to be a pedestrian underpass. It must be leading us into a tunnel where trains were supposed to run. I've heard that about thirty shafts were built before the siege in early 1941. But, like everything else, construction came to a stop because of the war.

We walk down the narrow corridor, descending into the gloom of Leningrad's unfinished metro.

Something skitters into a corner, a rat, I'm sure, and I scream. Luka swings the beam of his flashlight, blinding me.

"What is it?"

"A rat." I point in the direction I think it ran.

He shakes his head. "There are no rats here. They've all been eaten. Trust me."

Of course. There are no rats left in the city. Not since last winter. But what else could it have been? I don't believe in ghosts, but something is definitely moving down here.

Luka turns, and we follow his flashlight beam deeper into the tunnels. The echo of our shoes shuffling against the path accompanies our silent stroll. The sharp chill from the stone walls seeps into my bones. I shiver and wrap my arms around my shoulders. It's going to be a long walk in darkness.

"Watch your step. It can be slippery down here," Luka throws over his shoulder.

"Why do you live here? Who are you hiding from? The secret police?" I whisper into his back.

Luka stops and looks at me. "People. We're hiding from people."

People? What does he mean? "I don't understand."

Luka's free hand clutches into a fist briefly. "People prey on the weak. They steal, raid, and kill. Haven't you noticed?" His tone is sharp. Almost angry. "When Katya and I lost our home, we had nowhere to go. We spent a few nights in empty, destroyed buildings, and we ran into other homeless gangs. They chased us away. And then one day we came upon Boria, our old neighbor. He took us in." Luka swipes his forehead as if trying to erase bad memories. "The party doesn't care about any of this as long as there's no one on the streets after curfew. Everyone's trying to survive the siege. Most do it at the expense of others."

There's no shame in surviving.

Mama was a thief. So am I. But some lines cannot be crossed. Certain things can't be undone or forgiven. Can't be forgotten. Like a naked girl covered in bruises. Or golden hair scattered on the carpet. A pale limb on the pavement.

Luka holds the flashlight over me for a few more seconds before turning away and continuing down the tunnel.

The shaft we're in expands, but I feel like the damp, mossy walls are closing in on me. I should be more careful with my words. Luka trusts me enough to take me to the camp where he and his sister live. He trusts me enough to share his secrets. How do I explain to him that survival to me means smashing someone's head with a shovel? Stealing from starved people and trading their meager possessions for food? How do I find the right words to tell Luka that staying alive isn't just helping one another but using one another as well? He goes to the Mansion. He knows what's happening there. He should understand, shouldn't he?

My mother's boots make small scuffling sounds on the rough concrete under my feet. The light in Luka's arm bobs jaggedly in front of me.

"I saw something in the streets this morning," I say. "A severed arm."

Luka halts so abruptly I almost run into him. "Oh *chyort*."

I can't stop now. "This morning, on my way to the Haymarket, I stumbled on a group of people gathered around something on the pavement. It was an arm." The words pour out of me like a stream of water from a broken dam. "I've never seen anything like it before. It was just lying on the ground. Not torn off from an explosion, but sliced off. The cut itself was so clean. Neat." My voice croaks and I barely manage to finish my thoughts. I stop walking, sink to the ground, leaning against the wall. Suddenly I'm exhausted. "You're right. People are more dangerous than hunger."

"Did anyone notify the militia?" Luka hovers over me.

I shake my head. "I didn't stay to find out."

Luka mutters under his breath.

"What?"

"I wish you hadn't run into Maksim. And God knows how I wish he'd never taken you to the Mansion. A lot of things would've been different now." Frowning, Luka extends a hand. I put mine in his, and he pulls me up, keeping a tight hold on my arm. Gently, he pushes my chin up with the butt end of the flashlight. The cold metal feels surprisingly refreshing on my skin. Luka's jaw juts out, but his voice has softened. "You'll be safe here. With me."

I nod and hold on to him for a few seconds longer.

"Ready?" Luka asks.

A weak smile stretches my dry lips. "I am."

"Let's go. A few minutes more."

We continue our somber walk through the shaft, but a constant prickling along the back of my neck makes me twitch at every sound, until Luka says, "I never took you for a skittish type."

"I was just checking to make sure no one is following us," I say, and tuck a loose chunk of my hair behind my ear.

His jaw clenched, Luka studies my face, then his eyes scan the blackness behind me. "There's nothing to be afraid of down here."

He thinks I'm imagining things. I should stop acting like a frightened goat. We move on, and a few long minutes later, we come to a fork. The passage in front of us stretches out in two directions. A cool breeze blows from the left. Luka turns to the right. Tripping forward, I reach out to steady myself against a mossy, damp wall. My foot connects with an object.

An empty bottle rolls loudly down the passage.

"Who's there?" a man's voice says. "Name yourself." Did I trigger some kind of crude alarm system?

A tall, skinny figure stumbles toward me and picks up the bottle. His glassy gaze moves over me and settles on my face. "Who the hell are you?" The man's hand goes slowly to his back pocket and reappears with a knife. He's a thin, hard-faced man with round glasses. His head is bald, decorated with oddly shaped brown patches, and his teeth look alarmingly jagged. Time and hunger have etched deep lines onto his cheeks and around the corners of his mouth and eyes.

"She's with me, Fyodor." Luka steps around me and lifts the flashlight higher, illuminating both of us and the man.

"Luka," the man says, and lowers the knife. "Finally. Where have you been? Did you bring food?"

"It's a long story. This is Liza." Luka waves in my direction, ignoring Fyodor's question about the food. "She needs a place to stay. She's gotten herself into trouble with the NKVD."

A short, surprised whistle. "What kind of trouble?" His tone tells me he thinks I bring problems, and he's probably right. Fyodor takes a step closer and to the side, out of the light so I can't see his face.

"Minor thing. A misunderstanding of sorts." Luka shrugs, downplaying my assault of the NKVD officer. "No one followed us. We're safe."

"Let's see what Galina says to that." Fyodor turns around and beckons us to follow him.

We head deeper into the tunnel toward a flickering light and an echo of muffled voices. The space opens to a large rectangular chamber with high ceilings and a crumbled concrete landing, an unfinished passenger station. There's a firepit in the middle. A small group of people sits in front of it. A scrawny young girl, with painfully protruding cheekbones, looks like she's either half asleep or semiconscious, but she stirs in her seat as we approach. Still, I'm not even sure her vacant eyes register me. A few other children around the fire cradle their sunken bellies, chewing on something that looks like sticks of wood.

With a sudden jolt of dread, I turn to the adults. Bone-sharp, sunken cheeks and hollowed-out eyes. I try to smile but no one smiles back.

It was a mistake to come here. They're not cannibals. But they're not friendly. They are starved, weakened, and angry. These people won't accept me.

They don't know it yet, but they need you more than you need them, my mother notes.

A stench of unwashed bodies and cigarettes saturates the air.

"Luka brought a guest," Fyodor says to the woman who sits closest to the firepit. One of her hands is holding a lit cigarette rolled with what looks like strips of old newspaper; the other is wrapped around a cup.

"Luka, like an old cat, always drags something in," she says. Someone giggles. Most of the people nod. The woman obviously commands the attention of everyone around her. Her lips curve into what I might have considered a smile if there were any kindness behind her eyes. She's about my mother's age, midthirties, maybe a bit older.

"She needs to stay here for a few days, Galina. That's all I ask. She'll be in our tent," Luka says.

The woman takes a drag on the cigarette and lets the

smoke trickle out. It curls and disappears into the murkiness above us. "She will also need to eat . . ."

Voices around the fire mutter in agreement.

"And we have nothing to share," Galina's cold voice speaks above the murmurs.

"I do." I walk around Luka and step closer to the fire so that Galina can see me. "I have something I'll share if you let me stay here."

Luka is right behind me. "What are you doing?" he whispers.

I ignore him and take another step forward. "I want to help. To contribute. I won't eat your food, but I can help you to buy bread."

Galina tilts her head to the side and studies me with an expression I can't read. "The city doesn't have bread."

"Trucks are coming," Luka says. "Maksim told me. There will be a new shipment in two days. The stores will distribute bread on Tuesday morning."

"To those who have ration cards," Fyodor barks. "And money. And we don't have either."

A skinny boy by Galina's side stands and comes up to me. A short wooden stick hangs loosely in the corner of his mouth like a toothpick.

I stop breathing for a second, and I take a step back.

The boy is a man, all bones and pallid skin, nothing else. His skin is so tight around his face it looks like a skull. "You eat," he says with a slight whistle that sounds more like a hiss. He has only three teeth and when he opens his mouth, it looks like a big black hole. "Not too often and not much, but you eat. Where do you get food?"

Now that I know my mother took ration cards from the sick and the dead, I think back to those seldom occasions when we did have more bread than the allotted daily 125 grams per person. I don't want to think about what it will cost me to get those back from Kaganov, but I can still steal in the market. I'll get by—how did Luka put it?—at the expense of others.

"I . . . I . . . go to the Haymarket. My neighbors help when they can. We all help one another." The lies tumble over each other as they come out. I wasn't prepared for this type of questioning. Is he trying to make me feel guilty for eating better than these people?

"You have a home," he says. There is a sad longing in the way he stretches the word *home*.

My heart beats against my ribs like a bird trapped in a cage. "I do."

"Go home, then. There's nothing for you here, girl," he says.

"Let her speak, Boria." Galina gets up from her chair and strides toward me. She's taller and stronger-looking than I expected. "Tell us, Liza, what you can share with us, and we'll see if we'll let you stay." She puts a hand on Boria's arm.

Maybe before the siege, and hunger and death, Galina's hostility would've silenced me. But not now. Not after what I've seen and done. "I'll share my ration cards with you if you let me stay," I say in a firm voice, and stand a little straighter. "I have a couple of hundred rubles as well." The money in my pocket can buy a ration of bread. No one needs to know about the bundle in my left boot.

Luka steps closer, his nostrils flaring. "You never said you had anything of value. You never offered any help."

I turn away.

You don't owe him anything.

Galina and Boria move toward me until they stand uncomfortably close. Galina smells of stale ashes and cat piss. Boria smells of vodka and rot. They take me in from head to toe, and I suddenly realize they're trying to figure out where I keep my ration cards. Can they see through me and down to my boots and wool socks? Would they kill me and take my money and the cards?

"Do we have a deal, Galina?" Luka is right by my side, squaring his body between me and the pair. "Ration cards and a couple of hundred rubles in exchange for a place to stay?"

Galina crosses her arms. "Give me one good reason why I shouldn't take it all, throw her out, and feed my people?"

My head spins. I bunch my fists, afraid and angry at the same time. "I offer you help, and you want to hurt me?"

"No one said we want to hurt you," Boria says.

"Don't do anything stupid." Luka's whisper in my ear is surprisingly calming. He shakes his head slowly as if warning me to stay quiet. He and I both know my temper can get the best of me, and right now, it would be awfully inconvenient. We look at each other for a few long seconds: me unable to fight the pull of the deep blue, and he, probably, making sure I don't do anything foolish.

"You two are adorable," a croaky and familiar voice says from the farthest corner of the cave.

"Katya," I breathe her name, bend my knees, and open my arms.

She staggers across the cave but stops midstep and a violent cough washes over her. She lets it pass and stands shakily upright when the spasms are over. Then she spits something thick and dark on the floor. It colors her lips.

I think it's blood, but I'm not sure, because there's not enough light for me to see clearly.

I run to Katya and embrace her. Her arms wrap around my neck. She's sharp and bony and warm—too warm. I didn't realize how desperately I needed a hug until her thin arms come around me.

"Now that you're here, maybe Luka will stop talking about you," Katya whispers into my hair.

"Katya, go back to bed. You must rest."

The tenderness in Galina's voice takes me by surprise. I release Katya from my arms and turn to look at the woman. Sadness flickers across her pale face, but it's replaced with coldness the moment she notices my attention. "You can stay with us until the bread comes. That's all we'll give you. In exchange, we want your ration cards. And two hundred rubles. That's all we ask," she says.

12

KATYA TAKES MY HAND AND WHISPERS, "Let's go to our apartment." Her smile is weak, but her eyes glimmer with mischievousness. "That is, our tent."

I scan the group in front of the firepit. Luka's whispering something to Galina; his injured hand moves in the air, emphasizing his words. Galina replies, her face raw with anger. They're probably discussing my presence in their camp. I can feel Boria's leer drilling into the back of my head. I turn and our eyes meet for a short second. I can practically hear his thoughts spinning, assessing me. He doesn't trust me, and why should he?

"Don't mind Boria," Katya says. "Or Galina. They'll warm up to you. They don't know you yet." Katya pulls my hand. "Let's go."

One last look at Luka to see if he's coming with us, but he continues to whisper to Galina. What are they talking about so intently? With no answer in sight, I follow his sister deeper into the tunnel.

The siblings have their own space. We crouch on our knees and look inside their tent. It's small and dark, and smells of moss and stale water. Near the farthest edge of the tent, an oil lamp in the corner casts geometric shapes onto the place where Katya and Luka sleep—a pile of clothes and rags that lost their colors ages ago and now serve as their mattress.

"We don't have much. We lost everything in the bombing. Even those clothes on the floor aren't ours. We scavenge and use what we find." Her voice is small and sad; it's breaking me into pieces.

I have so much compared with them.

Comparing yourself with others won't save you, Liza.

"Let's wait for Luka outside." Her arms encircle my shoulders, and her fingers squeeze them lightly.

We get to our feet.

There's a small wooden bench beside their tattered brown tent. Random pieces of wood hammered together by a few rusty nails. Beneath my fingers, it feels like tree bark with rough ridges and prickly burrs. Another lamp on the ground in front of the tent illuminates a high arched ceiling above our heads. Katya sits down and pats a space close to her. I carefully lower myself, not sure the seat will hold both of us. My back muscles relax a bit when the construction doesn't sway under the weight of my body.

"Boria made it for me. He used to build things around here." She pauses, and I sense a deep sadness in her voice. She sighs and folds her hands into her lap. "When he had the strength. Now he's so weak he doesn't come out of his tent most days. Today was an exception. He doesn't have much time left."

I choose not to respond. What can I say anyway to make her feel better? I've seen people die in the streets. My mother told me about the dead lining up the long hallways in the Hotel Astoria. Death and hunger are our constant companions. They follow us wherever we go and leave only void and desperation in their wake.

My feet are so cold, even in Mama's boots, that my toes are about to curl into themselves. The smell of mildew and wet stone lingers between us. How do these people live here in this constant cold? In this humidity that seeps into your bones?

Katya studies my face. "You look good. You look like you've been eating."

Boria said the same thing, but Katya's tone isn't accusatory. I don't say anything as I examine the deep cracks that run through the wall in front of us, shafts of light from the lamp forming a variety of oddly shaped figures.

My hand goes to the pocket where the piece of bread from the Mansion still lies. It's dry and crusty already. I should share it with Katya. But if I do, wouldn't the girl expect me to share it with the others? The piece isn't even enough for one person. What if I'll need it later myself? I don't know anything about these people, and I have no idea when my next meal will be. My mama taught me to always save food for later. At some point, when the hunger got worse and people started dying every day, she asked me to not share my rations with Aka. "Aka's not alone. Her family will take care of her." The war has changed us in ways we never expected. Before, it was considered rude not to invite your friends for a meal. Now the same act of kindness is deemed stupid and reckless.

My hand falls away from the pocket.

"It's all right," Katya says, and takes my hand, as if she knows I'm hiding food. I want to pull away, but her skin is hot to the touch, and I leave my hand in hers. She's burning up.

Voices echo in the tunnel, but I can't distinguish any words.

"We're having supper soon," Katya says.

"Supper?"

The people sitting around the fire looked like they haven't been eating for a long time.

"Galina rings a bell when it's ready," Katya says. "Anytime now. Let's wait." She shuts her eyes. Conversation over.

I look at my feet. The beam from the oil lamp by the bench cuts through the humid darkness of the tunnel. With my boot, I dislodge a crumble of rock underneath my feet. I study it. Then I dislodge another one.

Finally, the bell rings, shattering the silence between us, and Katya gets to her feet. "Let's go."

I shake my head. "I don't think so. I haven't earned it yet."

"Don't be stupid. They let you stay." Katya pulls forcefully on the sleeve of my dress. "No one will say a word."

"I'll wait here," I say. "You go."

She hesitates for a moment. Her face seems to sharpen and I'm sure she's about to say something, but she doesn't. She turns away and leaves.

As soon as she's gone, I pull out the bread. Whatever these people are eating for supper won't be real food. They don't have any. Of that I'm sure. They chew on the wooden sticks to trick their bodies into thinking they're being fed.

I break the piece in half with my numb-from-cold fingers and quickly shove it into my mouth. When I swallow, it scratches the inside of my throat.

Compassion is a weakness. It'll get you killed. Food is all that matters now.

Food. The word lost its meaning a long time ago. Anything giving an ounce of energy is considered food. Things I wouldn't think of eating before the war—candy made of glue and dirt, smelly fish, bread full of sawdust—now seem normal. Before, caviar was a delicacy. A couple of years ago, my mother brought it home for a New Year's Eve dinner. A gift from a music fan who we later found out was an informant. Its salty, rich taste lingers in my mouth as I remember slathering a piece of white bread with butter and sprinkling red caviar on top of it. We passed a small plate between us and chewed in silence, the fish eggs popping on our tongues.

The bread from the Mansion lies in my gut like a rock, and I can't stop shivering. I rub my arms to get my blood flowing.

To rely on other people for protection is frightening. It goes against everything Mama taught me. But I should make the best of this situation and try to accept this place as my new shelter. At least for the next few days.

They made a home here. They built benches and tents. They created a community. Luka and Katya seem to feel safe here. It's me who doesn't belong with them. But I can't go home. My insides twist into a tight knot when I think about the officers and Aka. At least here, in this gloomy place, I'm safe from the NKVD. Safe from *him*.

Someone laughs in the distance, and I hear the clacking of plates and glasses. I can't see anything from here. Maybe I was wrong. Maybe they do have something to eat.

Luka emerges out of the darkness. The light flickers and changes the outline of his face. He holds two steaming mugs in his hands. A sweet smell wafts in waves toward me. He hands me a cup and sits on the bench.

"What's this?" I ask, and sniff the liquid. It smells like water spiced with herbs. No sustenance.

Luka deliberates for a few seconds before he says, "This is our supper. Boiled water and dried *zveroboy*."

I try to keep my face neutral. "*Zveroboy?* I've never heard of it."

Luka smiles and looks down, shuffling his shoes against the dirt. "It's a plant. Boria knows how to find it. He says just one or two teaspoons of *zveroboy* will settle your belly and give you some energy. It tastes bitter, but it's safe."

"How does he know this?"

"You'd never guess from his current looks, but he was a professor of biology before the siege."

"A professor?" I picture Boria's skull-like face.

"Boria knows a lot of things," Luka says. "He's the reason we've survived this long." He looks at me and nods at my cup. "Trust me, drink it. You'll notice the difference."

I take a sip. The liquid is bitter, but not overwhelmingly so. "Where did Boria find *zveroboy*?"

"It grows in the cemetery," Luka says in a low voice. "We have it every night."

So this is what Katya meant when she mentioned supper. The churning of guilt is fading away. I made the right decision not to offer my bread. There's no need to hate or shame myself. I had to do it. If I'm to stay here a few days, I'll need it.

"What do you have for breakfast?" I whisper.

Luka doesn't reply for a moment, and I don't push for an answer. I think I know it when I see Luka deflate. He suddenly looks years older. He tips his head back a bit and takes a few big gulps of his tea. I watch his throat move as he swallows. He catches my eyes and says, "Nothing. On most days all we get is this. But I used to be able to get a few pieces of bread, potatoes, and once even eggs from the Mansion. A couple of times Maksim sneaked cheese for me. When I played there." He lifts the cup to his lips and takes another sip. "Those nights we had a party here. Cheese and vodka." He chuckles. "But mostly, if we're lucky and someone finds something edible in the streets, we share. But it's getting more difficult to scavenge."

The bread in my pocket pulls me down toward the ground. They scavenge and share. I steal and lie to make sure I have something to eat, almost every day.

I think about Kaganov's offer to share his food and shudder. I can't even stand to be in the same room as him and, like everyone else, it seems, he'd expect something in return.

Whatever it takes.

My mother's voice echoes in my skull. After a year under siege there was almost nothing she wouldn't do to survive, but still, she always said there were lines we could never cross if we wanted to keep our humanity.

I shove the thoughts away and direct my attention to the boy in front of me.

Should I tell Luka I can take him to the market and teach him to lift things from one stall to trade at another? Would he see me as a lesser person? Would revealing how I survive make him think I'm foul? Cruel?

Unworthy of him?

He'll define you by your actions before you'll ever have a chance to explain.

"I'd like to meet the others," I say in a low voice. I need to be around people. I crave a distraction so I don't have to think anymore.

A broad grin starts in one corner of his mouth and spreads

to the other. "I thought you'd never ask." He gets up, holding his mug in one hand and offering me the other. "They want to meet you."

They want your money and your ration cards.

I put my hand in his, and he gently pulls me up. Together, we walk over to the firepit. The air is still laden with mildew and moisture on this side of the cave. But it also offers warmth.

"Come and sit." Katya gets up from her chair. "Take it. I'm going to lie down now."

I take her seat, and we watch her leave.

"She needs fuel," Galina says in her raspy voice. "She won't last long. Not with that fever."

I feel like I'm supposed to say something, to offer a solution, but I don't know what to do, so I study my cup.

"Our guest could go and get us bread. She offered her money and her ration cards," Boria says, his eyes latched to my face.

"Liza can't be seen in the streets." Luka shakes his head. "The NKVD is looking for her."

Boria leans forward as if trying to see me better. "She promised us. So, she goes." He sits upright and coughs, a deep cackling sound. Like Mama's. His head drops down, his chin resting against his caved-in chest as he waits for the air to return to him. A thin sheen of sweat glistens on his skin. He finally looks up. "And what did you do to disappoint the secret police?"

"I hit an officer in the head with a candlestick," I say sharply.

Luka winces, as if remembering the chaotic scene. Boria chuckles in amusement, and Galina leans back into her chair.

"No shit," someone says.

"They have lots of food. The officers. They conceal it from us," I say, and take a sip from my mug. A cold fury stirs inside me at the memory of the table set in the center of the living room.

"Food's not being distributed equally," Galina says slowly. Anger, hot and all-consuming, hardens her face.

Fyodor snorts into his glass. "Survival of the fittest. Only those with power will survive the siege." His glasses steam up from the hot tea, and he takes them off and wipes them with the sleeve of his dirty brown jacket.

Power's one way to survive. Keeping to yourself and doing what's necessary is another.

"It was disgusting. Atrocious, really," I say loudly, trying to talk over my mother's voice and the snapping of wood in the fire. "All that meat and cheese. Potato salad. Fresh cucumbers. Rye bread." With every memory, with every word, the hate grows dark in my heart. "And the girls. All these young girls . . . the things they must do to get food."

"And you were there," Galina snickers, shaking her head. "Just watching it all? Like some kind of royalty?"

Everyone laughs at her stupid comment, as if it's the funniest joke they've ever heard.

I look down at my boots. These people don't understand why I did what I did. They don't know why I went to the

Mansion. And now they're judging me, thinking me a girl who is willing to sell her body for scraps of food. I feel helpless and exposed telling them what I've seen, and yet fury, like a tick, bores under my skin, burning me from inside out. If I could hit Scarface all over again, I would.

Boria draws himself up. "I wonder if anything can be done about that."

"About what?" Galina asks.

Boria gives us a small shrug. "All that food came from somewhere. Maybe there are deliveries we don't know about."

"What good does it do for us?" Galina barks. "We can't track down and rob military trucks."

I shift in my chair. "You don't have to rob the trucks. You can get food from the Mansion. It's already there, isn't it?"

Boria spits in the dirt by his feet and gives a pointed look to Galina, who gawks at me like she sees me for the first time.

"What are you saying?" Luka turns to me.

I have no idea what I'm saying. Why am I even talking?

I pause for a long minute, scanning the hollow, starved faces around the fire. I didn't think anyone would take me seriously. Who in their right mind would want to break into the NKVD's quarters? But the intensity of their faces suggests otherwise. "We . . . we can take that food away from them." I stumble over my own words. Why do I keep saying *we*? I don't want to be a part of this group. "We could break into their kitchen. It's located downstairs." Is there a kitchen downstairs? It must be. Maksim brought me food from somewhere. "There's got to be a back door, a servants' entrance. We could use it to get inside."

Boria whistles and a broad smile appears on his face. The thin skin wrapped around his skull crinkles like dry paper. "Let's go and get what we can from the NKVD's lair. Eh? This is the craziest thing I've ever heard." He chuckles. "But it does sound interesting."

Luka doesn't move. He doesn't seem to breathe. I silently beg him to agree with Boria, to tell his people how stupid my proposition to rob the Mansion is. He inspects me with an expression I can't read, and suddenly dread blooms inside me, its sharp, cutting vines rising to my heart. What if he thinks my idea could actually work?

"Go on, girl," Boria barks, and then leans back, a wooden stick clamped between his teeth. "Tell us your plan. Amuse us."

Luka nods. A small sharp nod, and the vines squeeze so hard I can't breathe. I don't have a plan; I want to scream. Why are you listening to me? I'm just some girl who uttered a few stupid, stupid words without thinking.

"It's . . . it's dangerous. Are you sure we should even talk about it?"

Galina's mouth opens and closes soundlessly as if she were a gasping fish out of water. She waves for me to continue.

"Well, we could go through that back door. At night. After the curfew, when the streets are empty but not dark. And we could take what should've been shared with the people from the beginning. Then we would distribute the food equally among us."

Above, the explosions start. How did we miss the sound of air-raid sirens? We can't be that deep underground, can we?

I must escape this place before the shells drop.

13

I JUMP TO MY FEET, READY TO FLEE. BUT where would I go? We're already underground.

None of the others react to the sounds of the attack.

Fyodor, who sits across from me, stretches his long legs in front of him and closes his eyes. But there's a tension in his posture that tells me he's still paying attention to the noise in the streets.

"I can't sleep with this racket," a boy mumbles. His voice is so weak I barely hear it.

"It'll be over before you know it," Galina says.

The boy looks up and smiles at her.

"It might take longer than you think," Boria says.

Another explosion, and I drop to my knees, lean forward, and hold myself tight.

The thundering roar makes the earth quake, and we all stir and sit up straight. The Nazis' shells are landing right above us.

Two explosions in a row, and the walls around us vibrate. "So loud," I whisper. I clutch myself tighter.

"They're close," Galina notes calmly.

"They won't hit us," Luka says, then reaches out to me and pulls me up. "We're safe here. We've survived worse." He nods at the chair behind me. I slowly lower myself into the seat.

Galina snorts. "Why do you think we're here? Tunnels are indestructible. They protect us. No matter what happens above, we won't die from the bombs."

Another explosion, the loudest one yet. The sound reverberates through the walls, and a cloud of dust descends from above us, clogging my airways. I choke on it, but part of me is relieved that, at least with the bombs, we've stopped talking about the Mansion. I wish I hadn't said anything in the first place. It's a mad idea to try to rob the NKVD. We'd be more likely to get ourselves all killed than walk away with food from the pantry. The bombing stops as abruptly as it started. I wait for another discharge, but it doesn't come.

As if propelled by some invisible sign, everyone gets up and shuffles to their sleeping spaces. Children head to small shacks—resembling actual tents, even though their walls and flaps are pockmarked with rips and holes—in the farthest corner of the cave. Adults fold themselves into wobbly makeshift structures built from tarps, trash, and dirty rags. They've obviously established their own routine as if their life in this damp and dark place was the only life they ever knew.

"We should go," Luka says. "Let's get some sleep."

Their space is small. We'll be close to one another.

In the tent, Katya shifts farther into the corner and pats the rags, inviting me to lie down. I lie by her side, my arms wrapped around my midsection. Luka lies down by the exit.

A complete dark envelops us. The outside silence is interrupted by the occasional shuffling of footsteps and hushed voices. Katya falls into a restless sleep, tossing and turning. Her breathing is ragged.

I remove my boots, careful not to wake her, and shove them under my head. It's strange to be sharing such a small space with Luka. If I stretch my arm, I can touch him.

We remain silent. The rumble of voices in the background is a soothing sound. Katya whispers something under her breath. I scoot closer to her. She needs warmth and care. She needs a home. I shift my body, putting more weight on my right side. The ground is firm and unforgiving under the rags. I bet I'll wake up as stiff as Aka's grandfather.

I used to dread dark nights. I thought of them as a place of uncertainty and fear. A place of madness. In the beginning of the war, the nightmares invaded my dreams. Bottomless black holes would open under my feet and I'd fall, fall, fall into an abyss, bones vibrating, arms flailing, my mouth agape. Mama was always the one to wake me up. She'd smooth my hair, her eyes glistening in the night. She'd look down at me and whisper about the upcoming morning and the light and our plans for the day. She'd tell me to concentrate on the future ahead of me. The darkness would recede, and I could sleep again.

My heart swells with an ache I cannot escape.

I still hate darkness and what it brings. But tonight, I want the night to last as long as possible so I can remain close to the boy next to me. Listening to his breathing. Wondering if he's thinking about me.

I stretch my hand. Luka's farther away from me than I thought because my fingers don't touch him.

He has turned to face me, and I can see the glimmer of his eyes. Then his arm reaches out to me, and my heart responds, wild and uneven. Our hands meet in the middle, and I lace my fingers through his. Then I steady my racing mind, close my eyes, and fall into a dreamless sleep.

I wake up to a bright light shining into my face and confusion.

My first instinct is to hide under the rags Katya and I share. I want to retreat, but instead I bolt upright, staring wildly around, shivering with cold.

Someone touches my shoulder and I shriek.

"Shhh . . . don't wake her up," a familiar voice says.

Luka's leaning over me and Katya. He's wearing a white shirt that is open at the neck. It's fresh, not wrinkled, and smells of wind and soap. No jacket. No sweater. How's he not cold? And why's he so dressed up?

He beams his flashlight into my face. I cover my eyes with a hand. "What are you doing?"

"I'm waking you up. I want to show you something."

I glare at him through my fingers. "Now? What is it?"

He keeps right on grinning. "Get up and follow me."

I don't want to leave the tent. It's warmer here than in the tunnels. I like the safety of our shared blanket. Even as these thoughts run through my head, I know I'll follow Luka. I groan, push the rags to the side, and carefully get to my knees, trying not to wake Katya. I don't have to touch her to know she's burning up with a high fever.

As if feeling my presence, her eyes fly open.

"Sleep. I'll be right back," I whisper to Katya. "Your brother wants to show me something."

A weak smile appears on her pale face. "Something?"

"His words, not mine," I say.

"Go then. Tell me all about it when you come back." Katya nods, and her little, pointy chin moves slowly, as if it requires energy she doesn't have. As I watch her battling to stay awake, I lean over and hug her skinny shoulders.

"We'll be back soon—Liza, come on," Luka says, and disappears from the tent.

The temperature in the cave seems to never change—a constant ten-degree drop-off from the streets above us. I wrap my arms around myself. At least now I'm more awake.

"We'll walk fast; you won't freeze," Luka says.

Wherever he's taking me, it better be warm. "You're dressed for a day on the beach." My eyes slide up and down his lean frame. "Definitely not for a stroll through the tunnels."

"I'm taking you somewhere else." His grin widens. He's bouncing on his toes. "Ready?"

Luka leads the way. The light of his flashlight dances around us, casting peculiar shapes on the wet, mossy walls. I'm starting to get used to this never-ending play of light and darkness. The shadows don't appear angry and foreboding. Instead, they make me feel like I'm surrounded by old friends.

"The heat wave will continue for a while," Luka says.

It's an odd thing to say unless we're going into the streets, and I don't believe we are. If anything, Luka's leading me deeper and deeper into the tunnels.

"There it is," he says, and stops, pointing the flashlight at a pile of rocks.

"Is this what you wanted to show me?" I croak sarcastically. I can't stop the trembling in my body.

Luka shakes his head. "Not that. Come on." He waves a hand and grins at me again. "I promise, you'll like it."

I'm intrigued, all right. I bite down on my lower lip and raise an eyebrow at him. I know Luka's toying with my curiosity.

He takes my hand. "Let's go."

My skin tingles under his touch as we make our way to the rocks.

"One night, after a bombing, they crumbled down from

the ceiling. Katya and I climbed over the rocks to explore. That's how we found it," Luka says.

"Found what?"

"Come see for yourself." His eyes meet mine, a strange gleam in them, like he is about to share a secret with me. A secret only he knows. A special gift only he can give.

Luka pushes his hair back, and his fingers trace the top of his ears. His hair sticks out at different angles, as if he forgot to comb when he woke up. I suppress a smile. He looks disheveled, and so at odds with his ironed white shirt. But the messiness makes him more handsome.

Without waiting for my response, he starts climbing the rocks. And of course, I follow. I step on the large boulders, avoiding the ones that look loose and unstable. We climb up, up, up. The air grows warmer and sweeter, as if we're ascending into the city. We reach the top of the stones and pause, assessing the view below.

At first, I see nothing at all—just unexpected bright light. Colors. Then a warm breeze makes me blink in surprise.

The view below is like a scene in a movie. It's unexpected and vibrant.

An unfinished train platform rests below us. Pearl-white columns, thick and strong, are holding up a ceiling of stained glass mixed with white ceramic. The big, jagged-edged hole in the center of the ceiling doesn't spoil the view. Instead, the rays of light coming through the opening enhance the picture below.

"*Bozhe moi.*" My God. My voice breaks from all the emotions stirring in me. "This is beautiful. I didn't know we'd built so much before the war." If these remnants of beauty are not a divine intervention, then what is?

Luka smiles and starts descending onto the platform.

I want to follow him, but I can't move. Seeing the ruins of what was supposed to be the most amazing underground system in the world suddenly makes me want to scream. It hurts to look at the light, at the ceiling, to know all this might not survive in the end, God's intervention or not.

With a heavy sigh, I trail Luka to the platform.

When we come down, he takes my hand and leads me to the center of the floor underneath the gap in the ceiling. Small puddles of water scatter the platform. The wet patches look fresh. It must've rained recently.

"I lie here and watch the sky and the sun." He nods at a dry spot beneath the opening.

We settle there, our backs pressed into the floor. The concrete is cold and hard, but I don't care. My anger at Nazis fades away. Being with Luka right here and now is all that matters.

The rain must have stopped a while ago. The clouds have parted to reveal a pale blue sky. "It's about to start," he says in a low voice.

"What?"

"Shhhh . . . Don't talk. Just look."

I do as he asks. A small white cloud crosses the gap in the ceiling. Then another, fluffy and white, appears, a bright spot against the pale blue. I smile and tilt my face to the sky above us, happy to see the daylight, happy to be out of the cold cave. It feels like we've stepped out of a world of nightmares and come back home.

"What do you think?" He turns his head, and his warm breath washes over my skin.

"I love it."

The sun is higher now because the sky in the gap turns pale pink. It reflects in the blue of Luka's eyes like small flames of warmth. Dawn in the city. He brought me here to show me the sunrise.

We are so close to each other, our shoulders almost touch. It takes all I have to fight the urge to touch his face, to tangle his hair between my fingers.

As if reading my mind, Luka finds my hand, brings my palm up to his mouth, and presses it to his lips. Right in the center of it. Then his mouth moves up my wrist. An electric current buzzes through my arm and moves lower into my core. I can't resist him anymore. And why should I? We might not survive this week or this month or this summer. Why waste a single second? I let go of my reservations and turn toward him. My hair tumbles over my shoulders and encases us. I run my fingers around the back of his neck and inhale the smell of him—deep forest and June sun. And soap. He came prepared.

He doesn't kiss me, and for a moment we just look at each other, two people inhaling each other's scent and searching each other's faces with need.

"Can I kiss you?" he whispers.

I can't speak. I nod, and his expression is surprise, then amusement, and then something else. For a few seconds, I'm sure I made a mistake—I misread him, and the butterflies turn into rocks. But then Luka turns me onto my back, and his lips press against mine.

He tastes of fire and rain. Bitter *zveroboy* and something salty. His tongue slips between my lips and explores me without shame or hesitation. I thread my hands into his hair, wrapping myself around him. He responds with such greed, I moan against him. His mouth leaves my lips and nips my jaw, then my neck. His tongue travels down to my collarbone, and my back arches under his weight.

When he suddenly pulls away from me, I want to cry out in despair.

"If I don't stop now, I might not stop at all," he whispers into my neck. His hot breath sends me into places I want to stay forever.

Then don't stop, I want to say. Don't ever stop.

He takes a deep breath, and his tongue trails the side of my neck. I shiver. His tongue is soft and firm at the same time. His hands run up my shoulder into my hair, pull my head back, and he kisses my exposed throat. It's almost too much. A whimper escapes me, and I can barely catch my breath through the roar of desire surging through me.

He lifts his head. "We must go back to the camp. I must check on Katya," he says.

I wince.

Luka brushes his thumb over my lower lip. "She likes you a lot. You know that, right?"

We look at each other. But neither of us attempts to move. Then Luka slowly rolls off me, but instead of getting up, he remains on the concrete by my side, stretched on his back, his eyes on the sky above us.

"Were you serious last night?" Luka shoves his hand into his pocket, but not fast enough. I see how his hand curls into a fist when he asks me. "About robbing the Mansion?"

"It . . . it was just an idea that crossed my mind." I turn to him and bury my face against his shoulder. I was hoping no one would bring it up again. It was a stupid and dangerous idea. I don't even know where they keep the food. "Why do you ask?"

"It's foolish," he says with a smile in his voice. "It could make a good movie, though." He chuckles.

"In real life, it'd be a suicide mission," I mumble into his shoulder. "Do you think they took me seriously?"

"No. It was fun to entertain your idea for a few minutes. Did you see Boria's face?" He scoffs. "We're starved, but not crazy."

My chest lightens up at his words.

His fingers find my chin and softly push my head up. He watches me for a long second. "I can barely breathe when I'm with you." He kisses me again, his lips firm and sweet and bitter.

A minute later, he buries his face into the side of my neck. "We should stop. It's not right."

"It feels right."

Silence stretches between us. Endless and heavy.

"Katya's sick, and I'm here with you. I must be with her," Luka finally says. His words give me a sharp jolt, like an electric shock. Of course we must return to Katya.

Luka sits up. "I'd give my life to stay here with you. But we need to go back."

We get up and look at the sky above us. It's bright blue now.

Luka takes my hand and gives me a small smile, his eyes full of sadness. "We'll be back. We'll bring something to eat and drink. We'll put blankets on the floor. We'll make a picnic." There is a hitch to his voice that cuts me in half. He squeezes my hand. "And we'll stay here all day and all night."

"I'd love that." I pull my hand away from his and start walking toward the rocks. "Thank you for bringing me here." I stop in front of the pile of boulders. It only takes a few strides for him to catch up with me. His presence, the paleness of his face, the blue of his eyes, stir something raw and throbbing inside me. A premonition? Because deep down, I know we'll never have that picnic. "It was . . ." I pause as my bottom lip twitches treacherously. "It was wonderful. I needed something like this."

Luka nods. His mouth curls at the edges but doesn't form a full smile. "I wanted to show it to you the moment I knew you were coming with me to the tunnels." The words shift something inside me, and I'm blushing again.

"Katya's waiting," I say to Luka. "Let's climb."

14

WHEN WE RETURN TO THE CAMP, GALINA pulls Luka aside. Boria is nearby, his hands in his pockets. He's wearing a thick wool jumper in a dull green color. A new wooden stick hangs in the corner of his mouth. His face is ashen, but he looks better than he did last night. Galina shoots a few quick glances my way when she speaks, and I'm sure they're discussing me again. My ration cards. I linger, waiting for them to call me over, but they don't.

I might as well go back to the tent.

Katya's lying in the same position we left her a couple of hours ago. I touch her forehead. Her skin's so hot under my fingers, the heat radiating off her warms up the tent. Her breath is more labored, as if something is stuck in her lungs.

My presence wakes her.

"Liza . . . You're here . . ." Her voice comes out in a throaty whisper.

I can barely hear her, so I lean in closer. "Sorry I woke you. I didn't mean to."

"You didn't. I've been awake for a while, waiting for you to return." Her eyes open a little wider, and the smile that spreads on her dry lips cracks me open. "Did he show it to you?"

I nod, unable for some reason to form the words.

"It's beautiful," she says. "I wish I could go with you. It's been a long time since I saw the sunrise through the ceiling on that platform." She puts out her hand and touches my upper arm, as if making sure I'm listening to her. "He really likes you." Her eyes catch mine. "Do you like Luka?"

I nod again, remembering Luka's hands on my face, his breath on my skin, his lips on mine. "I like him."

"Good. I don't want him to be alone," she whispers.

I want to lean forward, cup her face, and tell her Luka won't be alone. I want to promise her we'll take her to see the sky soon. Instead, I swallow, and something hot and liquid trails down my cheek.

"Please don't cry, Liza," Katya says, and her hand brushes gently over my face, burning my skin. "I'm not dead yet."

I reach out, take her small hand, and squeeze it gently. The words are stuck in my throat.

"I'm not crying." My voice cracks. "I have something for you." I pull out the piece of bread from my pocket. "Here, eat this."

I put the bread to her lips.

Her eyes fly open, and she takes the bread from my hand. "*Khleb?*" Her voice is small and weak and full of wonder.

She chews with difficulty. When the bread is gone, Katya closes her eyes. "Will you stay with me?" A shallow breath. "I think I'm falling asleep again."

I nod, even though she can't see me.

She takes another breath. "I'm so tired," she says, and falls into a slumber that might be sleep. Might be something entirely worse.

You just wasted a piece of bread on a dead girl.

I shut the door on my mother's angry face and stay and watch Katya for a while. When I'm sure she's breathing evenly, I tuck the rags around her and crawl out of the tent. The realization of how isolated the tunnels are makes me shiver, not with cold but a deep fear for the girl. I wrap my arms around my shoulders. It doesn't help, so I peek inside the tent and grab something resembling an old sweater. I pull it over my head, and it feels warm and soft around my torso.

We must do something. Katya needs medical attention, and she needs it now. Maybe we can make a stretcher and carry her out of the tunnels. How far is the hospital? I'm helpless and disoriented in the never-ending gloom of this place. I can't pinpoint where we are under the city. Is the Neva River to the east of us? Where's the Haymarket and my house? I'm not even sure where east or west are.

I go back to the firepit. In the farthest corner of the cave, Luka's washing something in a big pan. From where I stand it looks like a set of clothes. When I see his moving shoulders, the long lines of his back, the spring that has been coiled inside me all this time relaxes. We'll talk about Katya, and we'll figure out what to do.

Galina sees me and waves me over. "We've heard news about a delivery truck. Stores might have bread tomorrow. In the morning, Boria and you will go to the store and use your cards. Where are they registered?"

"At the corner bakery on Volodarsky Prospect. A few blocks away from here." I look around for Boria, but I don't see him. "Why Boria? I thought he wasn't feeling well."

"Boria wishes to go up into the streets. In his own words, he wants to see the sun and feel the wind on his face." Galina pauses for a second, and her eyes narrow on me. "He also wants to make sure you come back with the bread."

I scrunch up my nose, about to say something brusque, but I realize she isn't snapping at me. She just sounds tired, and she looks smaller and thinner than I remember from last night.

I feel hands on my shoulders, and someone spins me around.

"I'll go with you," Luka says.

"No." I shake my head. "I'll go with Boria. You must go and get help for Katya." As I say her name, my eyes start to burn. I ignore it, and trying to distract myself, I ask, "Where's Boria?"

"Back in his tent," Luka says.

I don't even realize how close he is until his fingers brush my hand.

I wait for him to add a sentence, but he doesn't, and we stand and look at each other for a few seconds. Until the silence starts to feel heavy, and Galina sighs and says, "Hate to interrupt, but where exactly do you think Luka could get help for Katya?" She lowers herself into the chair behind her. Her eyes are dull and half-closed. "The hospital's useless. I've heard they ran out of medication last winter. They won't have a single Analgin. And none of us has money to buy anything in the Haymarket. I don't even think they sell medicine there."

"I can help with that," I say. As soon as I admit to it, I know there's no way back. But Katya needs help. Without it, she'll die.

"You're not thinking the Mansion again, are you?" Luka says.

He sounds angry, and I don't understand why. Did I say something to make him react this way? "I'm thinking about the market. For the right price, you can get penicillin there. And I have some money. If you go to the market, look for a boy who sells candy. Ask him where to get medication. The boy sells information. Bargain hard because you'll need money for the antibiotics." As the words leave me, my confidence leaks away. "Don't let him rob you."

I lean down to my boots and pull out three bills from my socks. "Here, take this. I still have enough to buy bread tomorrow."

"And why do you have so much money on you?" Luka's voice has an edge to it that stings. "Did Maksim—"

"He has nothing to do with it," I say. "It's my inheritance." The practiced lie comes easy.

Luka's head jerks back. "Inheritance?"

"Mama had some money saved up." I glance at Galina but she seems half asleep. Her lashes are unexpectedly long, dark crescents against the white skin of her face. She seems to have drifted off while Luka and I talked. "Luka, is she all right?" I nod at the woman.

He grimaces. "No one's all right here. We're all weak and tired. We fall asleep in odd places at odd times."

I know what he means. Hunger carves at your body bit by bit, and when there's nothing left, it shuts you down, and all you want to do is sleep. All you can do is sleep.

"I think we should go to the Haymarket. Today. We can get Katya penicillin and something to eat before the bread arrives tomorrow," I tell Luka.

"You shouldn't be in the Haymarket. The NKVD and militia patrol it. Maksim goes there with a group of his comrade officers all the time." His chin points at the bundle of rubles in my hand. "And you should save your money for the bread."

He's right about the patrols. But a good disguise would work. What if I borrow Galina's clothes and wrap a scarf around my head? How do I tell Luka about options that don't involve spending money? I shift my weight and scratch my chin. He won't approve of stealing from people. I clear my throat. "There are other ways to get . . . things."

"Other ways?"

I shrug. For some reason, I don't feel like telling him about stealing. "Scavenging?"

Luka sighs. "Lena and Tolik left this morning. They might be able to bring something back."

"And if they don't?" I ask in a raised voice. "Why waste time? Katya—" I almost say *might not last that long*, but I catch myself. "She isn't well. She needs medication now. Not tomorrow."

Luka takes my face in his hands, and his touch calms me down. The fire and flickering light make his blue eyes look darker, giving him a different feel. He looks older again. "We have rules. We always wait for our people to return before someone else can leave. It's safest that way. No one gets lost in the tunnels."

"I don't need to follow your rules. I can go by myself," I say, stepping back and pulling the sweater tighter around my chest. It would be great to get out of this cold, damp place and into the sunny streets of the city. "Maybe Galina can lend me her clothes. I need a scarf to cover my hair. I'll be careful. I'll avoid the main streets."

"When we go to the market, we go in pairs. Another rule. And if you leave by yourself, you won't find the way back," Luka says. "It took me a dozen times to memorize the turns. You've walked with me just once."

So many rules, as if they've built their own *kommunalka* where they follow the assigned schedule—twenty minutes to use the bathroom, no more than ten to use the toilet, and don't forget to wash hallway floors on Monday.

But he's right, of course, about being lost in the tunnels. I should've paid more attention when he brought me here. Defeated, I nod and sit down on the chair beside Galina.

I watch Luka go back to his laundry. This is odd. Why isn't he more concerned about Katya? She's been sick for a while. Does he think it's a simple cold that will go away soon?

As my eyelids get heavy, my thoughts slow down. I sit still, too tired to move.

I drift off at some point.

Loud noises, shouts, and laughter startle me, and I jump up from the creaky chair. My mind comes back to me piece by piece as I watch people move around me. Luka's pouring water into a small kettle. Galina, full of baffling energy, stirs something in a big pot over the firepit. A small smile lingers on her face, making her look younger. I swear I hear her hum "Katyusha" under her breath. Boria's sitting in the chair opposite me, his eyes half-closed, his jaw slack. A string of drool slowly drips onto his bony chest. He catches me staring and wipes the dribble off his lips. A short, scrawny girl with a messy bun is standing by the pot, her hands on her hips, intently watching Galina's every move.

"What's happening?" I ask and sit down in my chair, pulling the sweater tighter.

Luka turns at the sound of my voice and grins. "We've got dinner. Thanks to Lena." He waves at the girl and the pot where something's cooking. Chunks of white and red, and something brown float around in a dark liquid. "I told you they'd come back with food."

Galina looks up at me and says, "We're having meat. First time, since . . . since . . ." She stops for a few seconds and shakes her head. "I don't even remember. Maybe since the beginning of the summer."

Meat? My arms clutch to my core. To stop the tingling in my chest, I start to rock slightly in the chair. Where did they get meat? I can't stop staring into the pot as acid slowly makes its way from my gut to my throat. I'm going to be sick. There's no meat in the city. Unless . . . "What kind of meat is it?" I ask. The tinge of panic is obvious in my shrill voice, but no one seems to notice.

Boria shrugs. "Who cares? It's food."

"Not rats. That's for sure." Galina chuckles. "None are left in the city."

Time stills.

They don't know what they're about to do. I get up, clutching my sweater for balance, and take a step to the firepit. "Tell me where this meat is from," I say to Galina. "Please." My voice is raw, as if I've been screaming all day.

"Lena got it in the Haymarket. Some woman was selling ground meat for three hundred rubles a jar, can you believe that? Three hundred rubles used to get you a whole cow. Not that we have that kind of money anyway."

Lena steps forward, straightening her shoulders. She doesn't smile but there's a look of triumph on her face. "There was a raid and, in the commotion, I snatched a jar. The potatoes and beets are from the market, too. Someone dropped them running from the militia."

Galina pulls the spoon out of the pot and takes a small sip. "Needs salt and maybe some pepper. But we'll do without."

The world slowly shifts around me and I squeeze my eyes shut to refocus. Ground meat is banned and for good reason. Cannibalism runs rampant in the city. I open my eyes and the words are out of my mouth before I know it. "We shouldn't eat that meat. The woman shouldn't have been selling it. It's banned."

"Since when do we care if the meat is banned?" Boria barks.

"We shouldn't eat it?" Galina snorts and looks at someone over my shoulder. "Is she mad?" Her face twists into a grimace as she keeps on stirring.

"You don't know?" I ask.

How is it possible that these people don't know what's happening in the streets above the tunnels?

Lena gapes at me. "I don't understand why you're so upset."

It's difficult to form any thoughts. They're like flies, scattered in my brain, buzzing and buzzing. I straighten up and shake my head.

Suddenly, Luka takes my hand into his. "What's going on, Liza? You don't look well."

For a while, all I hear is my own breathing. "The government banned selling ground meat last winter," I say. "They raid the Haymarket regularly to arrest those who sell it."

"Why is it banned?" someone asks, and I turn around to look at Katya, who's somehow made it out of bed. She looks a little better. Less flushed. A thick brown shawl is wrapped around her bony shoulders. She smiles at me and points at the pot. "It smells so good."

I take in a deep breath through my nostrils. The stew does smell good. Maybe it's easier to pretend it's not happening. Because the reality is so horrifying you can't admit it.

There are some lines we must never cross, Liza.

I swallow hard and my hands roll into fists. "Don't you know what's happening out there?" I ask, my voice a rasp. My words seem to echo around the campfire, like a cry for help begging to be heard.

My question is met with silence.

"It's not beef," I say in a low voice. Almost a whisper, but it's loud enough for them to hear. No one says a word. My mind screams that something is wrong, but I don't want to piece it together. Boria shifts in his chair, but his face is expressionless. I turn to look for Luka, but he's slipped into the gloom, away from the fire.

"But you already know that." I feel sick, a rotten taste in my mouth.

Boria breaks the silence. "We don't kill." His voice is steely. "But we eat whatever we can get our hands on. And we never talk about it."

My legs go weak, but I manage to get back to my chair.

I watch Galina walk toward me.

She holds out a plate.

An acidic tang floods my mouth. I snatch the plate from Galina's hand and throw it into the wall behind her.

The plate explodes with a crash. I leap to the pot, and using all my strength and the heel of my boot, I kick its side. The pot flies off the hook, overturns, and crashes into the ground, sending the cascade of potatoes and chunks of meat into the darkness.

Someone screams, "No!"

Galina wails.

Then nothing, only the fire cracking in the silence.

I turn around and go back to the tent.

15

MUCH LATER, LUKA FINDS ME ON THE BENCH
in front of their tent.

"They want you out," he says.

Our eyes meet, and for the first time there's no pull, no
energy radiating between us. All I feel is a bone-crushing
cold. "Now?" I ask.

"Not yet."

That's unexpected. My pulse speeds up. "How mad are
they?"

Luka grimaces. "Oh, they're raging. You're not allowed
by the campfire anymore."

A punishment. No, an exile. "I understand."

"I don't think you do." His voice breaks. "Katya can
barely stand on her feet. Boria's half dead. Galina's so weak
she falls asleep standing. And you . . . you . . . destroyed
our dinner." He sighs and looks toward the firepit. "We
scraped it off the ground. Whatever we could salvage."

"Did you still eat it?" I whisper, my voice hoarse, strained with disdain.

His shoulders twitch, but he doesn't reply.

Of course they did. You can escape the thoughts of what you are consuming, but you can't escape the hunger. Even Aka, who in the beginning of the war used to bad-mouth the girls who were selling themselves at the railway station for scraps of food, who rolled her eyes at them, is now doing the same. Anything to fill her empty belly.

"I talked Galina into letting you stay another night." Luka sits down by my side. "We need your ration cards and money. All of it. I saw a thick bundle in your socks last night. You'll have to give it to us. I know it's a lot, but they don't trust you. And you need a place to stay."

My limbs go limp. Giving away my money means giving away my freedom. I'll have nothing left. I clutch my middle as if trying to hold myself together. "What happens tomorrow?"

"You go and get us bread. Boria will go with you. He'll bring the bread here and you can go wherever you want." He puts his hand out, waiting for the money. "It's for the greater good, Liza. We share our resources. It's *collectivism* here. That way we survive. And you're not willing to share."

Luka's teaching me Stalin's doctrine on the collective way of life. A group over an individual.

You threaten his community and his comrades. You need to leave.

As if I'm in a thick winter fog, I pull out a stack of rubles from each sock and hand them to Luka. I sit up straight, my spine tight. "That's all I have."

He nods, and we don't speak for a few minutes after that. Luka's chest rises and falls. He doesn't look at me, preoccupied by whatever socialist theories he's contemplating.

"I'm going to lie down," I finally say.

He doesn't answer, so I climb into the tent and curl into a fetal position. This tent felt like the safest place in the world the night before. Now it feels like a desolate and lonely slum. I want to go back to my apartment, lock the door to my room, and sink deep into the sheets until I feel warm and safe again.

Sometime later I hear, "Liza." Luka's voice outside the tent. It's soft but direct enough to let me know he knows I'm awake.

"Yes?"

"Do you really think I can find penicillin for Katya at the Haymarket?"

By now he's wasted an entire day. I crack my eyes open but don't see anything but blackness. "Yes."

"I'll go tomorrow then."

I close my eyes, shutting Luka out.

He crawls into the tent and lies down by my side. "It's too cold outside." He shifts closer to me, a silent invitation. I can lean against him if I want.

But I can't turn off the memory of how he treated me. I can't forget what happened tonight. Me smashing the pot with their outrageous excuse for food. Galina chasing me away with furious shrieks. Them taking away all my money.

And . . . Luka not standing up for me and acting like their way of life is true communism, and I'm ruining it.

"Do you hate me?" Luka whispers in the dark.

"What?" My heart feels like it's cracking under the hurt. "No."

"Are you afraid of me? We don't kill. We just . . ." His voice trails off.

I stiffen by his side. "My mother used to say that survival justified almost anything, but that we still needed to keep our humanity through this war. Otherwise, it wasn't worth making it to the other side."

With a heavy sigh, Luka turns to his back. His jaw is clenched, and I notice his right hand is curled into a fist. I inch away a little.

We don't talk anymore, and eventually I drift to sleep.

In the early morning, Luka hefts Katya's rucksack over his back. "I should be back by nightfall, if not sooner."

Katya and I sit on the bench outside the tent and watch Luka tie his shoes.

Katya's still burning up, and she looks weaker and paler than the night before. It's my fault. I shouldn't have reacted the way I did. Maybe Luka is right. I don't understand what it means to share. To survive together. He thinks I'm a selfish girl who doesn't take responsibility for her actions.

Suddenly, I feel homesick. I miss my mother, who always knew what to do. I listen for her voice, but she remains silent.

I follow Luka back to the campfire where Boria's already waiting for me. The cave is empty. Everyone must be asleep. Or they don't want to see me.

After the winding walk out of the tunnels, Luka hides his flashlight in the leaf pile by the door. He checks the street to make sure no one can see us exiting, and we leave the damp air and the suffocating tunnels behind. A warm breeze greets us as soon as we enter into the streets. My eyes burn while adjusting to the brightness. I'm vaguely aware of Luka's hand on my arm, steadying me. Of Boria's snorting. Of the sun, now shining above us through the tree branches.

"Liza, I must go." Luka's voice brings me back. "Be careful."

In the bright daylight, everything that happened in the tunnels seems like a drawn-out, feverish nightmare.

Boria grunts, but Luka and I ignore him.

"I'll be all right," I say. My voice is hollow and distant. The rapture between us is gone. His touch doesn't feel the same. His face doesn't light up the way it did just yesterday. I'm different, too. I want to be left alone. I want to go home and take my chances with the NKVD. With *him*. Maybe Aka is back, and she'll know a place where I can hide. But mostly, I don't want to spend the rest of the day with Boria in a food line. "Make sure to bargain."

Luka squints at me. "You don't trust my bargaining powers?"

"It's just that the Haymarket is a dangerous place."

"I'll manage."

"We don't have all day," Boria croaks, and pulls on my sleeve. "Luka, just go already." He turns to me. "Let's move."

I look at Luka's face and force a whispered goodbye. "You stay safe, too."

Luka nods and turns left, while Boria and I go the opposite direction and walk down the street.

"He still really cares for you," Boria says, eyeing me sideways. "Despite what you did." His face is hard. Watchful.

I lower my head, my cheeks on fire. The bakery is a few blocks away from here. "Can you walk a bit faster?" I glance at Boria, who shuffles slowly by my side.

"This is the fastest I can do." There's a cutting tone to his voice.

I slow down and adjust my steps to his.

"Luka's family and I used to be neighbors. In the other life," Boria says, and stops to catch a breath. "He's a good boy."

"That's kind of you," I say.

"Last winter, he and Katya were attacked by a cannibal. They barely got away from her."

The memory of the severed arm on the ground stops me in my tracks. "A cannibal?"

"Yes." Boria studies my face with his dark eyes. "It was an older woman, but she had more strength than two starving kids."

I shudder, and he pats me gently on the arm. "People with nothing left are the most dangerous."

Boria and I walk in silence until we reach the end of the street. Before we cross to the other side, I stop. "He never told me he and Katya were attacked."

This time, Boria's pause is long and full of dark meaning. "Last winter was the worst. Hunger, bombings, everyone going mad from starvation, turning on one another. We fled to the tunnels. We created our own refuge. We collected food. We . . . stole some food, too. For the children mostly."

He's so thin and weak, there's no doubt they starved through the winter and most of the summer.

"At some point, we were happy—we had something to eat, somewhere to hide. It didn't last long. The children were the weakest, so they died first. Some went outside, into the streets, and never came back. Adults went looking for them. Some of them never came back, either. Those who did come back told stories of people who hunted in the night. They wore black clothes. They came out after curfew. They hid in empty buildings. In the dark. They're strong and fast. Deadly. The Hunters."

My mouth goes dry. Is this what Luka and Katya faced? That's why Luka told me there were no cannibals in the tunnels. He knew they roam at night, in the streets. The tunnels were always safe for him. Why didn't he tell me about this?

Would it change anything if he had?

"Our government doesn't care. No one cares. When Luka and Katya returned to the tunnels, bruised and bleeding, I knew. Luka's back was slashed with a knife. He was protecting his sister. It was a miracle they escaped. Katya said the woman called for help, but then the Hunters got distracted by an approaching car and fled. After that, we decided to stay in the tunnels until we ran out of food." He stops and looks up at me. "You know how many of us were there in January, in the beginning? Seventeen adults and eleven children. Now we have twelve people left." He starts walking again, and I trail behind him. "Luka doesn't talk about it because it's too hard. We don't talk about those who died anymore."

I don't talk about the dead, either. I've seen emaciated bodies in the streets. Frozen in the winter. Rotting away in the summer. I've walked by, pretending it was normal to walk among the dead. Ignoring the fear in the eyes of those still alive.

"Survival of the fittest," I whisper as my hand flies up to my throat, my fingers wrapping themselves around it.

"No. It's survival of the savages," Boria says. His own fingers tug on the button of his shirt as if trying to rip it off.

"Have you been able to find out who these people are? These . . . Hunters?" My voice breaks. I can't bring myself to say the word *cannibals*.

Boria shakes his head. "Most likely families banded together in their determination to live. The ones who attacked Luka and Katya are not the only ones. There are many more in the city." His voice is flat, distant. "Enough of this talk. We must hurry. As I said before, we don't have all day."

An endless queue of people, a sign bread *has* been delivered, circles around the bakery. We stand at the end of the food line and wait.

It moves slowly, and the sun shines brighter and hotter with every minute.

"I need to go and sit down," Boria says in a hoarse voice. He nods in the direction of a tree on the sidewalk. "I'm not well." His hands shake so violently he drops his wooden stick and doesn't try to pick it up.

I lean over to get it for him, but he whispers, "Leave it. I'm falling asleep. Wake me up so we can go inside together." He wipes his face with his hand.

I straighten myself and nod. "I'll call you when we get closer to the door."

Boria staggers to the tree and slumps heavily in its shade. A few minutes later, his head falls forward on his chest. Some rest will do him good.

I hope the Red Army brought plenty of bread. Would the government allocate enough to its own citizens?

Please don't leave us empty-handed.

The sun is higher now. There's not a single cloud in the sky. The crowd of people looms in front of me as an endless ocean of misery. My back's wet, and my dress clings uncomfortably to my skin.

A heavy hand on my shoulder startles me. I turn, expecting to see Boria, but a clean smell washes over me. No one should be allowed to smell so fresh. Maksim, in his militia uniform and polished black boots, narrows his green eyes at me. "I didn't expect to see you so soon. And so close to the scene of the crime."

I try to step back, ready to run, but my body moves as if I'm submerged in deep water. I push his arm off my shoulder. I'm so tired, I don't care what comes next. "How did you find me?"

"Find you?" A cocked brow. A thin, cutting smile. "You think I've been looking for you?"

I don't know how to answer that, so I just stare at him, trying to figure out if I should run.

"I patrol the streets with my comrades. We usually start with the stores where the bread is distributed. A lot of crime is committed around bakeries."

There are others with him? I quickly scan the surroundings but don't see any other officers. Even if they are here, I can't lose my place in the line. I need that bread. Maybe if I talk to him, try to be nice, he'll leave me alone.

I glance over Maksim's shoulder at Boria, who lies on the ground, peacefully sleeping under the tree.

Maksim follows my gaze. "A friend of yours?"

"Yes," I say, and falter. Should I explain how I know him?

"You have some interesting friends," Maksim notes.

Being cornered by him like this, in the bright daylight, should've made me more scared. But Maksim's expression is not predatory. It's rather mischievous. And, to my surprise, I feel at ease.

"His name's Boria," I say. "He was supposed to be with me in line, but he's too weak to stand."

"You don't have to explain," Maksim says. "It was an observation. Not a question." He inspects the long rows of people in front of us. "You'll be in line for hours. Too many people."

"It's fine. This is not my first time." When the siege started, Aka and I spent hours in lines like this. Until the winter came. Until the bread ran out and the lines disappeared.

"There won't be enough for everyone," he says in a low voice. "I know another way and can get you a full loaf."

Not standing in line for hours under the heat of the summer day would be a relief, but getting a loaf of bread instead of two 125-gram pieces would be a miracle. Boria, most definitely, would approve. And Luka . . . would he think of me differently?

We study each other for a long moment. Offers like this come at a price.

"What do I have to do for this?" I ask.

He smiles, and this time it's a wide smile. "Go with me to the back of the store and leave your friend under the tree," he whispers. "That's it."

"That's it?"

Maksim takes my hand and squeezes it. "That's it. I don't want anything from you."

I want to believe him, because despite his arrogance and forcefulness, he hasn't lied to me. But what if Scarface and the other officers are waiting for me at the back of the store? Would Maksim do that to me? The steady way he gazes suggests he's attracted to me, but the last time I listened to him, I ended up on the run from the NKVD. There are always consequences.

Don't be stupid, Liza. Take the bread and go.

I try to pull my hand away, but Maksim holds it tight. "You're safe with me, Liza," he says softly.

"All right," I concede, and finally pull free, wiping my sweaty palms on my dress.

Maksim turns. People part around us as I follow him. We've almost left the line when I'm stopped by a woman. She obviously either guessed or overheard what's happening. Her clawlike hand tugs on my sleeve. I look into her sunken eyes with deep, inky shadows underneath, and almost gasp at the palpable hatred in her face. "What about the rest of us?" she hisses into my face. "What are we supposed to eat?"

Around me people nod and point and make remarks I can't understand. A dark and scorching shame burrows under my skin. I lower my eyes, turn away from the woman, and make my way toward Maksim, who's waiting for me at the corner.

My face is on fire. My chin trembles.

I must get out of here.

Someone grabs me by the shoulders and spins me around. "I hope you choke on it," the same old woman says, and spits on me. The dribble lands on my shoulder.

In a flash, Maksim appears in front of me. He raises his hand and slaps the woman across the face. Her head jerks to the side. She screams and falls to the ground, her arms flying to her cheek. Maksim leans over her and his cold voice cuts the air, "One more word, and I'll put you under arrest."

The woman whimpers and tries to crawl to the side of the road, distancing herself from us. I dig my nails into my thigh to keep clearheaded. Maksim takes my hand and hauls me out of the crowd.

I follow obediently.

16

MAKSIM DISAPPEARS INTO THE BACK OF THE store.

I wait, leaning on the wall by the door. I might have a whole loaf of bread to give to the tunnel people soon. I don't remember the last time I saw a loaf of freshly baked bread. In my dreams, perhaps.

The faces of the women and men in the food line come and go in my mind like a kaleidoscope. I press the heels of my hands into my temples, chasing it all away. If I continue to obsess over the look on that woman's face, her hatred, her spiteful words, I'll do something stupid. I'll walk away. I'll abandon Boria, forget the debt I owe Luka and Katya for destroying their dinner, and go back home.

I push the image of the old woman spitting into my face to the back of my mind.

We do what we can to survive.

A clatter inside the store clears my mind. A female voice rises and falls, suggesting different stages of desperation. There's a yelp, and Maksim's stern voice says something I can't understand.

A few seconds later, Maksim emerges. He's got a wide grin wrapped across a face gleaming with pride. In his hands he holds an undersized loaf, burned on the sides. It doesn't smell freshly baked; still my mouth waters. It's bread. Food. Life. He did it for me. And suddenly, I feel at peace.

"Stop staring at it. Take it. It's yours," Maksim says. His voice is nothing like I heard a few seconds ago inside the store. The cold and commanding tone is gone. Now it's low and kind. "Have you eaten anything since the Mansion?"

I shake my head and take the bread. My dress pockets are too small for it. Luka took Katya's rucksack. If I openly carry the bread through the streets, I won't make it far. Boria won't be much help, considering his size and physical exhaustion. "I don't have anything to put it in. I wasn't prepared for a whole loaf."

Maksim's smile slips. His chin dips down, and he rakes his hand through his lush hair. "What a fool I am. I didn't even think about it. Of course, you can't march through the streets with a whole loaf of bread in your hands. Wait here." He goes back inside.

I sit on the sidewalk, cradling the bread to my chest. One of my hands touches the warm stone underneath me. It almost burns my skin. I must give Boria the bread. But the crowd outside the store will see me handing it to him. What will they do? I just cut their bread supply short. The thought makes me dizzy. Again, I see the old woman's accusing eyes when she spat at me.

Seconds turn into minutes. When Maksim opens the door, he has a crumpled page of a newspaper in his hands. He hands the paper to me. "Wrap the bread. At least no one will know what's inside." His jacket is unbuttoned, and his white shirt is open at the neck. I guess the heat's getting to him as well. He catches me looking and smiles.

I wrap the bread in the newspaper.

Maksim watches my hands and nods with approval when I'm done.

"Thank you. For the bread," I explain for some reason as if he wouldn't know what I thanked him for. I shift my weight from one foot to another. "I must go."

"I'll walk you," Maksim says, and extends his hand to me.

I shake my head. "It's all right. I'm not alone, remember? Boria's waiting."

"He's coming home with you?" One brow raised, his eyes inspect me.

"I'm not going home until I know I'm safe."

"I'm missing something. Why don't you think it's safe?"

I step away from him. I can't believe he's asking this. "I assaulted an officer. I'm pretty sure your comrades want to arrest me."

"Oh, that." He waves his hand in the air, dismissing my words. "I never told them your name." The smile that hits me is slow and inviting. "Anyway, Andreyev passed out from too much vodka. Did you really think you had knocked him out?"

I nod and don't say anything. This doesn't make any sense. I wasted valuable time hiding from the NKVD underground while I could've been outside looking for Aka. All for nothing.

"Shall I escort you home?" Maksim offers me his hand again. "To keep your precious loaf safe?"

I shake my head. "No. I'm not going home."

"Where are you going?"

"I need to help someone."

"So mysterious." His voice low, he steps closer. "Who needs your help?"

I hold my breath, force myself to stay still and smile. "Luka's sister. She's sick."

"Katya?" He drops his hand. "Luka said he needed food. He didn't say the girl was sick. Why didn't he come back to play piano?"

"We didn't know we were safe."

"We?" His perfect brow arches. "You spent all this time with Luka?" His broad shoulders roll back.

"We thought we were about to get arrested. Luka took me down into the tunnels. He kept me safe."

A muscle tics along Maksim's jawline. "Safe and starved, by the looks of you. I don't remember you being so pale."

"Katya's very weak." I draw away from him, millimeter by millimeter. "I must go. She's waiting for me."

Maksim wrinkles his nose and shakes his head. "All right, the least I can do is take you back to that . . . dirty and desperate man under the tree. But first, I'd like to ask for a favor."

Maksim's words stir something hot and dark in me. "Aren't we all desperate?" I ask, and thrust my chin higher. "Luka? Katya? Me?" I pause and search his face. "And you . . . offering me help and then asking me to return the favor. Nothing's ever simple and easy with anyone."

Maksim steps away from me. "Where is this coming from? I'm trying to help you. That's it."

My hands turn clammy, and I almost drop the loaf. I shouldn't talk to Maksim this way. He can easily take the bread away. He can arrest me. He can leave me here alone to face the hungry crowd on the street. "I'm sorry," I whisper, and step closer. "I didn't mean it. It's just . . . I'm so . . . so tired. And I really must go."

He takes my hands in his. He isn't mad.

"Your temper will be your undoing, Liza." A wide grin spreads across his face. "Forget I asked for a favor. If any- thing . . . it was a stupid joke. I'll take you to Boria." He lets go of me, slowly turns around, and starts walking to the front of the store.

I follow him, pressing a hand to my chest to calm my pounding heart. Before we turn the corner, I stop. "Wait." I can't walk past all these people with the bread wrapped in newspaper pages. People will understand what I'm carry- ing, and they'll tear us apart.

"Come on, Liza. You're braver than this. No one will dare say a word." Maksim extends his hand to me.

The fear slithers, snakelike, under my skin, but I straighten my shoulders, raise my chin, and take his hand.

Side by side, we walk past the crowd and toward the tree where Boria's waiting for us. The murmurs in the line stop. Everyone's watching us pass, but I keep my eyes on Boria. A few more steps, and I can leave this street behind.

Maksim and I halt at the same time.

"Oh no," Maksim says in an odd, strangled voice.

A stench of piss and shit gusts over us. We cover our noses. My heart beats so fast I'm afraid it'll jump out of my chest. I walk up to Boria, who lies on his side in the grass. His eyes are closed. His skin is stretched tight around his skull.

I blink. I must not be seeing straight. Hunger has this effect on me—it numbs my mind, blurs my thoughts, makes me scatterbrained.

Boria's chest doesn't move. His skin is waxen. His lips have turned blue. It takes me an eternity to understand what my eyes are telling me.

"No, no, no. It can't be."

"He's gone," Maksim says.

I sink to my knees in front of Boria. The rancid stench hits me again and almost knocks me over. Boria's bowels and bladder released when he died, it seems. I shouldn't have left him. I should've done something. But what? I didn't know he was about to die. But the signs were there all along. I just didn't pay attention. Galina said he wanted to go out into the streets one last time to feel the sun on his face. That's why he came here with me. To die in the light, under the sun.

I can't stop looking at him, a starved man curled into himself while waiting for his life to seep away. Why couldn't he hold on a bit longer? I have a whole loaf of bread in my hands.

The air around me is still. Quiet. I don't hear any sounds.

My tears drip down on him. I sit back and wipe his face with my sleeve.

Maksim's hand on my shoulder interrupts my thoughts. "I wish you didn't have to see this. I wish things were different," he says in a low, soft voice. His eyes harden as he turns to me. "Go. Take your . . . package. Go to Katya. I'll take care of the body. I can't leave him here to rot."

I don't ask him what he's going to do. I don't ask if he needs help. All I can think about is Boria, lying on the grass—unmoving and stiff. Yet peaceful. As if he found whatever he was looking for.

I look down at the bread in my hands. The tears I try to hold back spill like a river, weakening my resolve. "I can't believe he's dead."

"God, the smell," Maksim groans. "I'll call the sanitary brigade to get the body." He nods across the street. "You must go."

But how am I supposed to find the camp? I don't know how to navigate the tunnels without Boria. I was supposed to leave. He was supposed to take the bread, not me. I'll never find my way back to the group. I grit my teeth. Why did Galina let Boria go to the store?

And it strikes me all of a sudden, the fact that I have

missed. Boria didn't know he was going to die. He wanted to see the light, then come back to the dark and die with his people. He was going to bring them the bread. His last selfless act.

I take a deep breath. Now what? Boria's dead. And there's no one but me who can take the bread to the camp. I owe Luka and Katya that much. I almost killed the girl by taking away her dinner. And Luka . . . what will he think of me if I don't bring bread?

The bright sun burns my face; its rays stab my sore eyes. The entrance to the tunnels is a few blocks away. I have a flashlight. There weren't that many turns. But my mind is hazy. I might not be remembering it right.

Maksim's hands slip under my armpits; he pulls me up to my feet and nudges me away from the tree. "Go now."

I take a step forward but then I pause, my mind focused on what lies ahead—a black labyrinth with endless turns.

"Are you all right?"

An uncomfortable silence cloaks us. My breath is shaky. Am I all right?

"I will be. Thank you for everything," I say. Surprising even myself, I grab the collar of his shirt, rise to my toes, and pull him to me. Maksim inhales sharply as I plant a quick kiss on his cheek.

Before I lose my composure, I let go, turn around, and run across the street.

Sweating on the outside, numb on the inside, I reach the entrance to the tunnels. I pause in front of the heavy metal door and grasp the wooden handle. I don't know how I'm going to find the right passage. I don't even know how I'm taking a step through the doorway that leads into the abyss. I cannot see myself finding the way forward, and yet I know I must try. There's no other option.

Survival is a lonely business. Take the bread and go home.

I look up at the sun and the blue sky sprinkled with shades of red and pink. Should I wait for Luka to return? But I don't know when he'll be back. Worse, I don't know how long Katya has left. After what happened to Boria, I don't want to waste another minute.

With a deep sigh, I let the door slam shut with a loud clang behind me. The heat of the streets, the hum of random traffic, the echo of people's voices all fade away. It's cool in here.

Just like Luka did yesterday, I find and turn on the flashlight. I must be smart and clearheaded.

I enter the tunnels.

17

I DESCEND INTO DARKNESS. AGAIN.

The tendons in my neck are as tight as metal springs as I try to remember the path I took with Luka two days ago. In the beginning it's easy—follow the long and narrow tunnel, then when one path turns into another, keep going. No junctions. No choices. No decisions to make.

There's too much quiet around me, and a throbbing pressure builds behind my eyes.

I track the narrow passage, my breaths coming loud and fast.

When I reach the first fork, I stop and try to recall which turn Luka took. I think it was the one to my right. Or was it left? Which one did we take?

"I don't remember," I gasp, my pulse roaring in my head. Hearing my own panicked voice doesn't help. My eyes dart to the walls on my right as I shine the light into the tunnel. I can see only a few feet ahead of me. It looks familiar, but then, most of the tunnels beneath the city look the same. Slimy walls, wet rocks, and brown dirt on the ground. There are no markings, no signs to distinguish this one from the others.

Maybe it was the other one.

I turn to my left and inspect the narrow hallway.

"I can't remember," I whimper.

I'm drowning in doubt and terror. All the emotions I carried since my mother's death bubble up and try to resurface. Loneliness. Overwhelming sadness. Fear. I can't allow it. Not now. I push it all down, down, down. Finally, I can breathe.

My fingers wrap around the flashlight so tight it hurts. The tunnel in front of me smells like wet dog and standing water. I don't remember this stench. But then I was with Luka, and I wasn't paying attention to the sensations around me. I was focused on his tall frame in front of me, the lean yet strong sweep of his shoulders.

I bite down on my lip and pause. What if I take the wrong tunnel and get lost? No one will ever find me. I'll die alone in the dark. At least Boria died under the sun in the street full of people.

Don't be daft, Liza.

The tunnels are an unfinished underground system. Each path leads to an exit. Even if I get lost, I'll find a way out eventually. I can always come back to this spot and try the other tunnel.

I walk on.

A darting movement startles me. Was that a rat? No, Luka said there are no rats here. The sound of claws on the stone. Talons digging into the ground.

I must act, pick a tunnel, and move.

I clutch the bread tighter and shine the light in the direction of the noise. Nothing. I hold my breath for as long as I can, but I don't hear anything.

So what will it be, Liza? Left or right?

I don't know, I want to scream. My legs feel as heavy as stone, but I must decide and move on.

Another movement in the dark, and a shadow fills the space on the wall behind me. I swear I hear a growl but I'm not sure it's real. My imagination is getting the best of me.

I turn right and rush down the path, putting distance between myself and the frightening echoes.

My boot catches on a rock and sends me sprawling to the ground. My hands hit dirt and rocks. The flashlight goes flying. I hear the sound of my dress ripping. The bread slides away into the blackness, and my head smashes into the ground hard. A cascade of white and red spots jump and scatter like sparks from a fire in front of me. The pain in my forehead slices me in two, and then everything goes dark.

When my senses return, I'm in complete darkness. Groaning, I roll onto my back and try to concentrate on my thoughts. I have to find the torch. Without it, I'm as good as dead. My fingers reach for it but feel only dirt and stones.

You should've gone home. With the other boy. You'd be safe.

I close my eyes and listen to the noises around me. Somewhere, not far, water's dripping. This is new. It wasn't there when Luka and I walked through the tunnels. I must've chosen the wrong turn.

My own panicked wheezing drowns out the sound of the water.

Find the flashlight.

I get on my knees and pat the ground around me. Nothing. My search is more frantic now. The blackness is thick. Hollow, yet suffocating.

Sweat keeps pouring down my brow, stinging my eyes. I wipe it off. The wetness feels thick and sticky. I smell my fingers, and the metallic whiff tells me I'm bleeding. I rip the bottom of my dress and wrap the fabric around my head, above the eyebrows.

I crawl forward, patting the ground again with my fingertips. The bread should be somewhere close. The flashlight is another matter. It could've rolled farther. A ragged, panting gasp escapes my throat.

Don't think. Keep looking.

Something cracks under my knees as I crawl. I touch whatever it is, and it feels like a dry, wooden stick. I stretch my hands out in front of me. Nothing. To the sides. Nothing.

The blackness around me has weight and shape. It's alive and determined to smother me.

My knee hurts so badly I can't crawl any farther. Maybe walking will be less painful. I scramble to my feet. One small step forward. Another one. My right foot hits something light and softer than a rock. I stop, crouch, and search the ground.

Newspaper pages. Then the dry crust of the bread like tree bark under my fingers. I grab the loaf and break it into two halves, shoving the pieces into my pockets so I don't have to worry about losing it.

Then I sink back down to the ground to rest, leaning against a wall. I cannot hold on to a single thought; everything seems to slide and move. I shut my eyes, trying to recenter myself.

In a moment, I'll continue searching for the flashlight. If I move forward, I'll either find it or find the way out of this endless passage.

A rustle. A gasp. The thud of footsteps crunching over the dirt and rocks.

I turn, hoping to see a blast of light. It doesn't sound like an animal. A person is coming my way.

"*Kto tam?*" I call out, my voice so weak and shaky I barely recognize it.

No response. No more footsteps. As if they heard me and stopped moving.

I can hear the thump of my own pulse.

My body freezes. Luka would've answered—of that I'm sure. The footsteps sound again, closer and closer. Someone is but a breath away from me.

"What in the world are you doing down here? In the dark." A bright light blinds me, but Aka's familiar voice makes me want to howl in relief. "You're bleeding, Liza. What happened to you?"

"You're blinding me." I shield my face from the unbearable brightness. I'm so happy I can barely talk.

Aka points the flashlight to the side, and I finally see her. She stands in front of me, feet planted wide apart for balance. She's dressed in her mother's long, wide pants held by a thick leather belt. The pants are tucked into her grandfather's battered shoes, and a dark scarf hides her glossy brown braid. She searches my face expectantly, her blue eyes narrowing at my expression. "You look like you've been through hell and came out of it only to run into a ghost. What happened to you? Why are you here?" Aka cocks her head at me, as though she expects me to give her a sensible response.

"What are *you* doing here?" I ask, still not believing she's standing right here in front of me. I want to hug her to make sure she's real.

"Saving you, obviously," she says with a wide smile. "I saw you walking across the street and called after you. You didn't hear, so I followed you." She pauses, licks her dry lips, and points the light down the passage. "Tell me, why are we here? This place stinks of rats and death."

"There are no rats," I say. "But there are people here. I'm delivering food to their camp."

"Since when do you deliver food to others?"

"It's a long story," I say, and look around, trying to locate my torch. "I fell, hit my head, and lost my flashlight. Help me find it?"

Aka holds her hand up, silencing me. "Wait a second. Are you telling me you're helping the rats?"

"What?" I look at her, puzzled. What is she talking about? "I told you there are no rats here. The people in the camp ate them all."

Aka shakes her head. "The people who live here are called the Rats. Haven't you heard that in the market?"

"I don't care what they're called," I say. "I need to find my light."

Aka shrugs. "We don't need it. I have a flashlight. Show the way." She waves it toward the darkest part of the tunnel. "How far is the camp?"

Do I tell her we're lost now or later? "I think we should go over there to the junction," I say, and point behind her. "I took a wrong turn."

"You don't know where you're going, do you?" She taps her foot a few times, takes a deep breath. "I'm trying to understand what you're doing. You came down to the tunnels to deliver food to a group of people. You took the wrong turn. You hit your head. You lost your flashlight." She cocks her head again and turns sharply to look at me. "Did I sum it up correctly?"

I nod and look at my hands.

"Liza, how well do you know these people?"

"Not well." My voice is so low I can barely hear myself speak.

"All of this," she says, and bounces her light off the walls. "Wandering in the tunnels, endangering yourself, is for someone you barely know? I'm having a hard time believing you." She steps toward me. "And we don't lie to each other."

"I wanted to tell you, but I couldn't find you." I recount how Luka saved me from the man from the cemetery, about meeting Maksim in the market and ending up needing to be saved by Luka again. "I did some things I can't tell you about right now. It's a long story. But now I owe him to help his sister and his friends."

"It's war. No one owes anyone anything."

My hands clutch so tightly my fingernails dig deep crescent moons into my palms. I inspect Aka's pale neck and thin arms. No bruises. No bite marks. "What happened to you? I looked for you in the Mansion."

"I'll tell you later. When you share your story with me. Let's go look for that flashlight of yours." Aka turns her head and gazes down the shaft intently, as if she's hoping to see it lying on the ground.

I'm so happy to see her I don't really care what she did in the Mansion. She's here, safe and unharmed, and that is all that matters. I follow her gaze and don't see anything but lingering blackness.

We search for the light for a long time. The air gets thicker.

My back is hunched, and I can't straighten it. It hurts too much. Drained of energy, I slow down my search. Exhaustion and anxiety tell me to go back to the intersection, take the tunnel on the left, and hope it will lead me to the camp. But my legs are too heavy to move.

Finally, I straighten my back, lean on the damp wall, and close my eyes. I'm so starved I'm about to faint.

"Weak?" Aka asks. I open my eyes and look at her pale face. I don't have the strength to even nod. Her eyes are rimmed with deep hollows I didn't notice before. The neckline of her shirt is soaked with sweat. She's as spent as I am. She leans on the opposite wall, and we study each other for a long minute. Then both of us slide down to the ground.

"Let's rest," Aka whispers, and closes her eyes.

"Let's eat." I pull a chunky piece of bread out of my pocket.

Aka's eyes fly open and glare darkly at the bread. "I thought you were taking it to the camp. Some dying girl is waiting for it. No?"

Somewhere in the back of my mind I wonder how she could know this. I haven't told her about Katya, have I? But then my hunger takes control.

"We're not going to eat it all. Just a few bites." I break off a few pieces for Aka and hand them to her. "They won't even know."

"You're probably right," Aka notes, and swallows a big piece of bread without chewing it. I watch her throat move up and down.

What we're doing might be wrong, but it's also right. If I'm to make my way back to the camp and deliver the bread, I need strength. And yet it feels like I ventured into the Neva River in the middle of winter. It feels like I'm about to fall into the glacial void. My heart stutters as I remember Boria's dead face. Katya's labored breathing. Luka's eyes when he asked me to be careful.

As if reading my mind, Aka says with a deep sigh, "It's not a crime to take a few bites."

18

WE EAT IN SILENCE.

I pull out the other half of the loaf. Hands shaking, we split it into small pieces, count them evenly, and eat. And eat. And eat. We don't talk anymore. There are no words left, just never-ending, unyielding hunger. It's an endless pit, a dark abyss in our stomachs, swallowing the rest of any decency we possess.

We don't stop, because stopping is impossible.

When the bread is gone, Aka puts her head on my shoulder, and I wrap my arm around her. "Let's sit here for a bit longer," she whispers. She pulls her knees to her chest. "Then let's go home."

"All right," I say. "A few more minutes and we'll go home." I should be ashamed of myself for eating food that wasn't mine. I'm used to stealing, but this feels different. The bread belonged to a dying girl. Unlike Mama, I never took anything from the dying and the sick. But for the first time in a very long while, I'm not hungry. For some reason, I feel at peace. I'm also tired. So very tired. My eyelids are heavy.

I close my eyes, and my mind drifts to places that are warm, safe, and bright.

Very bright. And scorching hot.

I wake up with a jerk and sit up groggily. It feels like I slept only a few minutes or less, and the sliver of rest has left me more exhausted.

Why's there so much light?

Luka and Maksim stare down at me. Maksim forces a smile, and Luka shines his flashlight closer to my face. I push it away.

I turn to check on Aka, but she's not by my side. I scan the tunnel, but I can't see her anywhere. Panic rises inside me. Where did she go?

I look down and freeze. Bread crumbs pepper my dress like debris of a shipwreck. I'm racking my brain, searching for something that will help me to understand why I'm covered in crumbs. Something small and dry is stuck to the corner of my lip. I sweep at it. A tiny bread crumb falls to the ground. My tongue runs over my teeth. I think I feel small pieces of bread between them. I angle my body away from the boys.

"Hey, we're right here." Maksim waves a hand in front of my face. "Do you see us?"

I blink a few times, slap his hand away, and scramble to my feet. I take a deep breath, trying to collect my thoughts. But they're a swarm of flies refusing to settle.

"We thought you were unconscious," Luka says in a low voice.

"Or worse," Maksim adds. "To be honest."

"I fell asleep," I say. "Where's Aka? Where did she go?"

Both of the boys raise their eyebrows at me.

"Aka. You know her." My voice is losing its confident note. "Brown hair. Wide pants. Dark scarf. A flashlight?"

"No one is here but you and us." Luka turns around and shines the torch into the darkest areas of the tunnel as if looking for something.

His words slice me in half. This is so much worse than I thought. Did Aka leave me here, alone in the dark? She wouldn't do that. Unless . . . unless she never was here. What happened to me? My mind is a raw piece of clay that my buzzing thoughts try to shape into a form. Into words. But I fail to comprehend any of it.

"What happened to your head?" Maksim carefully touches my right temple.

"I fell and hit it on a rock." I try to keep my voice from trembling. Suddenly, I feel dizzy. "I'm fine." I lean on the wall to steady myself.

"You don't look fine," Maksim notes.

"Where's Boria?" Luka asks.

My eyes catch Maksim's and hold them. I can't believe he hasn't told Luka.

Maksim clears his throat. "Boria didn't make it. He died under the tree by the store. Did you know how weak he was?"

Luka nods. "He hadn't been doing well for a while. I was afraid he wouldn't be with us for much longer." His hand is tight around the light. His eyes slant downward. "We must return to the camp. Katya's unwell."

"Did you get her any medicine?" I ask Luka.

His shoulders slump. "I didn't get anything. The market was closed. Something related to a raid."

Luka's words hollow me out. "Closed?" My voice cracks. I press a fist to my mouth so I don't scream. How will I survive without the market? I shake my head so violently I almost lose my balance. "I don't understand. Is it going to reopen at some point? The government can't close it down. We'll all die without it."

"People die every day with or without it," Luka says calmly. "Where's the bread? Maksim told me he got you a whole loaf."

Bread. A rush of frigid suspicion hits me. I shove my hands into my pockets. They're empty but for a few small and dry crumbs. Did I eat it all? Impossible. I wouldn't do that. No, someone was following me. Someone stole it from me. I heard odd sounds—scraping of claws, rolling hisses, and deep growls. Was I dreaming then? I can't tell any longer what is real and what isn't. My own mind has turned against me.

"I lost it. I fell, hit my head, and dropped it," I say, and look frantically around. "I also lost the flashlight."

"This one?" Luka waves the flashlight he's holding in front of me. "We found it back there." He points a few steps away. Only now do I notice Maksim's holding a second flashlight.

"I fell and I think I lost consciousness. I dropped the bread. It must be here," I whisper, swallowing the lump in my throat.

I look down the path but see nothing but the dark, crypt-like tunnel.

There is no good explanation for anything of what happened here.

Luka shines the light around. "It should be around somewhere." He wants to find the bread and go back to the camp. To his little sister.

Who's dying anyway. That bread wouldn't have helped her.

Feeling stronger, I walk in the opposite direction. "I think I fell right here," I say as I comb through the rocks and dirt.

Luka sits back on his heels and points his flashlight at me. "What do you remember?"

My body tenses, and I don't answer. I wish I could go back to when I entered the tunnels and undo everything.

Luka's eyes look bloodshot when he says, "You fell and lost the flashlight and then what?"

"Then I crawled around looking for the light." I force my shoulders to relax. He can't suspect what I did. It's one thing to fall, lose the light, and hit my head on a rock. It's another to admit to consuming the whole loaf of bread while . . . what exactly? Hallucinating? Dreaming? "I told you, I passed out."

As we continue to search, I watch Luka. His movements are rushed, jerky. Desperate. But there's nothing I can do or say to make it any better.

Suddenly Maksim is standing in front of me. "What about your friend? Aka? She could've taken the bread."

I brush the dirt from my palms. He's giving me a way out. I take in a deep breath. "I . . . I don't know. She was here when I fell asleep."

Maksim's pale face is grim. "Luka, I heard footsteps. I think the girl, Liza's friend, took the bread."

Luka stops, straightens, and glances at Maksim. "I didn't hear anything." Worry turns to fear on his face. "If she's taken the bread, we're doomed. All of us. Especially Katya."

Maksim turns to Luka. "Liza and I'll go back into the city. You go back to the camp. I'll see if I can get you some food." He pulls me gently by the sleeve of my dress. "Let's go."

I look at Luka. "I'm sorry."

He nods without meeting my eyes.

Maksim gives another tug on my arm, and I feel myself pulled toward the other side of the tunnel. Soon, he and I are ascending the steps back toward the streets. He moves in front of me at a steady pace.

When we reach the door, Maksim holds it open for a few seconds, then reconsiders and closes it, trapping me with him in the stairwell. We look at each other, eyes unblinking, lips pinched together. Finally, he's the one who breaks the silence. "I didn't hear any footsteps. There was no girl."

I don't respond. What's there to say?

"I know you spent time in the tunnels with Luka. I don't know what happened between you there. He was angry with you. He said you did something that he doesn't understand. A selfish act of a spoiled girl, he called it." Maksim continues in a calm voice. His words cut and scald their way through me. "Liza, you must understand that no matter what you do, his family and his friends in the camp will always come first. He will think about them before he thinks about you. He won't protect you. You're better off without him."

"I don't need anyone's protection," I say, and my voice cracks.

"What happened to you in that tunnel?" He steps closer and tucks a lock of loose hair behind my ear. "You can tell me. I'll understand."

We both know this is not the question he really wants to ask. He really wants to know what I did with the bread.

"I don't know what happened to me. I think I hit my head and passed out. I think I might've eaten the bread. Every single piece of it. I think Aka was only a dream."

19

WE WALK IN SILENCE MOST OF THE WAY.
After my admission about the bread, Maksim doesn't ask
me anything else. His face is somber. As we navigate the
streets, he doesn't even cast a glance in my direction. What's
there to say, anyway? Words can't make this better.

Around us, the streets are humming with life. It doesn't
surprise me. Summer, even during the siege, brings people
outside either in search of food or to escape from the warmth
of their apartments.

My eyes dart to Maksim, and I stop in my tracks. He's
grinning.

"What's so funny?"

"You." He takes a step closer. His fingers brush over my
hand, a mere breath of a touch. "Not everyone would come
out and say they ate a whole loaf of bread meant for someone else. It takes courage."

"Not courage," I say, and in spite of the grim topic, I

smile. "Desperation." I take a few steps and pause. "What happened with Boria's body?"

"I called the sanitary brigade. They said they'd send someone for him."

"Have they?"

Maksim shrugs. "I'm sure they wouldn't leave his body on the street in the heat of the day."

I'm sure they would. I've seen bodies left abandoned on the streets. Maybe if militia calls it in, it will be taken seriously.

Sweat soaks the back of my dress. I can't wait to get home and take a bath. Then a cold chill races down my spine. Is *he* home, waiting for me? Is he going to interrogate me about where I spent the past few days? Kaganov's all-knowing eyes will see right through me.

"I live close by." I turn and start walking down the street. "Aka and I used to go to that café for ice cream." I wave at the boarded-up windows. "She'd have vanilla, and I always had chocolate." It was such a relief to see her back in the tunnels. But I know now it was all a dream that my feverish mind conjured. I want to believe Aka's back home with her family, but my heart tells me she's still locked up in the Mansion.

Maksim pulls me by my hand across the street, to the café. We stand in front of the building and inspect its dark, gaping windows. The wooden frames around what used to be the front door are blackened from the fire caused by a shell. Someone drew a red star on the wall with chalk. In addition to the huge windows, big holes in the wall open a wide view into the room next to the door.

"Let's go," I say.

Maksim pulls away from the window with a slight shake of his head. "One day it'll be restored to its previous glory."

I don't believe him. Nothing and no one will be restored to its previous state.

A car pulls up to the sidewalk and stops in front of us. The window on the driver's side rolls down, and a young man's face peers out at us.

My feet are rooted to the concrete. I almost grab Maksim's hand, but he walks to the car and leans forward.

"Sasha, what are you doing here? The curfew is two hours away."

Sasha examines my pale face, my ratty dress spotted with blood, my mud-crusted boots, and slowly turns to Maksim. "Your father's looking for you. Something about the market. Are you coming back soon? With your girl?" He snickers, and I'm suddenly reminded of the ogling and the girls in silk slips and the stench of stale sweat hanging heavily in the air.

A faint waft of vodka and cheap perfume drifts back to us. Shrill, female laughter sounds from inside the car, and a girl's head appears in the back window.

"Maks, we miss you," the girl drawls, and flashes a wide grin at Maksim. "You're so elusive. Always busy patrolling the streets." I don't recognize her from the Mansion. A new addition, perhaps. "Who's that with you?" Her eyes are hazy. She's drunk out of her mind.

"A friend of mine. You don't know her," Maksim says to the girl. "I'll be back soon." He casts a look at me over his shoulder. "We should get going. I'll see you later."

"Where are you going?" the girl addresses Maksim. "I wouldn't mind joining you."

"Shut up." The officer's cold sneer is enough for the girl to retreat into the back of the car.

"Sasha, tell my father I'm on my way," Maksim says.

Sasha gives me an appraising look and wrinkles his nose. Does he recognize me from a few days ago? I don't remember seeing him. But I was so scared everything was a blur. He might've been there all along and I wouldn't know better.

I keep my expression neutral like my mother taught me and stand still by Maksim's side.

"Can I borrow a couple of hundred, Maks?" Sasha pinches his lips into a thin line. "I was unlucky last night at the card table. Lost everything."

Maksim chuckles and pulls a fat fold of banknotes from the pocket of his uniform coat. He counts five hundred rubles and hands the money to the driver. I guess he's replenished his never-ending supply of rubles already.

"Thanks, friend. Don't take too long," Sasha says. "Your father won't be pleased."

"Is he ever?" Maksim whispers under his breath, and waves at the car as it pulls away.

The relief washing over me is almost a tangible cloud.

"How much farther?" Maksim asks me, his attention fixed

on the departing car, his broad shoulders stiff in his militia uniform.

"A few blocks," I say.

He shakes his head, takes my hand, and starts strolling. I don't pull away.

My apartment building looks dark as we approach it. The sun is sitting low in the sky, its orange and pink rays cast deep shadows on the building. Still, it's a place of safety and warmth for me, no matter the gloom. No matter *who* waits for me inside. That is, if he hears me coming back. I bite down on my lip. Sneaking into the apartment might be the only way in for me. If I was alone.

"We're here," I say, and point at the building. "You don't need to come inside. I'll be fine."

"You won't get rid of me that easy. I want to see where you live."

There's nothing I can do, so I push the heavy door open, and we enter the stairwell. With the daylight fading outside, the inside is cooler than I expected.

"Nice building," Maksim notes. "Your parents must be important."

Not important enough to give us a separate apartment. Instead, the government shoved us into a *kommunalka*, where

strangers cluttered the space with their bodies and their meager possessions.

"I'm on the fifth floor," I say, not responding to his
comments about the building. "It's a long way up."

"Can you climb? Not that long ago you were passed out
on the ground."

"I ate a whole loaf of bread. I can run up the stairs if I
need to."

He chuckles and runs his hand through his thick, dark hair.
"Is that a challenge?"

I look up at the stairwell in front of us. The wide and
steep stairs sweep through the building. They turn around
the center of each floor. The elegant old banisters, shiny
and polished before the war, are now as dry as dust and
scraped. The shabby chandeliers exhibit cracked crystals,
exposed light bulbs covered with grime, and extensive
spiderwebs.

The once-beautiful building now looks haunted.

Without warning, I bolt up the stairs, my feet light as I
match my stride to every step. My body floats up the stairwell as if I were a kite.

Fast and heavy footsteps are close behind me. I skip every
other step, trying to get an advantage. I make it to the third
floor. Heart in my throat, I double over, trying to catch my
breath. Black spots float before my eyes.

"You're faster than I expected," Maksim says. His breath
is even. He doesn't sound like he just ran up three floors.

Dizziness sweeps over me, and my knees buckle. I sit down on the first step and close my eyes.

"This was a stupid idea." Maksim lowers himself on the floor by my side. The smell of cinnamon and stale cigarettes is familiar yet overpowering. I might be sick.

We sit in silence for a few seconds.

Maksim stands up first and reaches out to me. "Can you walk? We still have two flights."

I take his hand and let him pull me to my feet.

Slowly, we make our way up. I reach for our front door, but my hand freezes on the handle. I don't want Maksim inside. I want to be alone, in my room, with my disheveled thoughts. But before I say anything, the front door swings open and Kaganov towers in the doorway, looking down at me with a harsh expression on his face. His arms folded across his chest. His eyes narrowed.

"Where have you been?" he asks in his guttural voice. "You haven't been home for three days. I thought you were lying dead in a ditch."

A tiny bread crumb in the corner of his mouth distracts me. Has he just been eating something?

"Good afternoon, Comrade," Maksim says.

Kaganov's focus slides away from me and settles on Maksim, who stands rigidly behind me. Kaganov's jaw moves as if he's about to greet him, but no words come out.

The air turns heavy. Suffocating. He's making us wait on purpose.

I'm not ready for this confrontation.

Kaganov's attention returns to me. He moves closer and reaches out, as if he wants to pull me into himself. "Answer me. Where have you been these last few days?"

What am I supposed to say? The truth would sound insane.

"She was with me, Comrade. I apologize for keeping her longer than intended," Maksim says.

Kaganov studies Maksim, searching for something in his face, but his lips are pressed into a thin line. Then he notices Maksim's uniform, and his expression softens. "Would you like to come in, young man? And explain to me, please, where exactly Liza spent the last seventy-two hours?"

We stumble into the dim hallway.

"Has Aka stopped by?" I ask.

"I haven't seen her," Kaganov says. "Let's go to the kitchen." He waves down the corridor. "I was just about to have some supper."

If Aka hasn't been back, she must still be in the Mansion. I have to go back there. But who knows what they'll do to me if I just show up in that place? I shoot a quick glance at the boy by my side. If I go there with Maksim, the reception might be different.

"We'd rather go back to my room." I take Maksim's hand and pull him toward the door.

"Not yet, Liza. Please come along." Kaganov heads toward the kitchen. I follow because I have no choice. I know how the set of his shoulders looks when he uses practiced politeness to hide his displeasure. "Why don't you properly introduce your friend, Liza?" He throws the words casually over his shoulder.

Maksim looks at me, his brows raised, and nods toward the kitchen. "Shall we?"

Kaganov walks in first and settles himself at the table. He waves us over and points at the two chairs across from him. "Please, sit down. I put the kettle on just before you came."

Maksim takes a seat and looks around. His palms are pressed on the table.

I plop down on the chair and study the familiar speckled pattern of the tablecloth. The red, gold, and white lines crisscross and weave in odd angles. Yelena bought this tablecloth a few years ago for the New Year's Eve celebration.

I run my fingers across the delicate stitching. "Isn't this Yelena's?"

"She offered it to us since there are not many of us left," Kaganov says softly.

"Where is she?" I ask.

"Sleeping, I think," Kaganov says. "I invited her when I started baking. She said she'll come and join us later."

Maksim clears his throat and meets Kaganov's heavy leer. "I'm Maksim Nikitin."

"Nikitin?" Kaganov leans forward with sudden interest. "Is your father Major Nikitin?"

Maksim's head jerks back. "Yes, that's him."

"Your father's doing a fine job." An empty compliment. Kaganov never believed any of the NKVD or militia were doing a great job. Once he told my mother the NKVD's mission was not to protect but to subvert and eliminate. In reply, Mama whispered furiously that a true patriot would never say those words out loud.

"Thanks." Maksim nods. "And you are?"

A small smile stretches Kaganov's pale lips. "Comrade Piotr Andreyevich Kaganov."

Maksim turns to me. "Liza, isn't your name . . . your last name is Kaganova, isn't it?"

The floor at my feet drops away.

"Of course her last name's Kaganova. Liza's my daughter," Kaganov says, and pushes his chair away from the table. "I thought you knew that."

20

"WOULD YOU LIKE PIE WITH YOUR TEA?" MY father turns to the stove and fiddles with the kettle.

"What kind of pie?" A breathless whisper is all I manage. He sounds insane offering a slice of pie in a starved city.

"Apple pie, of course," he says.

I follow his movements around the kitchen, aware of Maksim's suspicious expression.

He's right: Something's wrong. Even before the Haymarket was shut down, it was impossible to find apples. I remember the food my father offered me a few days ago. It was a lot. I didn't question it back then; my mind was too preoccupied with thoughts of Aka.

Even as I inhale the warm scents of the kitchen, an icy chill makes itself at home in my bones. Like Mama said, my father has crossed many lines in the past few weeks.

And I'm not sure I want to know exactly what my father did in exchange for these apples. When Mama and I needed him the most, he decided it was time to do what others had been doing for some time—the most despicable, treacherous act of survival.

As sick and weak as she was, Mama stood strong. "That's not who we are, Piotr," she said. That same day she asked my father to move into a vacant room down the hall. My parents, who never spent time apart, now lived in separate rooms like strangers.

In the days that followed, the dark circles under my mama's eyes became more prominent. I swear she got grayer that week. And then, a couple of weeks later, I found her cold and still in her bed.

"What a delicacy," Maksim says. "Where did you find apples, Comrade?"

My father turns on his heels and looks down at Maksim with an expressionless face. The longer he stands there without replying, the more fear leaks from my pores. What if he says something that gets him arrested? That gets *me* arrested?

Maksim must sense my anxiety, because he shifts uncomfortably in his seat.

Say something, I beg my father in my mind. Your silence isn't helping.

As if hearing my plea, he smiles at Maksim. "I have friends who have their own small gardens in the city. They harvest what they can." He nods at me. "For us."

I have no idea whom he is talking about, but I know he is lying. There was that one woman who looked well rested and strong when she came traipsing through the apartment last week. Does he call her a friend now? I'm sure she is more than that. But maybe I misunderstand their relationship. Maybe they're not lovers. Maybe it is a transactional relationship. It still doesn't make any sense. No one gives anything to anyone out of the goodness of their heart. My father paid for the food one way or the other. Most likely by being an informant to the NKVD. But I have no clue whom or what he's reporting.

Maksim nods, satisfied. How easily he's deceived. "I've heard about people planting vegetables in their yards. Communal gardens." He nods at the *burzhuika*. "I'd love some apple pie."

My father stands in front of the white cupboard, a long shadow in the dim light of the summer evening. Beside him, the window is propped open and a breeze moves the heavy blackout curtain. I take a deep breath, feeling as if I'm resurfacing from deep waters. Maybe later I will ask my father what this is all about. For now I channel my thoughts into the extravagant treat in front of me.

My insides contract painfully as I watch my father cut into the fresh crust. With a shaking hand, I take a plate and sink my teeth into the softness of the pastry.

A few years ago, after school one day, Aka tossed her braid over her shoulder and suggested we bake an apple pie. We almost burned the kitchen down. My mother saved the pie and the kitchen. Old Yelena demanded I wash the toilet for a month as punishment, but Mama bought her off with half the pie. "It's magic," I remember my father saying after taking the first bite that night. He put his arm around Mama's shoulders, and she smiled and melted into him.

Kaganov now sits down and joins me and Maksim at the table. We don't talk as we consume the pie. We finish it all in one sitting.

As I swallow the last piece, I push away the memories of Luka's eyes and the way he looked at me when I smashed their pot full of stew into the ground. Because when I think about it, my gut performs an awkward spin, and the pie turns into tasteless mud. A needle is scraping at the corners of my mind. There is a thread that connects everything. I just need to pull on it, but for some reason, my instinct is to let it drop and run the other way.

"I didn't do a very good job with the pie, did I? *Burzhuika* wasn't cooperating. It took me hours to figure out how I could bake it." My father pushes his empty plate away and wipes his lips. "The apples are crunchy. Your mother wouldn't approve. She was a great baker."

How dare he talk about Mama? I pick at the ruff on my dress collar. The fabric rips under my tug, but I can't stop. I'll mend it later. I'm so tense I need to have something in my hands.

"Was?" Maksim asks, and my throat closes up.

"She passed away," my father answers before I can form a cohesive sentence in my mind. "A few days ago. It's just me and Liza now."

How funny. Your father knew all along.

"Oh, I remember. Liza did tell me," Maksim replies. His cheeks turn pink. "How could I forget . . . pneumonia, right?"

A dizzying pain builds inside my expanding heart. Did my father go to the Hotel Astoria to check on Mama, and when they told him she hadn't showed up for her shifts, he guessed? There's no denying it now. I'll have to tell Kaganov why I concealed her death, dragged her body through the streets, and buried her myself. It was all his fault.

My father throws a stern look in my direction. "Which is why I was so frantic when Liza was gone for days, with the fever and all. She should've been home, resting." I can hear the warning in his voice.

"My mother died last winter. Tuberculosis," Maksim says.

My father nods. "Last winter was brutal."

I swallow a sharp lump. "I'm sorry about your mother," I whisper.

"I'm sorry about yours. Most people I know have lost someone." His voice is low. His eyes don't leave mine, and the longer he gazes, the more his sadness melts into something else. Tenderness?

"Well, young people," my father interrupts our staring contest. "I think it's time we all turn in. Curfew's around the corner, though I guess that doesn't apply to you."

"No, I usually patrol the streets. But I should go." Maksim stands up and shakes Kaganov's hand. "Thank you for your generosity. It's so rare these days." He looks at me. "Will you walk me out?"

My father walks to the window, closes it, and pulls the

blackout drapes shut. "Don't stay out too long." His voice is hard, but he leans down to kiss the top of my head. I want to pull away, but I know Maksim is watching. There's already enough for him to be suspicious about.

I take Maksim by the hand and guide him into the hallway. "I'll come with you to the stairwell. But I won't go down the stairs." I push a stubborn strand of hair away from my face.

He chuckles. "I wouldn't ask you to. Not after what happened."

We step outside, and I close the door behind me. "Thank you for taking me back home." I lean against the cold wall and beam at him. "Can I go with you to the Mansion tomorrow?"

He cocks his head to the side. "Liza, Liza, Liza. Sometimes you don't make any sense." He pauses, assessing my reaction. When I keep smiling wordlessly, he asks, "Why would you want to go back?"

"Aka's still there. But I'm sure you know that. I want to bring her home."

"Are we back to that conversation again?"

I nod.

"How do you even know she went there? I haven't seen her, and I know almost all the girls by name now."

"Almost?"

He puts his hand on the wall over my shoulder. His expression sharpens. "They come and go. No one likes to stay for long. I don't think Aka's been there."

I want to trust him, but I can't. If Maksim is lying to

me, how would I know? He doesn't want to take me back because he feels responsible for me hitting Scarface. He's protecting himself and is trying to stay in his father's good graces. I bet his father is doing exactly the same—trying to look good in front of the NKVD. It must be a tedious and exhausting job pleasing the NKVD for extra rations.

"If I could take you there, I would. Just to reassure you." Maksim steps closer to me. "But I don't think it's a good idea. My father doesn't let go of his grudges easily."

My breath catches, but I don't pull away. He's keeping something from me. What if Aka is hurt and he doesn't want me to know? I saw what happens to the girls who talk back, who disobey.

"How about this? When I see her, I'll tell Aka how worried you are. Would that be enough?"

When. There is so much confidence in his voice. He has no doubt he'll see Aka.

"She's still in the Mansion, isn't she?"

"Liza, I haven't seen her. If I do, I'll talk to her. That's all I can do. I'm trying to help you, can't you see that?"

My nostrils flare. Why can't he admit the truth? If I can't make him take me back to the Mansion, I'll take his rubles instead. The fat stack should replenish everything I was forced to give away to the tunnel Rats. I'll share it with Aka when she's back so she never has to return to that place.

He leans toward me, and I feel his breath on my cheek.

Tart apples. A hint of cinnamon. "I care about you, Liza. You're beautiful. A beautiful and wild puzzle."

I grab the corners of his lapel and pull him slightly toward me. He follows my command and tugs me against him, tangling his hand in my hair. My lips part, and I pretend to let myself get lost in the heat of his mouth and the heady warmth of his body. My pulse quickens but my mind gains clarity. His hands roam up and down my back, his touch sending an electrical current through my skin. I pull away, but the heat and his firm hands draw me nearer.

I let him touch me, even as I remember different hands on my body. Different lips on my skin.

As Maksim hovers over me, my left hand slides up his strong neck. My right hand strokes his pocket, my fingers feeling for the edges of his folded stack of banknotes. I almost gasp when I locate it, full of promises and possibilities.

Maksim pulls away slightly, and I can't allow it. I arch my back, press my breasts against his solid chest, and my tongue slips into his mouth. The rhythmic beat of his pulse tells me to continue. My fingers trace down his chest, reach past a gap between the buttons of his shirt and find the skin. A small moan escapes him, and he deepens the kiss.

My hand slips into his pocket. My senses are on such high alert my body can't relax. I'm as taut as a board, but Maksim is oblivious to the rigidness of my back. My hand brushes over the bills. I curl my fingers around the stack and pull the precious thing out ever so carefully, pausing to assess Maksim's reaction. When I determine he's too busy dragging his tongue down my neck, I slowly pull my hand out with a relieved exhale.

His warm lips trail down my collarbone and slide lower into the opening of my dress. He fumbles with the buttons and, a second later, his hands cup my breasts.

I push his hands away, step to the side, and slap his face.

"I'm not one of your girls, Officer." The words come out sharp and cold.

His right hand presses to the spot where my palm connected with his cheek. His Adam's apple bobs sharply. He looks ashamed.

Secretly pleased, I turn away, pull the door open, and step into the apartment. Then I shut it in his flushed, shocked face.

His rubles safely rest in the pocket of my dress.

I hurry to my room, where I count to ten and then crack open the heavy blackout curtains. I watch Maksim cross the street. His shoulders are rigid. He doesn't stop to look up at my windows.

I suck on my lower lip. He must be replaying our encounter in the stairwell in his head. How long will it take him to notice the lightness of his uniform pocket? I'm sure he won't suspect me. If anything, he'll think the cash was lost somewhere along the way to our apartment. Or while he was running up the stairs.

With a sigh of relief, I pull the curtains closed.

Later, after a bath, and a failed attempt to sleep, I inspect my treasure. This is the most I've come across during my ventures in the Haymarket. I swallow and taste dirt from the tunnels. It fills the inside of my mouth, slides down my throat, and settles in my gut. My rib cage tightens. I'm going to use this money for something good. Something honest. When the market reopens, I'll buy whatever food I can find and take it back to Katya. I will find the words to explain what happened to me in the tunnels. Tears sting my eyes, but I blink them away. The memory of Luka right at the end when he stood unmoving—his back stooped and his lips in an angry thin line—splinters my heart into two aching, bleeding pieces. Will he ever forgive me?

There is nothing you can do about it now.

I force away the weight of my guilt and put the fold of bills under the floorboards.

21

MY FINGERS LEAVE A TRAIL IN THE DUST ON
the polished surface of the grand piano. I open the cover, sit
down, and brush over a few keys. A series of notes float to
my mind, and I strike. My hands glide over the keys rapidly,
desperately, yet not missing a note. The smoothness of the
tune is comforting. The rhythm is lively. My touch is light
but strong. Insistent yet gentle. I can't stop. All that exists
right now is music, and my fingers floating through the air
and pressing down on the keys. The melody spinning in my
head, sending out a tune.

Since I came back home, I have spent most of the time in
my room, coming out to eat and to warm buckets of water
for a bath. Twice I have gone to Aka's apartment. But no
one opens her door anymore. I don't know what to think,
because some thoughts are too dark. All I know is that I
must go back to the Mansion and find my friend. I must do
it now. Every waking moment, I try to come up with ways

to get back in, and every time I fail. Doubts, cold and sharp, chew on my mind, and I end up doing nothing.

I've barely spoken with my father, even though he consistently brings home food. Mostly vegetables. Sometimes big chunks of bread. We even had another apple pie. I ask him where it comes from, but his answers still don't make any sense. Farmers, friends, people who care. The weight of his gaze pinches something inside me when he talks about it, and I finally give up. If he doesn't want to be honest, so be it.

The house is quiet. Especially at night. This is when I hear my father pace his room, the floorboards creaking and groaning under his feet. He's been restless ever since I came back. I finally told him about Mama, and he just nodded in reply. Then he pulled me into his embrace, and I even allowed myself to rest my cheek against his skinny chest. Just for a few seconds.

Sometimes I hear him cry. His sobs are muffled as if he has a fist pushed into his mouth or a pillow pressed against his face. He prefers to grieve alone, in solitude. He doesn't want me to witness his pain. And I don't want him to see mine.

In the meantime, that woman visits my father again. Her knocks at the door are quiet but insistent. She never stays long. If anything, her visits are so short that my initial suspicions about her relationship with my father don't make sense anymore. The more I see her, the more I'm convinced I knew her, before the war, but no matter how hard I try, I cannot place her.

After another run of notes, I stop playing. I move my neck side to side to relieve the stiff feeling in my spine.

Yelena left this morning with my father. He offered to take her to meet a farmer who had vegetables for sale.

The knock at the front door is so light I think I imagined it. But then comes another one, a bit stronger, and the air around me stills.

Has that annoying woman come back again? My father isn't home, and I don't want to talk to her. She unsettles me. Her eyes are probing. Her smiles are fake. And she looks so healthy. Unnaturally so. My father denies she is the NKVD, the only reasonable explanation I have come up with. He keeps on calling her a friend.

I slowly walk out into the hallway. Another knock. Then I watch the knob turn slowly, catching in the lock. Could it be Aka? I rush to the door and swing it open.

Luka stands before me.

A wave of relief washes over me. If he's here, it means he isn't angry with me anymore. He has forgiven me.

"Luka," I gasp. "*Zakhodi.*" I step back, letting him inside the apartment.

The single naked light bulb swings from the high ceiling above us, splashing yellow light over Luka's pale face, and I take in his appearance. There's blood crusted in the corner of his mouth.

"Are you all right?" My voice comes out as a whisper.

He sways forward and I catch him by his shoulders.

"Tell me," I say.

"Katya . . . ," he whispers. "She doesn't get up anymore."

"Oh no."

"She's dying, Liza." His voice breaks.

I don't know what to say, except, "I'm sorry." As soon as the words are out, I realize how callous they sound. And that's not who I am. "There must be something we can do."

He looks at me as if expecting me to continue, to offer him a solution, but I'm not sure I have one. "What about Maksim? Surely, he can help. And what about playing the piano in the Mansion?"

"I went back," he rasps. "They wouldn't let me inside. They wouldn't even call for Maksim when I asked." A powerful cough bends him at the waist. When he stops, blood stains his lips. He has Katya's sickness. He wipes his mouth and looks down at his hand. It is stained with red streaks. "They threatened to arrest me if I ever came back. But I thought you might be able to help us."

He thinks I have money. Or food. Or both.

He isn't wrong.

"I have something to share," I say.

"I'm not here for that," Luka says, shaking his head. "Remember that crazy idea of yours about stealing the food from the Mansion? We're going to do it after all."

A sharp breath escapes me. It is such a reckless, stupid idea. I wasn't thinking straight back in the tunnels, and the group acted like it was all a joke. What has changed? "There must be some other way."

A muscle jumps in his neck. "Too many of us have died already. We can't wait any longer."

There is a short silence. I sense his utter desperation.

"It's a suicide mission."

"Not necessarily. We're going to sneak into the Mansion tonight. We need you to help us navigate the inside. I've never walked through that house. All I know is the front door and the dining hall. But you know the inside."

My hands turn clammy. I don't know anything about the Mansion. "Um . . . the inside. I've been there only once," I start to say, and pause as the realization dawns on me. This is it. This might be my *only* way back in. I thought about this numerous times, but I couldn't come up with anything. And here's Luka, offering me a chance. "But Maksim showed me around." The lie slips off my lips effortlessly. I don't know where the food is stored, but I'll figure it out when I get there. The building looked big, but not massive. Its hallways were long, drafty but brightly lit. It can't be too difficult to find the kitchen. "I will help. I'll take you right to the food pantry."

Another harsh coughing fit. "Later tonight, then. When everyone is drunk. We'll go in through the back door."

"The back door? It's locked, I'm sure."

"Galina is good with locks."

So am I. But I don't want to volunteer now. I can always help later. "Someone might hear us. The guards at the front door don't drink. They were very alert when I was there."

Luka shakes his head. "After the curfew, there are no guards at the front door."

"Who's coming?"

"Just a few of us."

They chose the strongest. But even their strongest can't outrun bullets from the guns of the police if they are caught. "Let's think it through, Luka. Maybe we should wait. Talk about it some more. The army will bring us bread soon. They won't abandon the city."

"Liza, we need you." He swallows. "You must help us. You must help Katya."

He trusts me more than I trust myself. But I'm going into the Mansion on my own mission, and I can't promise to be a part of his.

Luka's hand reaches out to me, but then just as quickly it drops by his side. "You need to promise me, Liza," he says. "Katya must live. She must survive the war. She's all I have left."

His shoulders are hunched, and he looks as if he's about to crumple. I take a shaky breath. "I promise."

He nods, finally satisfied. "We'll meet in the back alley behind the Mansion. Remember, we ran through it?"

I nod. Of course I remember. I was holding his hand. He was pulling me forward, guiding me to safety. So much heartbreak and loss has happened since then. So much has changed. I want to hold on to his hand, feel his warmth, but then I think about what happened in the tunnels, and I shrink away from him.

"An hour past curfew. Don't be late."

"I'll be there," I say.

"Where are you going, Liza?" my father's voice says from behind me. Both Luka and I turn around to look at him. His tall frame blocks the exit.

"I'm going to see Luka's sister, Katya. Remember her? She came here with Luka once."

My father rubs his chin. "I remember," he murmurs, and I know he's lying.

That woman is here again, by his side. She doesn't turn away from me this time. I can see clearly. Her face is round like a saucer. A coarse hair springs out of a small black mole at the corner of her lips. She nods at me softly, waking up a memory. I definitely know her from somewhere. She examines Luka's thin frame as if evaluating him for some weird contest.

"This is Larisa," my father says. No other explanation follows.

"I remember you," Luka says. "My mother used to go to your shop all the time. I'd come with her when I was little."

The woman's mute stare is the only response. I still can't quite place Larisa, the sharp angles of her face like an early sketch that's been abandoned, but I guess no one looks their best after more than a year of this hell.

Larisa shifts her feet and glances up at my father. For the first time since she's started appearing in our apartment, she seems unsure of herself. From a shop clerk to an NKVD informant. Quite a career path. The big bag in Larisa's hands looks heavy. Wrinkled newspaper pages cover the top, preventing me from seeing what's inside.

"I will see you later then?" Luka asks. An unruly chunk of blond hair falls over his eyebrow.

"Yes." I shift my weight from one foot to another. "Later."

He nods awkwardly and walks to the door. I seize his arm, the good one, and squeeze it. "Be careful, all right?" For a few seconds, I cling tightly to his arm, the warmth of it, perhaps a little too long because I sense a pull as he steps away.

"I'll be fine." He walks out the door.

I let myself take in the shape of his torso under the crumpled shirt, the breadth of his shoulders, the slight slope of his spine. Then I shut the door.

I turn to my father. The hallway fills with silence. All I hear is the sound of Luka's descending steps on the stairs.

My father studies me, as if I've truly surprised him.

"Are you in love with that boy?"

Larisa smiles, and for some reason, I want to hit her. My hands curl into fists. I shake my head. "I'm not."

"I saw how you looked at him. How he looked at you."

"Stop it, Piotr. They're kids. Let them be happy," Larisa interjects as she fidgets with her bag.

Who is she to me? What does she know about us? "His sister is dying. It's not about being happy."

My father comes up to me and puts a hand on my shoulder. "I didn't mean to offend you. But you must realize you cannot go outside at this hour." His fingers gently squeeze. "The curfew is almost here. Whatever you think you should be doing now, wherever that boy wants to take you, it all can wait. We must talk first." He lowers his voice. "Go to your room, please. Lock the door and wait for me. It shouldn't take me long. Please don't do anything reckless, all right?" He tries to catch my eyes, but I shake his hand off, turn around, and go to my room. A few minutes later, I hear the door to my father's room open and close.

Inside, I slump into a chair. I'm going back to the Mansion. I'm finally going to find Aka. God, I miss her so much. Her loud laughter always fills the emptiness inside me. My eyes start to burn. Between the two of us, Aka is the one who always looks for ways to brighten our days. She'll tell me stories to make sure long bread lines don't seem endless. She knows how to comfort me. How to make me feel needed and loved.

Longing sweeps through my body like a wave on Lake Ladoga. I need Aka by my side more than ever. She's kinder than me. Smarter than me. And she's definitely stronger than me. Together we can survive anything. I can't wait to tell her what happened to me in the tunnels. About the boys, and my confused feelings. She'll understand why I ate the bread. Because I know she'd do the same. I need Aka to hold me tight again so I can tell her how broken and lonely I feel all the time.

I run my fingers over the top of the table. I can feel her presence in the room. She floats against the window, her silhouette lit up by the light from outside. A lingering shadow that has the same questions as I do. How am I going to pull this heist off and save her? The kitchen must be downstairs, in the back. As soon as we enter the building, I will tell the group to search the hallway. I will go to the second floor, where I'll check every room. I can't think further than that because I'm getting dizzy from all the possibilities.

The break-in is impossible to think about. Acid stirs in my throat when I imagine the officers and their guns and their blank faces. If we're not careful, we can all die. My mouth goes dry. I'm terrified, even sitting here in my room. But Aka is there, and she needs me. I'm her only way out. Maybe if we're fast, everything will work out.

And being fast is my specialty.

I clasp my shaking hands together. No matter what happens, tonight, I'm bringing Aka home.

I crack open my door and listen. My father's low rumble tells me he's still dealing with Larisa. Their voices are hushed. The floorboards creak as they move around.

I tiptoe to the front door and slip out into the streets.

22

THE SKY IS HEAVY WITH AN APPROACHING storm. The daylight has dimmed, but the sun hovers over the horizon. Summer nights offer plenty of visibility.

By the time I reach the meeting spot, drops of sweat trickle between my shoulder blades and down my spine.

I spot them in the alley and stop. They're a group of ghosts hovering in the dusk, faces sharp, match-like limbs and bony frames held together with tattered clothes. Lena is holding a knife in her right hand, an unsettling sight. Her left hand is dangling by her sunken belly, an empty bag pressed to her sharp thigh. Galina paces back and forth, reminding me of a trapped animal. She's smoking a hand-rolled cigarette. She stops midstep, flicks ashes, and blows a deep, nervous breath. Luka sits on a sidewalk. His head is supported by his good hand. His eyes are closed.

Galina scoffs when I approach. "I could hear you from across the city. You're loud. Your steps are heavy." She scowls at my feet. I notice bald patches scattering her pale scalp.

"Must be the shoes." I look down at my mother's boots and kick gravel down the sidewalk. "They're heavy and a bit big for me. I'll be more careful not to stomp."

"Remove them. Everyone can hear you marching down the street. Your steps were thunderous."

"I'm not going to walk barefoot."

"You don't have a choice," Luka says. His voice is calm. Indifferent. He gets to his feet. "Galina is right. We could hear you coming blocks away."

"I'm not removing my boots. That is insane. I'll be careful."

"Why not? Because you think you're special?" Lena twists the knife in her hand, obviously smelling blood.

Luka doesn't say anything. He leans against a light pole and studies his fingernails. Lena gawks at me in disdain. A smirk stretches Galina's thin, pale lips. She nods at my feet, and I know I don't have a choice.

With a sigh, I remove my boots. "Am I supposed to carry them around?"

"Hide them," Luka says.

"Where?" My hands twitch, as if I'm about to throw the boots at him. I'm bitter and angry at his coldness toward me. "Here? Someone's going to steal them." My voice is loud. It echoes down the street.

He blinks and scans the street over my shoulders. "Keep your voice down. It's after curfew. Someone might hear you."

Galina waves her hand to a door leading into the abandoned building behind us. "In that arch, behind the door. Leave your boots there."

I study the building. It was bombed last fall. It used to be a school, and now it might be a shelter for the homeless. It looks dark and silent, but it doesn't mean it's empty. Someone might be there, watching us. Someone could find and take my boots. It would be inexcusable and stupid to leave my most precious possessions to random chance. Last winter, in a desperate attempt to get money to buy bread, we sold Mama's performance dresses, her jewelry, her other shoes, and the only fur coat she had. These boots are the only connection to Mama I have left. This and her piano.

When I don't say anything, Luka reaches out. "Let me."

I step away. "I'm going to carry them."

The finality in my voice makes him pause.

"She's a burden," Galina says. "I don't trust her. She'll get us all killed."

"She won't. She's with us on this. She knows the inside. And it was her idea, remember?" Just like this, Luka traps me.

"How easy you forget, Luka." Galina spits her words. "You asked me to trust her back in the camp. And what did she do? She wanted to kill us all."

"I didn't kill anyone," I hiss at the vicious woman. "Boria died from starvation."

"I don't mean Boria, you stupid girl. You ruined the only

food we'd had in days. We had to eat what was left from the dirt."

"How could you eat *that*?"

"*That?* It was food. Katya needed it. Have you thought about that? She can't get up anymore. Because you decided she should starve to death."

My throat tightens. "I didn't decide anything. Maybe I should go."

"You should've stayed to watch Katya crawl on her hands and knees and lick it off the ground."

I can't help picturing the horrible scene, and my hands start to shake. "It was wrong what I did."

She glares at me, unwilling to let me off the hook. "What about when you went to get bread and never came back? Was it *wrong*, too? Boria died on your watch. You left his body to rot outside. You stole our bread. Something is seriously wrong with *you*." She's mocking me.

"Galina—" I start.

"Enough." Luka's voice rings through the air. I'm not sure if he's addressing me or Galina. Maybe both of us. "We need to be united in this. Katya needs food. Liza knows how to get it. Whether either of you like it or not, we're a team now." He stops to catch his breath and starts coughing.

Galina shakes her head and puts her hand on Luka's back as if trying to comfort him.

My chest tightens. How am I going to tell Luka about

my true mission? About Aka? Suddenly, I'm not sure he'd understand.

"Pull yourselves together," he whispers hoarsely. "For Katya's sake."

Galina looks at me, her eyes cold and hard. "Keep your boots. Let's go."

We start walking down the street. The concrete is hard underfoot. I try not to step on anything sharp. My mama's boots are heavy, slowing me down. Maybe, when I'm inside, I'll put them back on. I don't think I was as loud as they make it sound.

Galina's feet shuffle behind me, scraping the sidewalk with her uneven gait. "Liza," she whispers. And when I stop, she grabs my hand, making me lean into her. Her rotten breath gusts over me. "You do anything stupid and I'll kill you." She spits on the sidewalk.

"I'm a part of the team," I whisper back. It sounds so simple when I say it. But the falsehood rests heavy on my shoulders. I wish I didn't have to lie to the group. To Luka. I wish I could tell the truth. But Galina looks like she's ready to stab me if I make a wrong move, and I have no choice, do I?

What about your promise to save Katya?

God, I wish I could take it back. But what was I supposed to do? Say no to Luka? I bite down on my tongue. None of this is fair. Katya has Luka. And the rest of the group. Whom do I have left? Mama's gone. And my father—he's gone, too, in a way, involved in something with the NKVD, of that I'm sure. Aka's all I have left. She needs me as much as I need her. Together we can survive anything. On the other hand, this group barely tolerates me. Even Luka is acting detached around me, as if he doesn't know me. As if that kiss never happened. I'd be doing them a favor if I leave.

Luka walks in front of the group with Galina right behind him. Lena stumbles at the back. I stop and wait for her.

"Need help?" I ask.

She shakes her head and doesn't look at me.

Finally, the Mansion comes into view. Luka stops at a corner and appraises it. We cluster behind him. The grand three-story building with its concrete pillars looms in front of us. I swear I can feel its eyes on my skin, as if the beast peers back, challenging me to reconsider. There are no guards at the door. The street is empty.

I blink rapidly as if that will make things disappear in my head. As if that will make the Mansion melt away and I'll be home with Aka, cooking up a stew. But the Mansion is still in front of me, and the group is by my side. As determined as ever.

Keeping to the walls, we walk around the building. In the courtyard, we stop and listen for a while; the only sound is the distant drunken shouts of the officers inside.

"Ready?" Luka asks no one in particular.

How could anyone be ready for something like this? A tide of dizziness rushes over me. I can't allow myself to collapse now. I must focus on finding Aka.

"Galina," Luka whispers. "Do it."

She fumbles forward and pulls out a long and thin metal tool with a curved shape at the end. She crouches, puts her ear to the door, and listens. Then she slightly pulls the door toward herself, inserts the tool into the lock, and twists it slowly, turning it to the left and to the right. Nothing happens.

Time expands, and it is getting increasingly difficult to breathe. We can't be caught. They'll shoot us on sight.

"Why is it not working?" Lena whispers.

"Don't distract her," Luka says. "She knows what she's doing."

Does she? I could probably do it faster with my hairpin.

"I can help," I say, leaning down to Galina's ear. "Let me try."

She sneers, shakes her head angrily, and her smoldering cigarette comes flying out from the corner of her mouth. It falls by my feet. Luka picks it up and rolls it between his fingers.

The lock finally clicks, and Galina pushes the door open. Luka hands the cigarette back to Galina. We step into the stuffy hallway. The air stinks of grease and vodka.

I swallow panic as we walk down the corridor. Luka's shoulders are hunched. His step is slow and heavy. A part of me wants to touch him and tell him we're going to be all right. But another part remembers Luka's eyes when he told me to remove my boots, and I don't say anything.

The hallway is narrow and long, but there is a white door with a dark brown wooden handle at the end of it. I hope it's the kitchen.

"There," I point. "Check that door. It's there."

"The kitchen?" Galina scowls at me.

I nod, and Galina and Lena move toward it. I fall back. So does Luka.

"Aren't you coming?" His voice is low.

I turn to face him and the world tilts. There are so many things that can go wrong when I tell him what I'm about to do. "I'm not coming with you to the kitchen. You go there. Load up on food. Get out safely. I need to find Aka." I step away from him toward another door, to my right. It must lead to the front of the building. "She needs me."

"I don't understand."

"There is no time for this now." I wave at Galina, who's waiting at the end of the hallway. "Go, get food and get out."

"It's so easy for you, isn't it? Leaving us just like this. You're so selfish you can't even see that Aka doesn't want to be found."

His words catch me like a blow to my kidney. I'm about to snap in half. I grip my braid and pull so hard it feels like I'm about to tear my scalp open. But pain recenters me, snapping me back into the hallway. "Go now, Luka. Save your sister."

"What's taking so long?" Galina half whispers, half hisses at us.

"Liza is leaving," Luka says.

In a few strides, Galina is back by his side. She still holds the sharp lock-picking tool in her hand. "What?"

"You were right; we shouldn't have trusted her," Luka

says. His eyes never leave my face. "She isn't helping us. As usual, it's all about Liza. No one else matters."

"You're not going anywhere," Galina says, pointing the metal tool at me. "Watch her, Luka. Don't let her go anywhere." She jogs back to the other end of the corridor, where it seems the kitchen door is locked as well.

I turn into a stone. "I took you inside like I promised, Luka. Why can't I go and save my friend?"

"Why are you so difficult?"

"I'm not difficult. Just let me go."

"When we get the food. We need to make sure you won't do anything stupid." He looks over his shoulder at Galina and Lena, who're trying to pick the lock. While he's distracted, I dash for the other door—terrified at the thought that it also might be locked. It swings open at my push and I glimpse a brightly lit hallway. Then a hand reaches out from behind and cold fingers coil around my shoulder. Luka jerks me back.

"Liza," he groans. "Don't."

A cold determination is in his eyes. He wants me to stay. At any cost. I can't let him stop me. I swing my boots and smash them into his face. Hard. He stumbles back. His hand falls away from my shoulder. There's blood gushing from his split lip.

Boots in my hand, I run. I dart into the unfamiliar hallway and shut the door behind me.

There is a lock on my side, and I turn it, cutting Luka off. Then I lean into the wall, trying to catch my shaky breath.

"Liza, open the door." Luka's hollow whisper comes from the other side. "Open it. We've got to talk."

I shut my eyes. This is getting tiresome. "I have to find Aka."

"Galina won't forgive you for this."

"And you?"

He doesn't answer.

"I'm sorry, Luka, but I must go."

"You're a traitor."

A strangled laugh escapes my throat. More of a crow's scratchy caw than a real laugh. "In the tunnels, you took all my money. You turned your back on me when I needed you. And then . . . then you threw me out."

There's a movement and a slight thud, as if he's leaning his head on the door. "You ate the bread," he says. "*Our* bread. You think I never guessed? I saw the crumbs all over your dress. All over your face."

I shut my eyes and push a sharp lump down my throat. "I didn't do it on purpose."

His chuckle is a bitter and angry sound. "How do you accidentally eat a whole loaf of bread?"

I slide down the wall, the boots awkwardly land by my feet. My fingers skim over the cracked, worn leather. How did this happen to me? How did I get here?

Your impulsiveness landed you here, Liza.

Or the sheer selfishness of survival, Mama.

I can't do this anymore. I inhale sharply through my teeth, and suddenly, I'm bursting at the seams. I've been suppressing the horrible reality of what happened in the tunnels for so long, it rushes to the surface like a bubble of oxygen in a swamp. "You're a cannibal, Luka. A flesh-eating monster. You and all your tunnel Rats. You've even tried to turn your little sister into one." Whether it's the hunger or the sickness or Galina's brainwashing, Luka isn't the same boy I thought I knew a few days ago—the one who blew air on my scraped knees, who showed me the unfinished metro platform, and who kissed me so deep and so hard I couldn't breathe.

"Go back to Galina." My eyes burn with tears as I push away from the floor, take my boots, and walk down the hallway.

23

THERE ARE STAIRS LEADING UP INTO THE house. I take them, and at the top I push open another door. It leads me to a hallway I know—Maksim's room is not far from here.

The familiar smell of vodka and stale smoke fills my nostrils. Men's voices, clinks of silverware on china or glasses on the table, and rough laughter drift from inside the building. From the dining room. By the sound of it, the party is in full swing.

I walk down the hallway and stop by the first door. Hearing footsteps echoing from down the hall, I turn the knob, and to my surprise the door swings open. I slip through and close the door quietly behind me.

The bedroom inside is in disarray. The floor is covered with empty bottles of vodka, wet towels, newspaper pages, cigarette butts, and other trash. I wrinkle my nose at the stench of rotten cabbage and dirty sheets.

"It's hard to keep it clean when there's no one to help," a deep voice says. A pair of expressionless, dead eyes glare at me from the unmade bed in the corner of the room. Scarface is lying half-undressed on the filthy sheets. He turns to the bedside table to pour himself a full glass from a half-empty bottle of vodka. Next to the bottle is his holstered service revolver. "Come, come, little chick. Don't be a stranger." His bloodshot eyes scan my face as I stand rigidly against the wall by the door. "How did you get in?"

Does he mean his room or the Mansion?

"The door was open. I think I'm in the wrong place."

"I think you're in exactly the right place."

I don't move an inch. I'm not sure where this is going. My voice doesn't sound as firm as I'd like it to be. Hopefully, he's too drunk to notice. I straighten my back.

Scarface sets his glass down next to his gun. "What's with the boots?"

"They're dirty. Didn't want to spoil the floors."

His drunken laughter roars through the room. "How thoughtful of you." His reptilian eyes size me up. "Why are you here?"

Maksim told me Scarface doesn't remember getting hit, but would he remember me? "I came to find a friend."

"I can be your friend," he says as he starts to get up off the bed.

My voice breaks and I clear my throat before I go on. "Her name is Akulina. But she goes by Aka. Looks like me." I clamp my lips shut while I scan his face to see his reaction. "Can you tell me where she is?"

He burps, wipes his mouth. "Never heard of any Aka." His eyes glide up and down my body. "Put your boots down and come here."

He pats his lap. Three slow taps. *Tap. Tap. Tap.*

"Come sit with me."

Bile rises in my throat as my eyes search the room for a weapon I can use against him. Again.

A heavy, exaggerated sigh from behind startles me. "Liza, there you are. I've been waiting forever." Maksim's voice is quiet, but there's steel in it. "Comrade Andreyev, Liza is here to see me."

My shoulders relax, my fingers unclench, and I almost drop my boots. I turn to look at him, and his green eyes get brighter when he catches my gaze.

"She said she's here looking for a friend. A girl. Not you," Scarface barks. Or was it a laugh? He pours another glass-ful of vodka down his throat and shakes his head. "You lucky bastard."

"Let's go," Maksim whispers, and pulls me by my hand.

We step into the hallway and he closes the door.

"I don't think he recognized me," I say.

Maksim ignores me. His expression is suddenly furious. "What are you doing here, Liza? Why are you in a room with that man?"

"I'm looking for Aka."

"Again? You're relentless." Maksim shakes his head and clicks his tongue, making a dismissive sound. "She isn't here, Liza. I don't think she ever came here."

Scarface said the same thing, but I can't believe a word any of them say. They're hiding her somewhere.

"You don't trust me?"

"Aka came here. I know that. She hasn't been home for days."

Maksim raises his hands in surrender, as if he's about to admit he has done something wrong. "Liza, they don't imprison girls here. Or keep them hostages. Girls come and go as they please." He drops his hands and shoves them into his pants pockets. "Have you thought about another option? That Aka never made it here because something else happened to her?"

His words shock me into silence. A thought is churning in the corners of my mind, like the insistent buzzing of a mosquito. What if Maksim is right? I never thought about the possibility of something else happening to Aka, because it would render me helpless.

"Prove to me she isn't here," I finally say.

His strong shoulders roll, hands clenched tight in his pockets. He rocks slightly on his heels. "You really don't trust a word I'm saying."

"I must see the girls with my own eyes. Take me to the dining hall."

"I can't do that, Liza. My father will be furious. Unlike Andreyev, he remembers who you are and what you did."

He steps closer, determined to drive me away from here. "Besides, he's busy discussing a raid."

"A raid?"

"We found . . . the kitchen." He runs his hand through his hair. "And a meat grinder. In the abandoned depot, behind the market."

I lean back away from him and swallow hard. "A . . . meat grinder?" I shake my head, chasing away unwanted images that flood my brain.

He says something else, but I listen half-heartedly as I watch the light from the ceiling glint and reflect in Maksim's eyes. Something else catches my attention.

"Are you planning to reopen the market then? After the raid?"

He shrugs. "Not sure. Why? Miss your playground?"

"Why would you ask me that?"

Maksim's head jerks back. Loud laughter escapes his throat. "You're quite good at stealing, Liza. Did you think I wouldn't realize it was you who lifted my money? Twice?"

I clamp my hands into fists, fighting the growing urge to step away from Maksim. He knew I stole from him, but he never asked me to give the money back.

I force myself to ask, "You knew? Why didn't you say anything?"

The air goes so quiet I swear I can hear the dust falling on the floorboards.

"Because I can always get more."

I chew on my lower lip. Maybe he's more of a friend than I took him to be. Maybe he's not lying about Aka.

My thoughts circle back to my mission. "What about the girls? Can I see them?"

"Liza, why don't you believe me?"

What am I supposed to do? Take Maksim's word for it? I slowly inhale through my nose, trying to slow down my thoughts.

"Please, take me to the girls. I must see them."

He smiles at me. "Are you going to put your boots on or are you walking in your socks?"

We look down at the boots in my hands.

"Whose blood is it?" Maksim leans down and studies the edges of the boots where a few speckles of blood stain the leather.

"No idea." My hands start to shake as I pull the boots on. "Must've bled over the boots when I scraped the knee the other day."

"It looks fresh. I don't remember seeing it before." He swipes his index finger over one dot and the blood comes off easily, not completely dry.

The hallway grows smaller and hotter. I might be a thief and a liar, but I'm not a traitor. I fumble with my socks, then my boots. I tug on my dress, brushing off invisible dust.

My throat tickles. I don't register it at first, but a few seconds later, a sharp chemical odor burns my nose and throat. Maksim coughs, I cough, and we both turn around.

Female voices scream. Men shout incoherently and curse. A pop of glass splinters somewhere in the house.

"Get out!" A wild roar from down the corridor. A voice I don't recognize.

Thick smoke rolls into the hallway.

24

LOUD SCREAMS AND THE CLOMP OF BOOTS
smacking on the wooden floor. Then gunshots.

"What's happening?" My voice is low, broken. Did someone discover the tunnel group?

All the blood drains from Maksim's face. He turns on
his heels, bangs at Scarface's door, and yells, "Comrade
Andreyev. Get out. We're on fire." When there is no response,
he swings it open and rushes in. "Andreyev."

"Wait, what are you doing?" I remain at the doorway. I'm
trying my hardest to remain calm as I peer inside and see
Scarface, stone-faced, lying on the floor. The vodka bottle
is still clutched in his hands. The clear liquid drips down on
his chest, his wool jacket soaking it in.

Maksim grunts, leans down to Scarface, and shakes his
shoulders. Nothing. He gives him another shake. Scarface's
head wobbles uselessly on the ground. Maksim slaps the
man across the face, and he moans in response but doesn't

move. Maksim shoots a quick glance at me. "Liza, get out of here. Go to the dining room and ask someone to come and help. I'll stay with this moron."

"I can help." I hurry inside the room, grab the drunkard by his ankles, and try to drag his unresponsive body across the floor. But, like a log of wood, he's too heavy and too stiff for my shaking arms. I drop his feet. Why do I even care if he lives or dies? But I know Maksim won't leave him. He's his comrade, after all.

Maksim gets to his feet and softly pushes me in the direction of the door. "Leave. Bring help." When I don't move, he roars, "Go!" I bolt out of the vodka-sodden room and into the smoky hallway.

A few seconds later, I turn the corner and I'm in the dining room. Everyone is scattered around, trying to get out. The heavy smoke oozes in. It's so disorienting I don't understand where it's coming from or where everyone is going. Dizziness turns my body into rubber, and I lean on the piano to steady myself.

"I need help," I scream into the smoke.

"Run. This way." A blond girl with red lipstick smeared around her mouth appears out of nowhere. She pulls me by my hand. "There's a door right there."

"I need someone to go and help Maksim. The major's son. He needs help. There are officers in the hallway who need help." I look around frantically, but I don't spot a single man in the room. Luka's face emerges from the depths of my mind. "There might be people trapped downstairs, too."

I grab the girl by her skinny shoulders. "Where's everyone? Where's Major Nikitin?"

"There." The girl waves to the opposite side of the room. "Let's go."

The ballroom's empty. How fast everyone fled the burning room.

Together we run. There's a door I didn't notice before. Smoke now pours into the ballroom behind us. It irritates our airways, and we both start coughing uncontrollably, the smoke too strong. We reach the door and hurry into a narrow hallway. There's no light in here, but the fire behind me illuminates the corridor. Without a single word, the girl disappears into yet another narrow hallway, leaving me alone. I peer into the dark ahead as panic surges through me.

Maksim might still be back there, helping Scarface. Luka could be trapped downstairs. And where are the officers? I must find them and send help. I follow in the girl's footsteps and turn the first corner. Flames roar, red and orange colors flickering behind me, but here it feels almost peaceful. The smoke hasn't contaminated the air yet, and I can breathe.

I make my way deeper and deeper into the building. I glance back; the fire is chewing its way toward me. If I don't keep moving, it'll catch up with me fast. Smoke slithers through the air and scrapes against my throat. My lungs expand, yearning for oxygen with every breath I take.

There's a small door in the wall. I yank on it, and it opens. It's so dark I can't see anything. I hold the door with my left hand and peer inside. The blackness is as thick as ink. It's impossible to see. The only light comes from the roaring fire behind me.

I leap back into the hallway.

The flames light up the corridor, and I see another door at the end of it. I run as fast as my weak muscles allow. I turn the handle and open it. The light is on in this part of the building. There are spiral stairs leading down. Maybe it's my way out of here. I enter, close the door behind me, and stagger down the stairs.

I pause by another door on my left. So many doors and hallways in this place. This one must lead outside because loud voices and the hiss of water against the flames tell me there are people fighting the fire. In the distance, something heavy—a ceiling?—crashes into the floor. I burst out through the door into fresh air.

Men, women, even children gather around the building. I don't recognize anyone. A hush falls over the courtyard as if everyone is holding their breath. Some throw a small, cautious smile my way. Others nod their heads and talk to one another in muted voices. But most of the people glare, their faces twisted in anger, hate sweltering in their eyes. The stench of charred wood and metal fills the air. Maybe it's the stench of revulsion. They think I'm one of the girls who entertained the officers for food.

An older woman spits in my direction. "You should've burned," she barks at me. "Whores and poachers don't belong in the city."

I want to tell her I'm not a whore. But definitely a poacher.

I turn away and stumble to the curb, dog-tired and weak. Frantically, I search for a uniform or a familiar face. Instead of officers, I see a group of girls in silk slips clustered by a tall linden tree on the other side of the road. I run across the street and approach the girls. They look almost identical—protruding bones, vacant eyes, and razor-sharp cheekbones. The girl who steered me out of the dining room scowls at me as if she thinks I'm going to spit on her like the woman in the yard. "What are you looking at?"

"I'm looking for my friend Aka. Akulina. I think she came here a while ago. A tall, dark-haired girl. Big blue eyes. A thick braid."

"You think she is here?" The girl laughs, a crackling, sad sound that pierces my heart. "Who wants to stay here longer than needed? I don't know about your friend. I've been here only a few hours myself. But let me ask." She steps in front of the group. "Anyone know any Aka?"

I examine the girls for a hint of recognition. But their faces remain vacant and gaunt. No one has heard of Aka. Most of them shake their heads. But one tall and dark-eyed girl steps forward from the tree. "Liza?"

"Sveta!" I'm so happy to see Aka's neighbor I almost squeal. My imagination is running wild. She'll tell me where Aka is. My search is finally over. "Thank God, you're here. Where's Aka?"

Sveta steps closer, and I gasp. The circles under her eyes are darker and deeper than the Neva River. She sways, and the stench of vodka is so sharp and acidic I flinch. Her lower lip is split. A front tooth is missing. "Aka? I don't know where she is." She shrugs. "If you see her, tell her to come home. Her mother and grandfather died. Their place got ransacked. Squatters are living there now."

Sveta is drunk. She doesn't know what she's talking about. "I know Aka came here."

Sveta shakes her head a little too hastily. Her eyes skim over me and then she looks away, toward the burning beast. "I'm pretty sure she never came here. Do you have any smokes? I really need a cigarette." Her hands twitch by her sides.

"I don't." Ignoring the stench of booze, I step closer to her. "Sveta, look at me, please. Are you sure Aka hasn't been here?"

Her eyes slowly drift back to me. "Listen, I'm here almost every day. I know for a fact she wasn't here." A great rumbling crash from deep within the Mansion drowns out the crowd around us. "I'm going to find a smoke." She stumbles forward.

I watch Sveta cross the street, her shoulder blades jutting through the thin silk. A dark bruise mars the white landscape of her calf. I press one clenched hand to my chest, feeling sick. What could have happened to Aka?

My stomach churns, and I run around the girls, behind the linden tree, and retch. When my body is done spasming, I wipe my mouth with my hand. A sharp movement, and someone is by my side; their arms hook around my neck and drag me into the alley behind the tree. Away from the

Mansion. Away from people. I try to scream but the air is cut off from my lungs. I dig my fingernails into their skin. A hiss. I claw and scratch. I'm kicking my legs, trying to get a foothold, but I have no strength. Then I smash the back of my head into their face. A wet crunch and the hold on my neck loosens. I whip around to face my attacker.

Luka.

Blood gushes down his face and into his shirt. He breathes heavily, the air is bursting in and out of his mouth in long gasps.

I don't know what I expected to see but not this. Not him. Suddenly, I'm so tired all I want is to sit down.

"You told them about us," Luka jeers at me.

Is that what he thinks happened? After everything we've been through together, he still doesn't know me. Why would he think I'm capable of something like that? It's one thing to keep them from eating their horrible dinner, but it's completely incomprehensible to turn them over to the NKVD.

"I'm not a traitor. Why would you think so?"

"There was no kitchen in that hallway. There was no food. We found canisters of kerosene, and that was it. You led us into a trap." He seethes. "They came and shot us. Galina's dead. Lena's dead."

My mouth is dry and tart as if I chewed on ashes. "I didn't tell anyone, I swear."

"Why did you take us to that hallway? What have we ever done to you?" His voice wobbles with rage. The muscles in his throat move as he inhales.

"I thought the kitchen was there. I didn't know."

"You're lying. You always lie."

The click of a gun behind me. I whip around.

"Liza?" Maksim's voice says. "Step aside."

I was supposed to bring help. How could I forget? Choking back my emotions, I move aside with slow, measured steps, letting him approach Luka.

"Whatever is happening here needs to stop." Maksim looks like he's been through hell. Soot is smeared over his cheeks. A deep cut over his left eye is dripping blood. His white shirt is burned in places. Buttons are ripped away, exposing his chest covered with blood and ashes.

"She's a monster," Luka whispers.

"And you need to disappear." Maksim rolls his shoulders back. His gun points at Luka's head. "Who set the building on fire?"

Luka doesn't answer.

"I thought so."

"Luka, please go." My breath comes out in gasps. I'm fighting to control it.

"I should arrest him." Maksim swallows hard, his hand shaking. It's obvious he's never arrested anyone in his life. Nor does he want to.

"No one needs to know what happened here," I say.

"Go." The gun now points into the sky.

Luka slowly turns around and vanishes into the streets.

Maksim holsters his gun and turns to me. His eyes are heavy with worry and something else I can't read. "You all right?"

"Yes. I'm fine. Where do you think he's going?"

"I suspect he'll go back to the tunnels. To his sister."

A breeze blows past us, and debris spreads in the air. I take a deep breath and sink into Maksim's arms. My fingers cling to his sides.

"What happened inside?" I whisper. "I got lost in the house. Everyone fled so fast I couldn't find help."

"My father came and helped me with Andreyev."

I close my eyes and listen to my own breathing. We stay like this for a long time.

He smooths my hair, running his fingers through the tangled mess of my braid that has started to come undone.

"Why did Luka call you a monster?" Maksim asks into my hair.

I pull away from his embrace. "I have no idea."

25

WE WALK AWAY FROM THE ALLEY AND THE burning Mansion. Maksim's hands are in his pockets. His shoulders hunch a little under the weight of everything that happened. Around us, the streets are empty as they should be, considering how late it is. A motor rumbles in the distance. Most likely, the militia patrolling the city. Somewhere far away a blistering sound of machine guns and artillery explosions split the air. The Red Army is attacking the Fascists. Or maybe it is the other way around. As long as we don't hear planes, we should be safe to walk.

For the first few blocks, we walk in silence, only the shuffle of our feet and the murmur of the breeze interrupting the quiet of the night.

"Did you know about Luka's plans?" Maksim finally speaks.

I hesitate, but then I hold my chin up and say, "I didn't." The lie is thick like oil, but it drips easily off my lips.

"I find it odd that both of you were in the house at the same time."

"A strange coincidence."

Maksim stops abruptly and turns to face me. I almost run into him. "I have a theory. Want to hear it?" He leans closer. "Look at me, Liza."

I tear my eyes away from his boots.

"I think you came with the group." His face is closed off, hard. "You used the back door. I'm not sure what happened, but the group stayed in the storage hallway, and you went upstairs to look for Aka. I suspect the group was looking for food. But they were in the wrong place. So, in anger and desperation, they set the fire. Another coincidence—a few of the officers were outside when the group walked out through the same back door. Then all hell broke loose." His voice trails off to silence.

I see it as clearly as the sky on a sunny day—the mistrust. The hurt. A part of me wonders if I had this coming all along. The way I promised Luka and the group to take them to the food pantry not knowing where it was. I could've told them the truth. I could've stayed and helped them search for the kitchen. And now . . . I either admit to everything and face Maksim's wrath or keep on lying and risk losing the only friend I have left.

It doesn't matter. You've lost him already.

"I'm not sure what you want me to say," I murmur.

"I want to know the truth, Liza. Why is it so difficult for you to stop lying?"

I stare over his shoulder at nothing.

"Please tell me. Did you come with the group?"

I nod, and my lower lip quivers.

With a deep sigh, Maksim starts to walk again. Trying to get hold of my nerves, I widen my steps, attempting to keep up with him. As soon as I catch up, he halts.

"Luka almost died because of you, Liza." He doesn't sound angry. Or disappointed. He sounds tired. "His friends were shot. He was about to get shot . . . I covered him." He turns his face away from me and inhales sharply. He pats his pockets and pulls out a pack of cigarettes. He lights up, inhales, and blows the smoke out to the side. "I could've helped him." Another huff. Then another. I've never seen anyone smoking so greedily. Desperately.

"Can I have a cigarette?" My voice is shaky and small.

He gives me his half-smoked stub. I pull on it deeply and let the smoke hit my lungs. My head starts to swim, a welcome sensation. I take another drag.

A muscle twitches in Maksim's jaw as he watches me smoke. "Why did he listen to you?"

I inspect the burning end of the cigarette between my fingers. The ground underneath me is solid, but I wish it could crack open and suck me down. "I don't know. Maybe he didn't trust you that much."

"Why wouldn't he? I'm his friend."

"You spend time in that place . . . with the girls . . . with the NKVD." I wave the burning cigarette down the road in the direction of the Mansion. "You call yourself the militia, but you're one of *them*."

"You got it all wrong, Liza." Maksim slowly shakes his head. "I never take part in any of it. I never stay, even though they want me to. Especially my father. He desires to be liked by them so much he loses his temper with me sometimes. I fail to inspire his confidence." He chuckles darkly. "I patrol the streets to get away from it all. I'm not them."

A surge of guilt and shame washes over me like a tidal wave. I feel like crying. How did I not see it? If I'd only paid attention to Maksim and what he was saying, I could've avoided so many mistakes.

"I'm surprised Luka trusted you instead." Maksim's face is harder than a rock. "And look what you did to him. And to Katya."

I always wanted the best for Luka and Katya, didn't I? But somehow it all went so wrong.

"Tears won't help," Maksim says softly. "Not anymore."

I touch my cheeks with a shaky hand, and my fingertips are wet. I hadn't even realized I was crying. "I've made many mistakes. Horrible, stupid mistakes." My voice grates like boots on loose rocks, but there's nothing I can say to undo it all.

Maksim clears his throat, like he's choking on something. He takes whatever is left of the cigarette away from me and throws it to the ground. Then he scrubs both hands over his face and up through his hair. "I understand why he called you a monster. Your mistakes are not stupid, Liza. They're deadly."

The silence grows between us, the finality of it all hovering like a heavy smoke.

With a shuddering sigh Maksim says, "Would you even have noticed if I didn't make it out? Would you have cared?"

He isn't being fair. I was searching for help, but I got distracted. Just for a minute. He's angry and hurt, and I understand why. "Of course, I care." I touch his face lightly, my thumb tracing his scruffy cheek. He pushes my hand away.

"Don't, Liza. Don't do it. People die because of you. And you come out unscathed. You're like a locust that sweeps through the city leaving nothing but ruins in its path."

Why is he so cruel to me? "What do you want me to do?" My voice shakes and I gulp, trying hard to hold back my tears. "I'll do anything. Just tell me what."

His expression switches from exhaustion to something darker. "I want you to leave. Go home." He turns away from me. His jaw is so tense I think it's locked up. "I want you to stay away from Luka. Stay away from me." Something catches in his throat when he takes a step away.

The breeze rushes over my face again. It feels alien against my skin. "I'm sorry, Maksim," I whisper. "For everything."

"For all our sakes, I hope you find Aka," he says. Then he turns around and walks back to the Mansion.

Something shutters inside me. A piece of my heart probably. I can't move, so I stand still, letting everything sink in.

Thoughts are buzzing in my brain like beetles trapped in a glass jar. I'm struggling to piece them together.

No matter how hard I tried to be careful, how hard I tried not to hurt anyone, I hurt so many. How did it happen? Maybe Luka is right. In my focus on Aka, I've become selfish. Not intentionally. Not like my father.

A strangled sound escapes my throat, but I bite it down. Have I turned into my father without noticing? No, I'm not *him*. That's not how my mama raised me. I'll make it right by the boys. By Katya. I don't know how, but I'll come up with something.

In the trees next to me, there is a snap of a branch. A call of a crow. I look up but see nothing.

When I don't hear Maksim's footsteps anymore, I continue my somber walk home alone.

My father opens the door. He blinks slowly as he takes in my appearance. "I was worried sick. Where did you go? And what happened to you?" he stammers. "Are you hurt?"

"I'm not hurt."

My father steps to the side, and I walk into the apartment.

I don't stop until I reach my room. My father follows me inside.

His eyes narrow on me; his nostrils flare. "You sneaked out of the house. After curfew. Do you realize how thoughtless it was? What would your mother say if she knew?" His pinched mouth twitches at the corners as if all the muscles in his face are pulsing with fury. "What's gotten into you, Liza? You've never behaved so . . . stupidly."

"Please close the door," I say.

He does as he's told.

"Where have you been?" His voice is even louder now. More insistent. "I heard sirens, but there were no planes. Has something happened in the city?"

"There was a fire. The NKVD's living quarters are burning down."

"You were there? Why? What happened?"

I happened. I almost laugh at this thought. I lower myself onto the chair by the table. I wave at the chair on the other side. I look down to find my hands trembling.

My father sits down, the chair groaning under his weight, his eyes now watching me with concern. I put my head down on the table and tell my father everything that has happened since my mother's death. About my exploits in the Haymarket. About the tunnels and the people who live there. I tell him about the Mansion and the girls. About the friends I betrayed and the friends I lost.

As I talk, my father leans over the table, drawing closer to me. The fine lines around his eyes and mouth settle deeper into the grooves. When I'm done, he says in a low voice, "I wish you'd talked to me sooner. I could've helped." But there's no conviction in his voice.

"Do you know where Aka is?" Saying my friend's name aloud is like digging a finger into a fresh wound. "I'm worried something horrible happened to her." I pull my head up and meet my father's eyes. He looks a hundred years old. There are deep, dark hollows on his angular face. He reminds me of Boria under the tree in the moments before his death.

"I don't know anything," he says. "I haven't seen Aka for a while now. I think you should stop looking for her."

"I can't stop looking for her."

"Liza."

"You think she's dead?" I sit up straight at my own words. "But why would she be dead?"

"We live in the times of war, Liza. People die every day in the city."

"But she was fine the day she left. I don't understand."

"Maybe as time passes, we'll know more. For now you need to think about yourself." My father leans forward, elbows on the table, and puts his head into his hands. He murmurs something under his breath, but I can't hear the words.

"I can't hear you, Papa."

"I don't understand why you didn't let me help with your mother." My father's voice is shaking.

"You know why." I stiffen.

Tears run down his pale face. I lean away from him. Nausea swirls in my throat. How dare he look me in the eye and pretend he doesn't understand me? The truth is the truth. There's no escaping it.

"I don't understand," he repeats. "I wanted to say good-bye. You robbed me of that."

"I didn't tell you about Mama because I didn't want you to use her body."

My father forms his words slowly. "Liza, I would never do that to your mother. Why would you think that?"

"I heard you. I heard you suggesting stealing bodies from the morgue—to eat. Mama was disgusted and horrified with you. She called you a madman."

His chest caves in as he leans over his knees. "It was a horrible, desperate suggestion. We were starving. Your mother was sick, you could barely stand on your feet. I wanted to protect you from everything. I couldn't just watch you both wither away."

"What was I supposed to think? You were so insistent. It was awful. We didn't want anything to do with you. I protected Mama."

"I loved her. I'd never . . ." He doesn't finish. His hands slide into his lap.

We sit in silence for a very long time.

"This war has changed everything," my father says after a while. "It has changed how we live. How we love. How we think." He stands up, walks around the table, wraps his arms around me. "I would never hurt you or your mother." I blink back tears and press my face into his chest.

"I'm sorry you thought that." He lifts my head between his palms. "We should be open with each other. Never hide anything. You understand me?" He makes a sound in the back of his throat. A sob? "All we have is each other. Let's get through this war. Let's survive. That's all I want for us."

26

THAT NIGHT I DREAM OF THE BOYS.

I waltz with Luka around a big ballroom with mirrors as high as walls. There are no windows. Hundreds and hundreds of candles light up the space around us. Luka's hand is on my waist. He twirls me closer, and I want to tell him how much I've missed him. He smiles at me and says, "You're not a monster. I was wrong. You're just lost."

My breath catches as a flock of butterflies unleash their wings within me.

Yes, I want to scream. I'm very lost. I open my mouth, willing the words to come out, but my vocal cords fail me. The only sound that emerges is a hiss. A snakelike hiss—sharp and cold and violent. It startles us both and we stop moving.

Almost all the candles blow out, only a few of them left in the dark corners. The hairs on the back of my neck bristle at the look in Luka's eyes. His gaze glides over my shoulder, an odd awareness in his face, and I turn around.

Maksim is behind me. He fixes his arm around my neck and nods at Luka. A knife appears in his hand. Maksim pulls my hair, exposes my throat. The blade slices the air, descending on my neck. I try to move my head away from the oncoming assault. I let out a scream, but it's too late. The knife slashes my skin.

Maksim lowers me to the ground.

In the distance, a crow lets out a caw. Wings flutter and a flock of black birds surrounds us. Their beaks drip fat drops of blood. Another croak. One of the birds leaves the flock and propels down, down, down. Another second and it will smash into my face.

I wake up with a start to the loud thud of the front door. My father must've left. The room is dim, the blackout curtains shut tight against the morning light. I jump off the bed and pull the curtains aside. The rain stopped sometime before dawn and now the sun shines through a tiny crack in the heavy, smoky sky. A few seconds later, a storm cloud covers the sun, and the rain is back. It patters against the glass, blurring the view of the city.

I go into the hallway. Not a sound but my own heavy breathing. I realize I haven't seen my old neighbor since my father took her to see his new vegetable-selling friends. I hope Yelena isn't sick. I walk over to her door and knock. "Yelena Stepanovna, are you home?" No one responds. I walk over to the kitchen. It's empty, too. Where would an eighty-year-old go? The stores are closed and even the market is still shut down after the raid.

My stomach gurgles. I haven't eaten anything for a long time. I wonder if there is still the vegetable stew left in my father's refrigerator.

I knock at his door. "Papa, are you there?"

No response. I knock again, and when a continuous silence greets me, I turn the knob. The door doesn't budge. I don't have his key. My mother asked my father to move out the night he offered to steal the bodies from the morgue. He offered us a key to his room later that week, and Mama threw it in his face.

I can work around it. I stick my mother's hairpin into the lock and wiggle it until it clicks. I push the door open.

I haven't been in this room for so long I've forgotten how appalling it is. A light yellow floral wallpaper decorates the walls with blue parrots and red roses. It is an assault on my eyes. Whoever lived in this room before my father had an odd taste. Who was that? An old veterinarian. A woman in her sixties. I vaguely remember her short silver hair and thick-rimmed glasses. A rectangular rug depicting proletarian masses gathered around Lenin covers most of the opposite wall. My father's failed attempt at covering the flowers and birds with socialist ideas.

If not for some scattered clothes and shoes, the room would feel unoccupied. There's a small round table by the window. One chair. A black cupboard by the bed, and a stocky refrigerator in the corner.

My father, being one of the most important professors at the university, brought home one of the first refrigerators manufactured in the Kharkov Tractor Factory. It replaced the icebox my family had used until then.

A big black padlock hangs on the refrigerator's door. When our apartment was crowded with people, Papa used to lock our old icebox in case our neighbors got any ideas about a quick grab.

I can wait for my father to return home, or I can pick the lock and get the stew.

I inhale deeply and go to work on the padlock.

A few long minutes later the padlock lies on the floor by my feet. My hands shake when I touch the wooden handle of the refrigerator and give it a slight pull.

I pause.

I listen and wait for something I can't define. With a deep inhale, I yank the door and peer inside.

My mother's dark blue pot is on the top shelf. My father used it last time he cooked a stew. I pull it out and put it on the floor by my feet. I take a step back. The floorboards creak—a long and muffled screech. It's not the usual sound of the wooden floor shifting and groaning under my weight. I have gained a special awareness in the war—I've learned how to feel a shift in the air and read odd sounds. I know when something is different. I lower myself to my knees and run my fingers across the wooden panels. They are scratched and lightly warped, as if they've been moved around constantly. Just like me, my father created a hollow space under his floor. In mine, I hide stolen money and trinkets I lift in the market. What does Papa have to hide?

With my fingernails, I hook a jagged corner of a floor-board and slowly lift it. Splinters dig into my skin. The wood is old and dry, and it feels like a whittling walnut shell under my touch. There's a hollow space underneath. I move two more floorboards. Ration cards, about eight of them, are arranged into a neat stack. I take the cards out and read the name on the first one. Yelena Stepanovna Sinicina. Did my father steal Yelena's cards? Or did she give them to him for safekeeping?

I spread the cards on the floor in front of me. The names are unfamiliar. All of them female. The last card is bent in half. There are brown spots on the paper. Something thick and crusted. I scratch at a spot, and the brown flecks come off easily. Blood? I unfold the card, and my breath hitches. A gasp is frozen somewhere in my throat.

The name on the card is Akulina Viktorovna Riabina. Aka. Why would my father have Aka's ration card? Maybe she dropped it in our apartment the last time she was here, and he found it. But why wouldn't he tell me about it? I look at the other ration cards again. The dates on the cards are recent—they're valid for the second quarter of July. These must be the cards Mama took from the dead in the hospital. But it doesn't explain Yelena's and Aka's cards.

I insert my hands into the black hole and carefully move them around, trying to avoid getting splinters under my skin. Something soft brushes against my palm. I hook my fingers around it and pull. A crumpled purple silk cloth. It is a folded female undershirt. Something is wrapped inside it, but I cannot tell what the object is. My spine stiffens when I unfold the material. A thin silver chain with a pendant slides to the floor. I pick it up and carefully spread it on my shaking palm. A small silver crucifix with a tiny *A* carved with a knife into the center. Aka's crucifix.

I slump to the floor. The silk is a purple cloud in my hands. "Slipped off a stall, it seems." Aka's words ring in my mind. As I brush my fingers over the silk, I remember how her eyes twinkled with giddiness when she told me about it. I turn the undershirt in my hands, and it catches the sun. There's dark gold woven in, and it glints like sunshine in Aka's hair.

My world darkens at the edges, and a tidal wave of thoughts crashes around in my head. My father's words, "I would never hurt you or your mother," echo through my mind.

But would he hurt my friend?

A chilling suspicion is growing inside me, overtaking my mind. It obliterates every other thought in its path. There is a gnawing ache somewhere inside my rib cage. My father's face emerges through the mist in my brain. He's been different with me for a while now. How could I not see it? His jaw still tightens the same when he is displeased with me. The skin around his eyes still creases when he talks. But his eyes are dull. There is no light behind them. When did the light go out? When Mama got sick? When he told her to steal a body?

Or when I asked him if he knew what happened to Aka?

Tears burn the back of my eyeballs, and the floor tilts. I feel like I'm waiting for my body to shatter. This is not possible. It doesn't make sense. There must be an explanation. The silver crucifix glares back at me, faceless and silent. I turn it in my fingers, inspecting it. It is Aka's, I have no doubt. What did she call it? Her cross of protection. It is cold and smooth under my touch. So different from the softness and warmth of Aka's skin.

I'm trying to find a way to explain it all. Maybe the thin chain broke, and Aka hasn't noticed. She lost it somewhere in our apartment. Maybe my father found it without knowing what it was. He kept it to trade later in the market. It could've been a mistake. Why do I think the worst of him?

Because of what he wanted me to do.

My thumb brushes over the chain. It's not broken. It was removed and carefully wrapped into Aka's undershirt. The realization that there is no explanation jabs at my brain.

I close my eyes and try to take deep breaths. But I cannot control my breathing. I must return to my room. No, not my room. I need to get outside. Away from the apartment. Away from *him*. But I can't move my leaden body.

27

FLOORBOARDS GROAN UNDER SOMEONE'S
heavy footsteps, and my father enters the room. His hair is
unkempt, greasy. A gray stubble outlines his jaw. Larisa
is behind him. At the sight of them, panic in my chest builds
up, readying to explode.

"Liza, are you all right?" My father wants to rush to me,
but Larisa jerks him back.

"Piotr," she whispers, and nods at my hands and the purple undershirt billowing between my fingers.

"Liza." A shocked, weak murmur.

We look at each other. I'm numb and breathless. He's lost
and speechless.

"Why do you have Aka's ration card? Why do you have
her jewelry? Her undershirt?" My insides are a sick knot.
I've never felt so scared in my life. I'm not sure I want him
to answer. But I have to ask. I must. "Do you know what
happened to Aka?"

His chin trembles. He takes a deep breath; his shoulders rise and fall with each inhale. "Liza, we will talk later. Now is not the time."

Rage turns my skin hot. I clench my hand around the crucifix so hard its edges cut into my palm. My knuckles go paper white. I'm breathing louder now. My voice is high. "We'll talk now."

The woman twists her mouth like she has something to say. But she changes her mind and remains silent. Suddenly, I remember where I know Larisa. She's the wife of the butcher and used to run the store in the back alley by the market. I saw her in the beginning of the last winter selling a fur coat. I even asked her if she had any meat to trade and she angrily chased me away.

"All these ration cards you have. Who are these women? Why do you have their cards?" I wave weakly at the opening in the floor. "Yelena's card is there, too. Where's Yelena? Where's Aka? Tell me, please."

My desperate plea for an answer to explain it all rings in the air, but my father is frozen.

"Why don't you tell her, Piotr. Tell your daughter how you saved her life."

Chill, mixed with sharp, broken glass, stirs deep in my chest. I grip the undershirt and Aka's crucifix harder, anchoring myself with them. "What have you done, Papa?"

My father takes an unsteady step forward. "You were very sick. Burning up, delirious. You were dying. There was no food. Larisa offered me help. In exchange . . ." He swallows hard, his Adam's apple moves up and down with each word he says. "Aka was here ... And I ... I ... did what any parent would do. I saved my child." A sob breaks out of his throat. A wild, frantic sound. "She ... Aka ... she helped you live. Liza." He takes a small step forward. "I had lost so much already. I couldn't let you die."

He doesn't even try to deny it.

"Aka wrote me a note when she left. You followed her?"

He runs his hand through his hair, not meeting my eyes. The tendons on his neck bulge out like ropes. "I didn't follow her. I told Aka there was a shipment and my friend, Larisa, saved food for us. Bread, vegetables, fish cakes. I asked her to go and get it."

His words catch me like the blow from a shovel to my ribs. I can barely find my voice. "You sent Aka to the slaughter?" The words burn my throat. My chest hurts so badly I'm not sure I will ever be able to breathe again.

My father doesn't reply. His shoulders start to shake.

I point a trembling finger at the murderous woman. "All this food you brought home. Your apple pies. Your vegetables and stews. Is that what she gave you in exchange for Aka?" I slowly pull myself to my feet. "When I was beside myself, looking for her ... you knew. All this time." I want to shower him with vile, hateful words. I want to hurt him. Make him bleed. But I'm so drained I can't muster anything.

"Liza." His voice breaks. "You must understand; I didn't want to do it. But I thought you were dying. I ... I can barely live with myself."

His every word stabs me like a knife. "You're a murderer."

"He's a survivor. And a good, loving father. You benefited from this, silly girl," Larisa interjects. Her face doesn't reflect a single emotion. She is a hollow, dark void. "You lived because of your father. Because he had the courage to do what needed to be done."

An abandoned depot at the back of the market. A meat grinder. The butcher's wife. It all falls into place—the sudden abundance of food at home, the woman's constant visits, my father's lies. She is the reason Aka's dead and my father is a murderer. I can see all the horror of her crimes pouring out of her.

"No one moves," Maksim's voice says from the hallway. A click of a gun, and we all freeze.

"Maksim, what are you doing here?" My voice rings through the apartment. How much has he heard? His unexpected presence, comforting yet surprising, is too strange. I didn't expect to see him again.

"I came to warn you." Maksim's eyes settle on my father's pale face. "About your father. About *who* he really is. My father showed me the list. Your father's name was on it. I rushed here as soon as I saw it." He aims the gun at my father. "As an officer of the militia, I'm placing you, Piotr Kaganov, under arrest for murder."

"I didn't kill anyone." My father steps away from the door and deeper into the room. His face shifts, his features sharpen. "Maksim, you're making a mistake. Perhaps we should talk, in the kitchen, and leave Liza out of it," he says calmly.

"I think I should go and leave you all to sort this out." Larisa's voice is as hard as steel. The look in her eyes, cold and calculating, tells me she won't be escorted out of this room. Not by Maksim. Not by anyone. The woman is pure evil, rotten from inside out. How did my father meet her? Did he go to the Haymarket in search of the Hunters? Did she somehow find him and reach out to a desperate, broken man offering him food?

I raise my chin. "Maksim, don't let her go. She's the one who made my father do it." I point at Larisa. "She's the real threat here."

"Your name?" Maksim's gun moves to the woman.

Larisa pinches her mouth but doesn't say anything.

"What's her name?" I turn to my father. "Tell us her last name."

He falters.

"Please, Papa. Don't you see it? She ruined us. She turned you into a monster."

"Yudina," my father says. His voice is strangled, as if he's struggling to speak. "Her name is Larisa Yudina."

"Larisa Yudina," Maksim says slowly, rolling the woman's name over his tongue. He shifts, the floorboards creaking under his weight. I sense a shocked disbelief in his tone. "The leader." With the mouth of the gun, he nudges Larisa inside the room. She reluctantly takes a few steps, puts her bag on the floor, and stands by my father.

Maksim remains by the door. His aim goes back and forth between Larisa and my father.

The space around us is getting smaller with every breath I take.

"Maksim, let Liza go. She has nothing to do with this," my father's low rumble breaks the silence.

"We'll wait for my comrade officers. They're on their way." Maksim slightly nods in the direction of the front door. "Liza, move to the side, please."

I don't move.

"There are more of you coming?" Larisa asks.

Maksim takes a step into the room, and a loose floorboard—the one I never had a chance to put back—catches under his foot, his arms fly up instinctively as he tries to balance his weight and not lose his footing. His grip on the gun tightens, and a shot rings through my ears, deafening me. I feel the bullet graze my cheek. The sharp pain is a welcome distraction.

In a short instant, my father is on him. He wraps a hand around his head and yanks Maksim forward so fast I hear the explosion of cracking bones as Maksim's nose connects with Papa's head. Maksim yelps and chokes on his own blood, the painful, desperate sound of an animal about to die. My father twists Maksim's hand, and the gun falls to the floor.

Larisa leans over and picks up the gun.

My lips move, but I don't hear the words. I think I'm screaming but I don't hear anything but loud ringing in my head. Maksim crashes into the wall behind him, loses his balance, and slides to the floor.

His nose is crooked and slanted to the side. Blood's gushing down his face and onto his shirt. His skin is ashen. He tries to grab my father's hands and hold on to them, but both of his hands slide down to his knees when my father elbows his head.

Larisa points the gun at Maksim.

"No!" My scream is audible but still muffled.

"We can't let him leave this room." My father's words float to me from afar.

And then Maksim laughs—bitterly and loudly. He takes his time laughing. For a few unending seconds, I think he has lost his mind. He has gone insane from fear. "Are you going to trade me for food? Isn't it what you do?"

"Liza, this is the only way," my father says. The tension in his voice is mounting. "We can still leave through the attic." When he meets my eyes, his face crumples and his lips tremble.

"Piotr, I thought better of you. You sold me out to the boy so easily. After everything I've done." The gun in Larisa's hands shifts from Maksim to my father.

"Leave," I croak, and step closer to the woman. "Go to the attic."

"Liza's right." My father's voice trembles, striking a desperate note. "You can leave. Put the gun away. There is no need for this. I'll take care of the boy."

My knees go weak. My father . . . he'll kill Maksim.

I've been through so much already. I've lost everyone I

loved. With my shallow inhale, a small breeze shifts my hair. The air is quiet around me as I listen for my mother's voice to tell me what to do. But she is silent. My heart turns over in my chest. I couldn't save my friend. It was too late for that. But I can do something now. I must.

My father remains completely still. "Larisa, go upstairs. There's a narrow staircase leading from the top floor to the attic. There's a back door at the end of it. Use it to get out. I'll handle the rest."

"What are you going to do?" The gun shifts from my father to Maksim. "They know who we are."

A car roars down the street. I hear it pull to a stop by the front door. Heavy boots run up the stairs.

All the blood drains from Larisa's face. She rolls her shoulders back and aims at Maksim.

"Don't. Please," I whisper.

The footsteps are getting closer. They must be on the second floor already. Thoughts race through my mind in cadence with my pounding pulse. The war brought out the most selfish parts of me, but Mama was my anchor to everything good. Aka taught me how to survive. Mama showed me how to remain human even in times of war.

I stand silently, absorbing it all. Larisa's hate. My father's hesitation. Maksim's terror. There should be a point to it all. There should be a purpose. And I think I can finally see it. I'm capable of more than just trying to survive. I'm so much more than a thief and a liar.

Larisa's arm tenses. The cold glint in her eyes gives away her decision.

"Liza, no," my father roars, and lurches toward me.

As Larisa pulls the trigger, I step in front of her, blocking Maksim.

The pain is excruciating. An all-consuming wave. It cuts me at my knees, and I hit the floor. The smell of blood hangs in the air around me. People rush into the room. Sounds of struggle. Shots ripping through the air. A shrill wail. I hope it's Larisa. Another shot cracks. Then another. They're not taking any prisoners.

Someone squeezes my hand, says my name. Maksim leans into me; his blood drips onto my chest, mixing with my own blood. He presses my hand to his chest. I smile. The world is getting smaller. The darkness spreads. From the corners of my mind, it creeps into the center. The pressure on my chest increases, as if concrete blocks are being stacked on my rib cage. Every single part of me is in agony.

Maksim slowly moves my head into his lap. I don't understand a single word he is saying. The pain is dull now. It's not so bad.

I look up at the ceiling and I think of my mother and Aka. Of Luka and Katya. Of my father.

"Papa?" I whisper.

Maksim slowly shakes his head.

My eyes start to close, but Maksim grips my shoulders, and I groan in pain.

"Don't close your eyes. Look at me, Liza. Look at me." His voice is full of sorrow and heartbreak. "Why did you do that?" He touches his forehead against mine. "Tell me why."

I want to smile but it's too much effort. "I finally did the right thing."

With a shaking hand, Maksim smooths my hair. At his gentle touch, something shatters inside me. I didn't think there was anything left in me to break.

"Liza," he whispers. "Don't close your eyes." Softly, so softly, he pushes a strand of hair away from my face. His lips touch mine.

A hint of cinnamon and tobacco.

And blood.

EPILOGUE

A THUNDERSTORM SWEEPS ACROSS THE city. The air is saturated with moisture. Heavy clouds block the sun, and a strong wind rattles the trees, making them bend back and forth. Some of the trees are short and stubby, like imps from the Brothers Grimm fairy tales. Their branches sliced and chopped away.

The city itself feels oppressive and washed out.

After the storm, by the wrought-iron fence at the end of the cemetery, we bury my father. Away from everyone else. Maksim does all the digging, and I just sit on the ground, watching the clouds and letting the wind whip my hair around my face. Every time I move, my shoulder hurts. My muscles are raw and sensitive to my every breath. The bullet is out of my flesh, but I still can feel its metal grip on my shoulder.

Maksim rolls my father's body into the wet hole. When he asks me if I want a cross, I shake my head. We leave his grave unmarked. Maksim helps me to my feet, and I brush the wet grass from my dress. For a few moments, we stand over the grave in silence. I don't think about my father. All I can think about is the people who died in this war. And now everything that's left of them are ration cards stored in the NKVD's file cabinets.

Lastly, we bury Aka's crucifix and her undershirt by the grave of her grandmother, who died of a heart attack years ago. Before Maksim covers the hole, he motions to me to say my goodbyes. I scoop up a clump of dirt, hold it in my palm, and close my eyes. "I love you," I whisper, and throw the dirt on top of the grave.

I ask Maksim to make a cross, and we go looking for something that can be used for the task. We can't find a single bench that wasn't chopped up and used for fuel, so Maksim climbs a tree and cuts down a couple of thick branches. He ties them together with rope and hammers in three nails. It will do for now, we decide, and stab the cross into the center of the small mound. I promise Aka, after the war, we'll get her a real cross and engrave her name on it—AKULINA VIKTOROVNA RIABINA, 1925–1942.

Maksim stands by my side. He's red-faced from the hard labor, sweating, breathing heavily. His swollen eyes slowly rake over the small grave, the cross, and then my face.

I inspect Maksim's broken nose, touching it gently with a finger. "You look awful."

He covers my hand with his and chuckles. "Everything heals. Eventually."

We look at each other, and for once I don't see Aka, and

I don't hear my mother's voice. For the first time, it's not the shadows of the past that surround me. It's not a long walk in darkness that lies ahead of me. It's something entirely different.

Something I'm afraid to admit I have.

Hope.

AUTHOR'S NOTE

IN THE LATE SUMMER OF 1941, THE GERMAN army severed the last railway connection between Leningrad and the rest of the Soviet Union. By early September, the city was cut off from the world. Though nearly 500,000 residents were evacuated before the city was surrounded, over two million remained trapped inside. The blockade wasn't lifted until 1944.

The siege of Leningrad was one of the most horrific events of World War II. The city was under German blockade for almost 900 days, from September 1941 to January 1944. Different sources report different numbers of deaths: between 400,000 and 1.5 million. Most civilians died of starvation. Many were killed in bombings. Some died of the brutal cold and diseases, and many were killed by others when so-called "crime for food" became rampant. The winter of 1941–42 was the deadliest.

To this day, the Russian government controls how the

siege of Leningrad is portrayed to the world, which is why there is a lack of reliable portrayals in Russian sources. The most dependable sources of information are the accounts of survivors shared with Western journalists and writers.

My interest in the siege goes back to my childhood. I was born in the USSR, in the country then called the Lithuanian Soviet Socialist Republic (Lithuania was occupied by the Soviets for fifty years). For the first sixteen years of my life, I attended a Soviet school. In our schools, the education was controlled by the Soviet government, which determined what we were supposed to know and what we were not supposed to know. The siege of Leningrad was mentioned. Mass starvation was acknowledged. But the textbook discussions were mostly centered around the Germans bombing and shelling the city.

Like everything else in the Soviet Union, stories about the blockade were heavily censored. The message derived from our Soviet textbooks was clear: Under the heroic leadership of the Communist Party, the Soviet people endured and behaved heroically. And that's what I learned as a kid—a story of a great survival under the leadership of the party.

Fast-forward a few years, and Mikhail Gorbachev's glasnost, a commitment to increased transparency by the government institutions of the Soviet Union, opened the door to the influx of information about the real story of the siege. What we learned was truly shocking. The real story was significantly different from the one presented to us in Soviet textbooks.

During the blockade, the city had no running water, no

electricity, no plumbing. Food rations were at starvation levels. A bread ration was 125 grams a day, roughly 400 calories. Crime was flourishing, and the food distribution system was corrupt, with massive theft of food and ration cards. There was looting, and there was cannibalism. Of course, none of it was mentioned in the textbooks because it didn't fit the Soviet propaganda image. For the survivors and their descendants, the siege of Leningrad redefined the meaning of life, love, family, and survival.

The Hunger Between Us was a very difficult book to research because the true story of the siege is dark and harrowing. While researching, I had to pace myself. I could only research so much at a time because it was a heart-wrenching and intensely emotional experience. I chose to set the story during summer because life during that summer of 1942 was a bit better, a bit more bearable than in the first winter of the siege. I wanted Liza, Luka, Katya, and Maksim to feel sunshine on their skin.

One of my main English-language sources was *The 900 Days* by Harrison E. Salisbury, a great, comprehensive source on the siege of Leningrad. It covers not only military actions but life inside the city from the beginning of the siege and into the spring and summer of 1942. For general information on the day-to-day experiences, I referred to *The War Within* by Alexis Peri and *Leningrad* by Anna Reid.

As the story unfolded, I realized I couldn't give the siege and its survivors the justice they deserved without digging deeper into some basic survival questions and moral intentions:

What lines could people cross if faced with inevitable death? What would they do if their family was withering away in front of their eyes? We all want to believe we can endure anything when it comes to saving our loved ones, but do we ever consider what price we're willing to pay? And most important, I wanted to explore what role our conscience plays when we decide to shift our moral compass to justify a crime in the name of love.

All the characters in *The Hunger Between Us* are fictional. Although the Mansion is a fictional location, corruption and sex work were widespread during the siege. The Haymarket is real, and raids to track down those trading human meat happened on a regular basis. The hunger was all-consuming and deadly, and many lines were crossed. People did unimaginable things to survive.

I hope I portrayed the experiences of the siege and people with the utmost respect. All historical inaccuracies or mistakes are my own.

ACKNOWLEDGMENTS

I'M ETERNALLY GRATEFUL TO EVERYONE WHO has helped me on this journey.

Special thanks to my fierce and fearless agent extraordinaire Melissa Danaczko, who pulled *The Hunger Between Us* out of her slush pile and saw the heart of this story. I'm lucky to call you my agent. Thank you for changing my life in so many wonderful ways.

I'm forever thankful to my editor, Wesley Adams, at Farrar Straus Giroux, who gave me this incredible opportunity. Thank you, for taking a chance on me, believing in this book, and being such an amazing champion of my work.

Writing a novel might be a solo pursuit, but it truly takes a village if not a town to bring books into the world.

My sincere gratitude goes to the outstanding people at FSG and the Macmillan Children's Publishing Group who worked tirelessly to make this book what it is today. Many thanks to my exceptionally talented cover designer,

Veronica Mang, who blew me away with her vision, and who created something so beautiful and so haunting it almost stopped my heart. I'm forever indebted to the foreign rights team, Kristin Dulaney, Kaitlin Loss, Ebony Lane, and Jordan Winch, for fiercely championing my book in foreign markets. Thanks to production editor Helen Seachrist, copy editor Kelley Frodel, and proofreader Tracy Koontz for all the hard work refining my novel. Your attention to detail is phenomenal. Thanks also to Hannah Miller for their fantastic work behind the scenes and everlasting patience with my questions.

I don't know how I could have ever gotten this far without the support from my insanely talented writing friends. Grateful acknowledgment to Marte Mittet, Amanda McCrina, Elizabeth Cooper, Ella Stallion, David Neuner, Jamie Nord, Rose de Guzman, Gabriella Saab, Olesya Salnikova Gilmore, and Jenna Aker.

Lastly, thank you to my mama for your love and your endless encouragement, especially at crucial moments.